*Skylar placed map and pen
in her satchel.*

Gilbert and Aldwyn stood on either side of her. Queen Loranella faced them.

"Find the Crown and bring it back to the palace," she said. "We'll assemble an army, and when the Fortress is summoned, animals and humans together will reclaim it."

The trio nodded.

"Familiars, for hundreds of years the safety of Vastia has rested on the shoulders of wizards," continued the queen. "Now its future rests on yours."

THE FAMILIARS
SECRETS of
the CROWN

Adam Jay Epstein
Andrew Jacobson

Art by Peter Chan & Kei Acedera

HARPER

An Imprint of HarperCollinsPublishers

Library of Congress Cataloging-in-Publication Data
Epstein, Adam Jay.
    Secrets of the crown / Adam Jay Epstein & Andrew Jacobson ;
[illustrations by Imaginism Studios]. — 1st ed.
        p.   cm. — (The familiars ; #2)
    Summary: When human magic is destroyed, familiars Aldwyn the
cat, Skylar the blue jay, and Gilbert the tree frog set out without their
wizards to seek the Crown of the Snow Leopard, the only object that can
save the kingdom of Vastia from the evil hare Paksahara.
    ISBN 978-0-06-196113-7
    [1. Animals—Fiction. 2. Shapeshifting—Fiction. 3. Magic—
Fiction. 4. Wizards—Fiction. 5. Fantasy.] I. Jacobson, Andrew.
II. Imaginism Studios.   III. Title.
PZ7.E72514Sec   2011   2011002086
[Fic]—dc22   CIP
                                                                 AC

Typography by Erin Fitzsimmons
14 15 16 CG/OPM 10 9 8 7 6 5
❖
First paperback edition, 2012

For my dad, my biggest fan and best friend.

&

For Olive, my daughter, this story is for you.

—A. J. E.

For my mom and dad,
who set the path I follow every day.

—A. J.

CONTENTS

1

TREMORS

Aldwyn had often wondered what it would feel like to have wings. As the wind blew through his whiskers and his claws dug into the linen collar of Jack's tunic, he was beginning to get a pretty good idea. Led by Jack's outstretched wand, loyal and familiar were soaring above the treetops, climbing higher and higher toward the clouds. Back in his Bridgetower days, before he had become the magical animal companion to a boy wizard, Aldwyn used his claws to scale the rooftops and chimneys of some of the city's tallest buildings. But having his fur graze the needles at the top of the mighty pine trees in the Palace

Hills was something different altogether.

"We're about to get wet!" exclaimed Jack.

Aldwyn braced himself as they blasted straight through a puff of white, sending rain pixies scattering in every direction. The tiny cloud fairies sprayed water with every flap of their wings, drenching the black-and-white cat's fur within seconds.

"Guess we won't be needing baths tonight," he shouted at Jack.

Bursting through the cloud right behind them was Jack's older sister, Marianne, gripping a wand of her own.

"Not bad," she called out, "for a beginner."

She flicked her wrist and made an upside-down loop in the air before coming up alongside her brother. Gilbert's bulging orange eyes peeked out over the edge of Marianne's shirt pocket, his webbed hands clutching on for dear life.

"Was that really necessary?" croaked the tree frog in a panic.

Jack used his free hand to brush the dirty blond hair out of his eyes, revealing a determined look beneath.

"Come on, sis," he hollered as if he had something to prove. "I'll race you back to the manor steps."

The young wizard siblings darted downward. Aldwyn felt his stomach do a little somersault as they hurtled through the air at an alarming speed. Dipping below the clouds once more, the grandness of the Vastian countryside opened up below them. Nearby, Aldwyn could make out Sorceress Edna's Black Ivy Manor, a regal estate surrounded by hedge walls and rose gardens. Beyond the manor was an invisible dam that held back the heavy waters of a mountain river. Through the enchanted barrier's sheer surface, fish could be seen swimming, as if a giant aquarium had been built into the side of the rocky peaks. At the base of the dam lay the grazing fields of Edna's fabled short-horned steers, whose silver-hued hides were tough enough to resist even a dragon's fiery breath. Farther down the hill was Bronzhaven, with Queen Loranella's palace rising into the sky at its center, surrounded by the floating torches that hovered just above the castle walls.

Marianne had jumped ahead to an early lead,

but Jack was quickly catching up. The two raced past Dalton and Skylar, who were practicing precise hairpin turns around floating wooden cones. Dalton, the eldest—at fourteen and a half—and maturest of the children, called out: "Sorceress Edna instructed us to work on mid-flight reversals!"

"Slow down," added Skylar. "You're not competing on the Warlock Trail, you know."

But neither Jack nor Marianne paid the boy or his blue jay familiar any attention. They were too focused on outpacing each other.

"Woo-hoo!" shouted Jack, as he pulled in front of his sister by a wand's length.

As they skimmed lower, they approached the living topiaries that guarded the outside of Black Ivy Manor. These enchanted shrubs had been sculpted less than a month ago to protect the teaching grounds, a precaution of great import now that Sorceress Edna had taken over the training of Kalstaff's three pupils and their familiars. The topiaries had been shaped like archers holding thorny bows at the ready. They swung their weapons from left to right, preparing to fire upon any unwelcome intruders.

"Shortcut through those columns," suggested Aldwyn from over Jack's shoulder.

Jack nodded, then barrel-rolled between two marble pillars on the edge of the estate's reflecting pool. The maneuver increased his and Aldwyn's lead over Marianne and Gilbert and seemed to make their victory to the steps inevitable. That is, until Marianne invoked: "Creeping vine, possum tail, make Jack move, like a snail!"

Suddenly, it felt to Aldwyn as if the air around him had gotten thick and gooey like molasses. He and Jack found themselves slowed to a near crawl. Marianne zipped past them and landed on the outdoor stairs leading to the manor's back door. Gilbert immediately jumped from her pocket and began kissing the ground.

"Ah, the sweet taste of gravel," said the tree frog, pressing his lips to the earth.

"Gilbert, aren't you being a little dramatic?" asked Marianne.

"No fair," cried Jack, still inching forward in slow motion. "You cheated."

"You could have countered the spell," replied

Marianne. "I don't remember anyone making a rule about no castings."

Jack's feet finally touched down, and Aldwyn leaped off his back. Marianne walked over to her little brother and gave his hair a ruffle.

"Next time," she said with a wink as Dalton and Skylar landed beside her.

"Thanks for the pointers, Sky. I think I'm finally mastering those turns," said Dalton to his winged familiar.

"Just remember, birds always keep their eyes on the horizon. I'd recommend the same for you."

As the familiars and their loyals continued their friendly banter, Sorceress Edna rose from her chair beneath the shade of a canopy and came toward them. She was a plump, middle-aged woman with hair dyed black and a pair of oversize spectacles. Her familiar, a mink named Stolix, was wrapped around her neck. Edna took short little steps like a penguin, sending splashes of blueberry tea from the top of her porcelain cup. And though her appearance would suggest otherwise, she was a formidable magician indeed.

"Sloppy, sloppy, sloppy," she said in a high-pitched, nasal voice. "At this age, your wand flight should be much more advanced. Tonight I want all of you to reread *Crady's Book of Aerial Wizardry* cover to cover."

Jack groaned. "But you said we could—"

"Another word out of you, young man," warned Edna, "and Stolix will put you in muscle stasis."

"Yes, ma'am," said Jack apologetically.

Stolix snapped her head to attention and exhaled what looked like steamy breath on a cold day. The vapors traveled straight for Jack's nostrils, disappearing into his nose and tightening his muscles into a temporary paralyzed state.

"Stolix!" scolded Edna. "What in Vastia did you do that for?"

"You said 'another word,'" replied the mink. Aldwyn knew that Stolix was a powerful and dedicated familiar, but she definitely wasn't the brightest. Edna shook her head.

Despite Jack's pained expression, Aldwyn knew his loyal would be back to his old self in no time. In the few short weeks of their tutelage here, all of the loyals and familiars, except for Skylar of course, had experienced Stolix's punishment.

Just yesterday, Aldwyn had been immobilized after accidentally knocking over one of Edna's prized crystal dining glasses while playing telekinetic catch in the house. And while the sensation of having every muscle in your body tighten, even for only thirty seconds, was excruciatingly unpleasant, fortunately the spell did no permanent damage.

With as little warning as they had come, the vapors that had slithered up Jack's nostrils wafted out of them, and the boy's body relaxed again. He clenched his fists and shook it off.

"You'll have to forgive Stolix," said Edna. "She has become a bit pea-brained in her old age. Anyway, better get your wits back about you." She turned her attention to the group. "Now, for the next part of your wand flight training, I'll be adding a new challenge. The skies won't be yours alone. You need to be able to face danger in the air as easily as you do on the ground. Especially if you wish to have any chance of defeating Paksahara."

Paksahara. The name gave Aldwyn the chills. It had been four weeks since he, Gilbert, and Skylar had faced Queen Loranella's traitorous familiar in the dungeon of the Sunken Palace. The shape-shifting hare had come very close to killing both the loyals and the familiars, and had it not been for Aldwyn's fortuitous discovery of his telekinetic abilities, she would have done just that. But even though the familiars had prevailed, Paksahara had managed to escape, and nothing had been heard from her since. Aldwyn could only imagine what new evils she had been plotting.

"And familiars, your assistance will be helpful, too," added Edna.

Although Queen Loranella had told Edna that Aldwyn, Skylar, and Gilbert were the Prophesized Three, the plump sorceress didn't seem to believe it. She still held to the old belief that familiars were second rate in their abilities compared to human wizards. Aldwyn couldn't really blame her; he himself still had trouble believing that he, a former alley cat who never dreamed he had even a whisker of magic, was destined to save all of Vastia. Aldwyn was just happy to know that the next time he and his fellow familiars faced Paksahara, they wouldn't be alone: Jack,

Marianne, and Dalton would be beside them to protect them with their years of wizard training and magical prowess.

Sorceress Edna dumped her tea on the ground and magically reshaped her cup into a porcelain piccolo. She brought the instrument to her lips and blew a melodic call. The sound echoed in the air.

"You'll have five minutes to cage them," said Edna. "How you do it is up to you."

"Cage what?" asked Jack.

That's when Aldwyn felt the air begin to vibrate. There was only one creature that could make the atmosphere rumble with such force.

"Tremor hawks," said Marianne with a bit of caution.

"Just be thankful I didn't call the winged rhinos," said Edna. "Off you go. Time's a-wasting."

Already a flock of the brown-feathered predator birds had emerged from the clouds. They beat their wings, leaving fissures of darkness in their wake like black veins across the blue sky. Dalton whipped out his wand and flew upward, with Skylar flapping beside him.

"I'll stay down here and man the—" Gilbert started to say, but before he could finish, Marianne scooped him up and shoved him into her pocket.

Aldwyn jumped onto Jack's back and hooked his claws into the already worn fabric of his loyal's tunic.

Sister and brother took to the air, led by their wands. Aldwyn felt a surge of excitement as they accelerated and rose higher. He looked ahead at Skylar, then at Gilbert, his two best friends, who had accompanied him on his incredible quest across Vastia. One was a blue jay with the talent of casting illusions, the other a tree frog who could see visions in puddles of water. Well, sometimes he could, anyway. Together, the three familiars had faced insurmountable odds and lived to tell the tale. And here they all were at it again, in the thick of danger, tremor hawks circling around them.

"*Trussilium bindus*," incanted Dalton. A silver rope materialized in his free hand, and he threw the coiled end around the neck of one of the hawks, lassoing it. "Got one! Marianne, conjure a glider cage."

"Giant clover, poison sage—" she chanted, but the spell remained half cast as Dalton was pulled into her by the angry bird trying to break free from his capture. The impact of the blow sent Marianne spinning downward. Aldwyn watched as she struggled to regain control. She was heading straight for the granite garden deck when an ethereal hand grabbed her in midair and tossed her back into the sky.

"Concentrate," called out Edna, whose spell had saved the wizard in training. "I won't always be here to catch you!"

Jack was quick to pick up where Marianne had left off.

"Giant clover, poison sage, trap that hawk, inside a cage," he shouted.

A golden bird cage formed in the sky. Its door swung open and Dalton was able to steer the thrashing tremor hawk inside.

"Good," shouted Edna from below. "Work together."

Two of the avian predators screamed toward Jack and Aldwyn, the shock waves nearly knocking Aldwyn off his loyal's back. Then from the clouds dove a northern fire-breather dragon, its copper wings shining in the sun. The pair of hawks immediately cowered, allowing Dalton the chance to rope two more.

Aldwyn knew enough not to be afraid of the dragon, because when he looked over to Dalton, he could see Skylar's wing trembling. It was one of her illusions. They had been getting more and more lifelike with every attempt.

Marianne summoned two more golden cages, and Dalton guided the ensnared hawks into their aerial prisons.

Now three tremor hawks remained, each sending skyquakes through the air.

"Aldwyn, reach into my pouch and pass me some blinding dust," Jack instructed his familiar.

Aldwyn grabbed Jack's pouch in his teeth and was about to open it when a burst of green light flashed over the eastern horizon. For a blink, everything around them took on an emerald hue, as if it were reflected in an algae-covered pond. Suddenly all three children were in freefall.

"My wand's not working," cried Jack.

"Neither is mine," said Marianne.

"*Gustavius rescutium,*" incanted Dalton, and Aldwyn could detect a hint of panic in his voice.

It was a simple wind gust spell. One that Aldwyn had heard him cast a hundred times. But nothing happened.

Then, suddenly, the cages that had held the tremor hawks disappeared, allowing the dangerous birds to go free once more.

Aldwyn watched as Sorceress Edna waved her arms frantically on the ground, but there was no ethereal helping hand to save them this time.

As the wizards and their familiars continued to plunge downward, gathering momentum with every second, Gilbert tumbled out of Marianne's pocket.

"Gilbert!" Marianne reached out to grab him just as a tremor hawk tried to snatch him out of the air with its beak. Fortunately, the bird mistimed its attack, and Gilbert landed on the hawk's back, clutching its feathers in his webbed hands.

"Ahhhhhhh," he shrieked.

Skylar seemed terrified as well, but if she was screaming, it must have been on the inside. She grabbed at Dalton's shirt with her talons, trying

in vain to slow his descent. Fortunately, her loyal was heading straight for the black ivy–covered hedge wall, which would spare him from a bone-shattering impact. Marianne looked to be headed for a safe landing, too, as she was tumbling toward the reflecting pool. Jack and Aldwyn didn't appear to be so lucky; they were on a collision course with the barren ground. Thinking fast, Aldwyn concentrated as best he could, given that he was hurtling toward his death, and focused on the nearby garden canopy.

Move, move, move, Aldwyn repeated in his head. He wasn't exactly an expert in this whole teleki-nesis thing yet. He had only recently discovered that he was a Maidenmere cat, one of the legend-ary black-and-white felines who had the power to move things with their minds. And while each day for the last four weeks he had continued to hone the skills borne out of this revelation, he wasn't in full control of his magical abilities yet.

At the very last second, Aldwyn managed to make the entire canopy and the frame beneath it drag across the dirt, and he and Jack landed safely on the cloth top. The frame collapsed beneath their weight, and boy and cat rolled to the ground. A nearby splash signaled that Marianne had had her own fall softened by the reflecting pool. And Dalton was climbing out of the shrubs with nothing more than a few cuts and bruises. In the distance, Aldwyn could hear the faint sound of Gilbert screaming from the tremor hawk's back.

"What has happened to my magic?" wondered Sorceress Edna, who was hurrying, or rather waddling, toward them.

There was no time to ponder the question, as the tremors were growing stronger. All six hawks were in attack formation now, and they were flying lower, heading straight for the manor, with Gilbert flailing atop the one leading the way. The day's exercise of capturing and releasing these normally reclusive creatures of the sky would have been routine—a simple and safe class lesson. But given the fact that the human wizards had suddenly been rendered powerless, the enraged birds had become deadly foes.

As the sky-shaking predators swooped down over the reflecting pool, the columns that lined its sides began to vibrate, cracking from the base to the top. The fissures of dark energy left in the hawks' wake finished the job, toppling large chunks of the pillars into the water. Marianne had to dive beneath the pool's surface to avoid the crumbling debris.

The bone-rattling birds flew over the group's heads, and Aldwyn could see Gilbert still clinging to the neck feathers of the lead hawk.

"Somebody get me off of here!" Gilbert shrieked.

"Without the ability to cast spells, we're powerless to stop them," said Sorceress Edna.

"We might be," said Jack. "But Aldwyn's not. His telekinesis moved the canopy."

"Yes," Edna concurred. "It appears whatever curse has affected us human wizards has no hold over the familiars." She turned to Aldwyn. "If you don't do something quick, they'll destroy all of Black Ivy Manor."

Marianne had barely pulled herself out from the pool, and Dalton had only just dropped down from the hedge wall, when the tremor hawks came back around for another onslaught.

"Don't worry, we'll handle this," said Skylar.

"What can we do to help?" asked Dalton.

"Just stay back. It's too dangerous for you," replied the blue jay. Upon hearing Skylar's words, Aldwyn couldn't help but think how strange it was to see that the roles between humans and animals had been reversed yet again. Normally, it was the wizards telling their familiars to stay out of harm's way. But now it was Dalton, Marianne, Jack, and Sorceress Edna who were forced to take cover behind a tall topiary.

In unison, the hawks let out another scream that sent a seismic blast reverberating through the air, causing the trees to bend and sway.

"You need to get Gilbert off the back of that hawk," said Skylar to Aldwyn. "I'll see what I can do about our rude guests."

Aldwyn nodded and looked up at Gilbert, who had an expression of true terror on his face. His eyes were bulging even more than usual. Aldwyn glanced over at Jack, then back to Gilbert.

"Gilbert, help is on the way," Aldwyn called out. He used his telekinesis to rip the flight wand out of Jack's hand and make it fly like an arrow toward Gilbert. "Catch it!"

As the hawk made a sudden dip, all Gilbert could do to grab the wand was shoot out his tongue. He snatched it out of the air, and the wand magically jerked Gilbert upward, off the tremor hawk's back and into the sky.

"How dugh I uthe thith thing?" screamed Gilbert, tongue-tied.

"Don't look at me," Aldwyn shouted back. "I was just supposed to get you off that hawk."

Meanwhile, Skylar had perched herself on the edge of a garden fountain, her wings outstretched and trembling. That could only mean one thing: she was preparing to cast another illusion. And indeed, a second later, a baby lamb was limping across the grounds, stopping atop the fallen canopy. And like vampire leeches drawn irresistibly to a pool of blood, the tremor hawks came down, eyeing the feast in front of them. Once they converged, the lamb disappeared. The hawks screeched angrily, clearly confused.

"Aldwyn!" shouted Skylar.

He knew just what to do. Aldwyn turned to the canopy and narrowed his eyes. A moment later, the cloth fabric was ripped telekinetically from the collapsed metal frame and was quickly wrapped into a bundle, trapping the birds inside.

Just then, from above, Aldwyn heard Gilbert, whose tongue was still wrapped around the wand, shouting, "Looooo ouuuu!" Although his friend was difficult to understand, Aldwyn knew enough to get out of his way.

Gilbert was coming in for a landing, and if he had any ambition to do it gracefully, he was failing miserably. The wand jerked him left and right, up and down. The tree frog smacked against shrubs and branches before hitting the ground and bouncing along the dirt as the wand magically dragged him to a stop.

Gilbert coughed up a mouthful of mud and dust as his tongue let go of the wand. Then he looked around dizzily. "Whoa. My life just flashed before my eyes. I've spent a surprising amount of time picking flies out of my teeth."

Sorceress Edna and the children came out from behind the topiary and rejoined the familiars. The tremor hawks remained tied up in the canopy cover.

Aldwyn could see by the look on Edna's face

that she was deeply unsettled. She stared blankly at the garden fountain, which was no longer flowing. Dalton was watching the topiaries, which were now motionless, standing as still as any common shrub. Jack's attention was on the sky.

"What's that?" he asked, pointing at a pillar of gray smoke that was rising into the blue in the distance.

Curious and with a growing sense of dread, Aldwyn hurried to the hedge wall and scaled it. From the top, he surveyed the Vastian countryside. It was worse than he had feared: the enchanted dam that stood beyond Black Ivy Manor was gone, and water from the lake above had flooded the grazing fields. Cows and horse carts drifted aimlessly, while fish swam in and around stalks of corn. Farther in the distance, the floating torches of Bronzhaven, which were always magically held aloft as a symbol of Queen Loranella's great power, had fallen, igniting the palace walls. And lightning storms and thunderclouds, normally held at bay by the queen's weather-binding spells, were forming over the lush green hills to the south, moving in on the great expanse of plains west of the Yennep Mountains and east of the Ebs River. This stretch of grassland, once known for its tranquility and peacefulness, was in ruins.

Aldwyn felt his stomach do a somersault for the second time today. But unlike before, it wasn't adrenaline or gravity that was twisting his insides. It was the realization that something terrible had befallen Vastia: all the spells and enchantments that wizards had cast upon the land had vanished. Human magic was gone.

2

A FACE IN THE GLASS

"Have there been any reports of humans casting magic since the *green flash?*" Queen Loranella inquired of the council and the concerned citizens who had gathered in the grand hall of the New Palace of Bronzhaven. Not a single voice called back from the room—the only response was a shaking of heads and anxious murmurings.

Aldwyn sat in Jack's lap in the back row of the high-ceilinged chamber, alongside Dalton, Marianne, Skylar, and Gilbert. The six of them had traveled here with Sorceress Edna, who had received word of the emergency meeting from one of the queen's courier eagles shortly after the disenchantment. By the time they had taken to the roads, most of the water released by the dam had sunk into the earth, so at least the group was spared having to swim to the palace. Instead, they made the short trip on foot, witnessing some of the profound effects already being felt by the loss of magic: the enchanted scythes that were responsible for chopping down the wheat and corn crops lay lifeless on the ground, awaiting human hands to manually use them; healing wizards were turning away sick patients from their doorsteps, unable to help them; and rock beetles were pouring out from the ground now that the bug plugs were broken—an unpleasant nuisance to everyone but Gilbert. While their old teacher, Kalstaff, would have surely kept his concern and worry hidden from his young pupils, Sorceress Edna wasn't shy about sharing her own. "This is bad, very, very bad," she kept repeating until they had reached the castle, whose walls were charred and smoking from the fires caused by the fallen torches.

Aldwyn looked to the front of the grand hall, where the queen was standing at the head of a long, crescent-shaped table, five chairs to her left, another five to her right. The men and women occupying the chairs wore different-colored wizarding robes, all distinct to their local region. Each was accompanied by their familiar—ranging from the common potbellied weasel to the truly bizarre wall-crawling dingo.

"Those ten sitting on either side of Queen Loranella are the council elders," Dalton whispered to Marianne. "They represent each of the ten provinces of Vastia."

The room itself was grand, with high-vaulted ceilings and stained-glass windows, the largest of which depicted a swirl of silver dust rising up above the Peaks of Kailasa. Hundreds of notables had gathered to fill the benches that stretched in long rows across the hall. Wizards and non-spellcasters alike sat side-by-side, waiting impatiently for answers.

"The spirits from the Tomorrowlife have come back to curse us," a voice shouted from the crowd.

"No, it's an *estriutus burst*," another citizen interrupted.

"I'll wager my goat farm that those ore miners in Kailasa struck a spell vacuum—sucked all the magic out of the world!" said a country villager. Aldwyn thought his theory even more desperate than the first two.

"I'm afraid it's worse than that," said Queen Loranella in a steady voice that was comforting in spite of the gravity of the situation. "This is neither a cosmic event nor an accident. It's a purposeful attack, and a focused one at that: not all magic has been displaced from Vastia, only that cast by humans. And it is no coincidence that animals have retained their gifts. I am certain that it is an animal who is responsible for bringing this dispelling curse upon our land."

Aldwyn knew just who the queen was talking about.

"Paksahara," Queen Loranella continued. "A spell so powerful and encompassing could only have been cast from the Shifting Fortress. And since she stole my wooden bracelet, Paksahara is the only one with the ability to harness its powers."

Aldwyn had been told of the Shifting Fortress, a secret tower whose location changed each day. From the top of the Fortress, powerful spells could be cast that affected all of Vastia. He knew that while under the control of the queen, the Fortress had been used to protect the lands— but he shuddered to think how Paksahara would wield its ancient magic.

"Well, I will not just lay down my wand and give up," a bearded wizard called from the crowd. "I'll defend myself with sword, and shield, and bare fists if needed!"

"Urbaugh won't be the only one. I'll be at my brother's side," said another citizen in the hall, who definitely shared a family resemblance to the bearded wizard. "Who here is frightened by a carrot-eating hare anyway?"

Defiant laughter briefly lightened the mood. They wouldn't be laughing, Aldwyn thought, if they had seen Paksahara's skills of sorcery or the coldness behind her pink eyes.

"Her spell will never hold!" shouted a towns-woman. "This will all be over by the morning's sun."

These boasts, as unsubstantiated as they might have been, still seemed to lift the morale of the masses and rally the hall.

Queen Loranella raised her hand to quiet the people. "I'd like to hear what the council—"

Just then, what sounded like nails scraping across a mirror screeched through the hall. Aldwyn looked up to see the pane of stained glass—the one that depicted the Kailasa mountains—begin to transform. The triangles of different-colored glass began to shift, rearranging on their own to form a different picture: that of the gray hare,

Paksahara. The image smiled down menacingly on the assembled, and then the lips of the stained-glass hare started forming words.

"Question: What's a wizard without magic?" Paksahara's voice taunted them. "Dragon food," she continued, as her nose twitched happily.

Dalton had to hold Skylar by her tail feathers to keep her from flying up, so spitting mad was the blue jay.

"Now, I'd love to take all the credit for this cruel turn of events, but you have Loranella to thank as well," continued the face in the glass. "If it wasn't for my old loyal foolishly underestimating me, I never would have been able to betray her."

"I know how much you desire my crown," said Queen Loranella, "but what good will it be if no one is there to follow you?"

"You may rule with the will of the people," replied Paksahara, "but I shall do it under the fear of clenched paw."

"When I find you, you'll face the sharp end of my blade," threatened Urbaugh, rising to his feet.

"And while you're off searching for me, who will be there to protect your family?" asked Paksahara, a frightening chill in her voice.

The word "family" made Aldwyn snuggle closer to Jack. It was perhaps the thing he longed for more than any other.

"We defeated you once," shouted Skylar, her voice bold and trumpeting. "Don't think we won't come after you again."

Gilbert cowered inside Marianne's shirt pocket. "Speak for yourself," he said out of the corner of his mouth.

The pink panes that formed Paksahara's stained-glass eyes turned to the three familiars in the back row.

"Such animosity," said the hare, "when we're on the same side. If you were smart, you'd leave your loyals behind and join me. Many animals already have."

"We're the Prophesized Three." Aldwyn jumped in. "It's our destiny to stop you."

"Prophesies are made to be broken," said Paksahara. "I won't underestimate you this time. I even considered disenchanting animal magicians, just to eliminate you as a threat. But that would have left me in a bit of a pickle."

Queen Loranella spoke up again, and this time her voice sounded fierce.

"Why do you choose to show yourself like this?" she inquired of her former trusted companion. "What is it you want?"

Paksahara turned her glass face back to the queen. "For all on two feet to bow down before me. For you to relinquish your throne and pledge your allegiance to the original rulers of Vastia. For you to let me enslave you, the way you did me: you called me familiar, but in reality I was nothing more than your servant."

"I was your loyal and you my companion. We were a team," said the queen. "I will never bow down to you."

"I was hoping you'd say that. I'm quite looking forward to hearing you beg for mercy." The sunlight gleamed through Paksahara's stained-glass visage—it was strange for something so terrifying to be so beautiful, too. "Upon the arrival of the next full moon, a new Dead Army will rise, one comprised of animals, and it will not stop marching and conquering until every human has surrendered to it."

The glass panes began to shake once more, but this time, instead of reforming into their original picture, the window shattered. Triangles of colored glass, sharp as knives, rained down upon the Queen and her councillors. Elders ducked beneath the table, while the gathered townsfolk covered their heads with their arms. With no magic to protect them, the shattered glass impaled itself in flesh and fur. It was only after the last shards had settled that humans and animals came out from their hiding spots. But they did so cautiously, fearing that Paksahara could return at any moment. A quick survey told Aldwyn that, fortunately, no one was badly hurt from the blast; as far as he could see, there were just cuts and grazes. Queen Loranella signaled everyone to return to their seats.

"Let's not panic," she said, trying to bring a sense of peace back to the grand hall.

"If we are to have any hope at all of regaining our magic, we must find the Shifting Fortress," said Sorceress Edna, rising to her feet. "It is the only way to stop Paksahara's plot."

One of the council elders, wearing a blue scarf

on her head, spoke up: "We can put together a team of trackers and a volunteer citizen army. Try to have eyes everywhere at once."

"No, Vastia is too big," responded Queen Loranella thoughtfully. "We have only eight days until the full moon rises. Without the bracelet, finding the Fortress is a hopeless task."

A hush descended on the hall, and there was a silence that seemed to go on forever, until the elder from the Estovian province, recognizable by his black gown, spoke up: "There might be another way," he offered. He had gray, lifeless skin and eyes sunk back deep into his sockets. Only patches of long stringy hair remained on his scalp, as if the rest had fallen out in clumps.

"If you hold truths, speak now, Feynam," said the queen.

"I have no knowledge of the Shifting Fortress's secrets. But if I still had my magic, there's someone I would talk to: the famed architect Agorus, the man who built the Fortress itself. Of course, given the circumstances, I'm unable to commune with the dead."

"Then why did you even bring it up?" shouted

a voice from the crowd. "You're just wasting our time."

"We need another plan," said a different citizen.

Out of the corner of his eye, Aldwyn saw Skylar whisper something into Dalton's ear. Then he watched as the fourteen-year-old boy slowly began to nod. Dalton stood up and cleared his voice. A familiar could communicate with their loyal and any master wizard, one who had the many years of training needed to become adept at comprehending animal tongue. But commoners and lesser wizards were unable to understand the words that animals spoke.

"My familiar can do it," Dalton told everyone. "Skylar has become versed in more schools of magic than the one her kind is born with. She has studied necromancy. She believes she can speak to the non-living."

Aldwyn knew his fellow familiar had experimented with dangerous magic. He had watched her try to bring a beetle back from the dead, with hair-raising results. He also suspected there was more to the mysterious bejeweled anklet she wore than she had yet revealed. But as every single head in the hall turned toward Skylar, he wondered whether the blue jay would really be able to do what she had just claimed she could.

"She is a blue jay," said Feynam. "Her talent is illusions. No animal has ever been known to commune with the dead. Why should she be different?"

"She strives for more," said Dalton, defending his familiar.

"Such conjuring is forbidden for non-humans," said another member of the council. "Look what happened to Paksahara!"

"Things are changing," said Queen Loranella. "And with our own magic gone, we have to put faith in our animal friends."

The queen left her spot behind the table and walked down the aisle toward Skylar, who remained perched on Dalton's shoulder.

"You familiars are just full of surprises, aren't you?" she said, a note of hope coming through in her words. "Perhaps this is the next step in your journey to fulfill the prophecy."

By mid-morning the next day, the queen's royal carriage was rolling south, across the Brannfalk

Pass and toward the rolling hills that hugged the east bank of the Enaj. Without the aid of Loranella's swift-step spell, the horses pulling the coach could only travel as fast as their own hooves could gallop. The queen had decided to leave at dawn, concerned they wouldn't be able to find what they were looking for by moonlight alone.

From inside the gold-trimmed carriage, Aldwyn stared out at the lush green slopes and flocks of sheep, whose wool had taken on the same lime color as the grass they ate. He sat on Jack's lap; his loyal looked eagerly out the window as well, for as little of this land as Aldwyn had seen, Jack had glimpsed even less. Dalton and Marianne were seated beside them, along with Skylar and Gilbert. Marianne had fallen asleep, her head slumped on Dalton's shoulder. Skylar studied a pocket scroll on necromancy, reading the words silently to herself as she prepared for the task ahead.

"Even muttering Wyvern and Skull's chants in your head comes at a price," warned Feynam. He stretched his arms out from beneath his black robe, revealing dark, twisted veins on his hairless arms. "I've read from those scrolls too often."

The elder was sitting on the bench opposite the young wizards, next to Queen Loranella, Sorceress Edna, and Stolix, who had dozed off around Edna's neck. Feynam had been invited along to lead them to the location where the Shifting Fortress had been originally built—the same spot from which it was believed Agorus could be summoned from the Tomorrowlife. Aldwyn hoped Feynam's expertise in necromancy would be useful, but right now the elder was just giving him the creeps.

Gilbert had his attention fixed on the charcoal-colored snake curled up on the floor across from him. This was Feynam's familiar, Ramoth, whose scaly body was capable of turning to flames at will.

"I don't like the way he's looking at me," Gilbert whispered to Aldwyn. "I know that look. He's picturing me between two slices of bread."

Normally, Aldwyn paid little attention to Gilbert's paranoia, but there was something about the way the reptilian familiar was licking its lips that made him think that perhaps frog wouldn't be the only thing on the snake's menu if it got hungry.

"It's just over this next rise," Feynam called out to the coachman who held the reins of the four horses.

The carriage pulled to a stop, and Dalton nudged Marianne awake. She looked at him with a shy smile, then spotted some drool left behind on his shoulder and quickly wiped it away.

"I don't normally drool in my sleep," said Marianne, blushing.

"It must be a side effect of Paksahara's spell," said Dalton.

Aldwyn had seen these two playfully tease each other before, and he was coming to learn that this was how young boys and girls showed affection.

Sorceress Edna pushed her way out of the carriage first, which was no surprise, since she had complained most of the way about feeling cart-sick from the bumpy ride. The others followed, Gilbert making very sure to keep his distance from Feynam's serpent as he hopped down to the ground.

They all walked from the road to the top of a small hill, where a large gray stone jutted out from the green. It was polished smooth and stamped with a circle with eight lines jutting out from it. Embedded in the ground beyond it was the sunken imprint of what looked like a long-disappeared castle. The massive indentation had four long sides and burrowed several feet deep into the earth. The architectural fossil had now been filled in with the same grass that covered the hillsides.

"This is the cornerstone of the elusive Shifting Fortress," said Feynam, gesturing to the gray obelisk with his bony hand. "It was left behind as a monument to remind all where the grand tower first stood."

"And you believe the spirit of Agorus resides here?" asked Loranella.

"Every departed soul has a gateway to the Tomorrowlife," explained Feynam, "a place of profound importance to them. I am confident this is that place for the mighty architect of the impossible."

Skylar fluttered from Dalton's shoulder to the base of the stone. She unrolled the scroll at her feet, then grasped a talonful of silver powder from her satchel.

"Silver dust is a weak substitute for obsidian," said Feynam. "You'll be lucky to hold this spell long enough to get any answers at all."

Skylar seemed undaunted and ignored the elder's words. She closed her eyes, concentrated, and then started her incantation.

"Agorus, hear my call and speak once more," she chanted to the sky. She tossed the powder into the air and intoned: *"Mortis communicatum!"*

Nothing happened for so long that Aldwyn thought Skylar's spell must have been unsuccessful. But then a bluish mist began to form in the air and curl around the stone. It grew more and more solid, and Aldwyn saw a faintly glowing figure emerge from it. As the spirit became more concrete, Aldwyn was taken aback: what had taken shape in front of him was not a man, but—a beaver!

"I knew it," said Feynam. "There is no way a bird could cast such a powerful spell!"

"I'm sorry," said Skylar to the four-legged creature. "I was trying to commune with someone else."

The beaver looked at her, exasperated.

"You mean to tell me you've woken me for nothing?" he said. "I was in the middle of the most peaceful sleep."

"Perhaps you can still help. Is there a man who lingers by this stone in the Tomorrowlife?" asked Skylar. "A famed architect who goes by the name Agorus."

"Now you've got me confused," said the beaver. "Are you looking for a man or for Agorus?"

"They're one and the same," said Feynam, growing impatient.

"Then you're out of luck," replied the beaver. "It's a shame, too. If you had been here looking for a beaver named Agorus, you would have found him."

The group stared back at him in disbelief. He smiled and gave a little wave.

"*You* are the famed architect Agorus?" asked Feynam.

Aldwyn had known at once that it was true, recognizing that yet again they had made a wrong, very human, assumption: that man was responsible for the greatness of Vastia's past rather than animals.

"You're a beaver," exclaimed a startled Gilbert,

giving voice to the surprise that could be read on everybody's face.

"Well, I should hope so," said Agorus. "That's how I left this life, and that's how I've stayed. Although if reincarnation were a possibility, I always wondered what it would be like to come back as a gazelle—a handsome, elegant creature indeed. Now tell me, blue bird, how many years have passed since the Turn? Two, three?"

"A little over four thousand," said Skylar.

"Huh. Time goes fast in the Tomorrowlife. It seems like just yesterday I was overseeing the team of Farsand lifting-spiders who built the Shifting Fortress. I'm sure you noticed their insignia carved into the stone." Agorus gestured to the circle on the cornerstone with the eight lines sticking out of it. "Amazing creatures. Ten times the size of regular spiders, with webbing strong enough to carry a boulder. But none of it would have been possible without my meticulous design. And the Fortress— what a miracle of engineering it was, if I do say so myself! Walls as strong as steel, a casting tower that could spread magic from Liveod's Canyon to the southern tip of the ever-flowing Enaj, and a teleportation globe buried into the glass floor, randomly spinning so the Fortress never appeared in the same place twice, making it impossible to ever lay siege to it."

"We come with a question in dire need of an answer," interrupted Skylar. "Is there another way to summon the Shifting Fortress beside the wooden bracelet?"

"Wooden bracelet?" asked Agorus. "I'm not sure what a wooden bracelet has to do with the Shifting Fortress."

"My bracelet," said Queen Loranella. "It was a relic possessed by my great-grandfather, the king. I retrieved it from the Sunken Palace during the Dead Army Uprising."

"You speak of a history I am unaware of. Back in my day, the Shifting Fortress was not summoned by some wooden trinket. There was meant to be only one way to bring forth the mighty tower. Seek the Crown of the Snow Leopard! That is how the First Phylum intended it."

"Please, slow down," said Skylar. "First Phylum, Crown of the Snow Leopard . . . knowledge of these things has been lost to time."

"The First Phylum are the seven tribes that ruled over Vastia," said Agorus with an exasperated sigh. Suddenly, his faint glow began to disappear. "The strongest and most powerful wizards of the . . ."

"Wait, don't go," pleaded Skylar.

But it was too late. The mist pulled Agorus away. His voice trailed off as his form dissipated into the Tomorrowlife once more.

"I'm afraid your components were too weak to hold the spell," said Feynam.

Aldwyn thought there was no need for the elder to rub it in: he could see that Skylar was disappointed in herself by the way her wings slouched and her beak hung down.

"But it was enough time to get a clue," said Queen Loranella. "The Crown of the Snow Leopard," she repeated aloud. "If we find this magical item, perhaps the tide can still be turned."

"In all my years of study, I have never heard of such a crown," said Sorceress Edna. "And my memory is like that of an elephant. Nothing escapes it."

Though Skylar had succeeded in contacting

45

Agorus, they were left with new mysteries: what was the Crown of the Snow Leopard? Where would they be able to find it? What did it have to do with the Shifting Fortress? And what was the First Phylum? Aldwyn knew he wasn't going to be of much assistance in answering these questions, seeing how his knowledge of all things magical was still in its infancy.

"Hmm-hm hm hm-hmm hm hm . . ." someone began to hum.

Everyone turned to see who the off-key tune was coming from: it was Gilbert.

"Sorry," said the tree frog when he felt everybody's eyes resting on him. "I don't do well with uncomfortable silences."

"We'll have to search through the dustiest of tomes to have any chance of learning about the Crown and its whereabouts," said Queen Loranella. "I suggest we start at the Vastian Historical Archives."

Skylar was still collecting her components, and Aldwyn couldn't help but notice that she looked rather drained, almost as if her blue sheen had lost a little of its luster. As she took to the air, a pair of her tail feathers dropped to the ground. Feynam walked up alongside her, and Aldwyn overheard him whisper: "Remember what I said, little bird. There will be consequences."

3

WIZARD ALMANACS AND WHISPER SHELLS

The wizards' and familiars' arrival at the Historical Archives, just outside Bronzhaven, marked a reunion with an old friend: Scribius. The enchanted quill pen, which had helped guide the familiars on their quest to the Sunken Palace, had spent the last month happily transcribing the details of their adventure on the Vastian time line. Upon seeing its former companions, the metal and feather writing tool glided across the long wooden tabletop where it'd been working and executed an elegant curlicue before them.

"Scribius!" exclaimed Gilbert. "So this is where you've been keeping busy. Pretty fancy for a pen from the Runlet."

Indeed it was. The Historical Archives was more than just the grandest library in all of Vastia; it was a two-story museum of the queendom's past—the most recent past, anyway. Hanging against the red velvet wallpaper were large tapestries of old kings and early maps of the countryside. Pear-shaped globes sat on pedestals around the room, and they would have been spinning had it not been for Paksahara's disenchantment spell. Open cabinets were stuffed with history scrolls. And there was no lack of books—shelves of them on the walls, piles stacked fifty high on the floor, and tables with tomes too heavy to lift. Only a handful of dedicated scholars were studying the folios during this time of crisis, so the team of magical animals and their loyals nearly had the run of the place. One or two of the civilians recognized the queen and bowed before her, but there was little time for formalities.

"Let's all split up," said Queen Loranella. "There's an awful lot of ground to cover if we hope to find some mention of this Crown of the Snow Leopard. Feynam, peruse the *Encyclopedia of Artifacts*. Edna, you and I shall check all the diaries of kings and queens of yore. Children, see if there's anything in the old Wizard Almanacs. Start with the earliest editions."

Everyone dispersed. Feynam headed for the second floor with Ramoth, his firescale snake, slithering behind him. Loranella walked to a far wall of sheepskin journals and started reaching for the ones at the very top. Sorceress Edna, much shorter than the queen, began at the bottom. Stolix remained coiled around her neck, fast asleep. Marianne approached the meek librarian who was sitting behind the front desk.

"Excuse me," she asked. "Could you point us to your Wizard Almanacs?"

The young woman looked up from the Archives' book roster, which she was busily updating. "Most of them are in the Reference section. I'd start there." The librarian was about to return to her administrative task but became sidetracked by a slither of bookworms crawling in through an open window. "Pesky little creepers," she muttered as she grabbed a broomstick to sweep the purple parasitic worms back outside.

Marianne, Gilbert, Dalton, and Skylar made their way through the stacks. Jack and Aldwyn followed behind. Jack slowed as he passed by a counter cluttered with conch and snail shells.

"Did you hear that?" Jack asked his familiar.

Aldwyn listened. Sure enough, he could hear faint voices coming from nearby. He approached the shelf with the shells resting atop it and the quiet murmurs got louder. Jack came up beside Aldwyn and lifted one to his ear.

"They're whisper shells," explained Jack. "I've heard about these. They preserve voices spoken from long ago. Put your ear up to one."

Aldwyn jumped up on the counter and leaned his left ear—the one with the bite taken out of it—up to a rose-colored spiral shell. Immediately, he could hear the sound of a voice speaking: "This is Derkis Toliver, local fisherman, speaking to you three years into the reign of the seventh king. I stand here at the port of Split River, watching the first spice vessel sail in, and I wonder if this will be a renowned harbor in the years to . . ."

Aldwyn pulled his ear away. Not the most riveting recollection, but just the fact that the words were spoken centuries ago made the otherwise mundane message become vivid and real.

"Maybe one of these shells will mention the Crown of the Snow Leopard," said Aldwyn.

Jack didn't even respond, as his attention was drawn to a shelf labeled *Tales of the Beyonders*. He quickly began lifting snail shells to his ears. "What if my mom's or dad's voice has been captured in one of these?" the boy wizard asked.

Jack had told Aldwyn how he and Marianne's parents were Beyonders, lost at sea while on a secret mission ordered by Queen Loranella. The boy wished to become an explorer of distant lands, too, one day, in the hopes of finding his mom and dad, who were perhaps waiting to be rescued on some deserted island. This desire to reunite with the family he never knew was one that Aldwyn could relate to, having only the foggy memories of his own parents that had come to him in dreams. He often wondered why his parents had abandoned him, sending him away from his home.

"No," Jack kept saying, as he listened to each shell

for a brief moment before trading it in for the next. "No, no, no." He moved through them quickly, then put the last one down with a defeated look on his face. "I knew it was a slender chance anyway."

"Don't be discouraged," said Aldwyn, trying to comfort his loyal. "I know how you feel." He nuzzled his head up against Jack's hand.

"I wish I could hear their voices, just once," said the boy, the words heavy with melancholy.

Dalton and Marianne walked up with arm-loads of books and scrolls, interrupting the shared moment between loyal and familiar.

"Hey, Jack, we're going to need your help getting through all of this," said Dalton, who dumped the selected materials onto one of the mahogany reading tables with a thud.

What chance did they really have of coming across some mention of this mysterious Crown? Just scanning this first pile alone could take a whole day. To Aldwyn, it seemed like trying to find a single flea on the back of a gundabeast.

Aldwyn had lost track of the time, but he could tell by the lack of light coming in through the windows that night was approaching. The only sound that he had heard in the past few hours was that of pages flipping and the occasional snore from Stolix, who seemed to steal naps even more frequently than Gilbert. Nobody had found any leads in their search so far, but everybody was determined to work through the night until they did. Without the convenience of Protho's Lights to illuminate the Archives after dark, the librarian had gone out to purchase candles, a magicless alternative that could still be lit despite the dispeller curse. No other visitors remained inside the crimson-colored walls.

"Hm hm hm hm hm hm," hummed Gilbert.

"Would you give it a rest already?" snapped Skylar.

"I didn't even realize I was doing it that time," said the tree frog.

Skylar returned to her reading, but the silence only lasted a moment.

"Hm hm hm hmm-hm hm." Gilbert had started in again.

"Gilbert!" snapped Skylar.

"I'm sorry. This stupid tune is stuck in my

head and I just can't get it out."

Sorceress Edna set down her magnifying glass and rubbed her eyes wearily. Feynam poured himself a tall glass of water from a pitcher on the table.

"Brannfalk's Crown, the Golden Crown of the Clouds, the Twin Crowns of Yajmada," said the Elder. "But nothing at all about a Crown of the Snow Leopard."

"Don't lose faith," said Queen Loranella. "An old friend of mine used to say, 'You always find what you've been searching for in the last place you look.'"

Aldwyn could tell by the smiles on the children's faces that they had heard this from the same source she had: Kalstaff.

The front door of the Archives opened, and the librarian entered. Curiously, she was empty-handed.

"You forgot the candles," said Jack. "How are we going to be able to see?"

"Yes," replied the librarian, somewhat sheepishly, "they're in rather high demand right now. The shops were all out. I'm so sorry, Your Majesty."

"No need to apologize," said the queen. "We'll work by moonlight if necessary."

The librarian walked back to her seat behind the front desk, stepping right past a trio of the slimy bookworms that had found their way back inside during her absence. Aldwyn found it curious that now she ignored them, seeing how quick she had been to retrieve her broom before. Perhaps the exhausting day of research had taken its toll on her, as well.

"You said most of the Almanacs were in the Reference section," Marianne called to the librarian. "Where are the rest?"

"Let me check the catalogs," she replied. Aldwyn was certain she was fatigued now, as this was the first time all day she hadn't had a ready response to one of their queries.

"I think I found something," said Dalton, sounding rather unsure about it.

"You did?" asked Jack.

"Yeah, right here, in the *Wizard's Almanac of Fables*," said Dalton, his excitement growing. "It's written in Elvish, but I think I can translate it."

"Move over, move over," said Sorceress Edna.

"I'm fluent in all dialects of the Wood People." She nudged him aside with her large rear-end so that she was sitting in front of the book and put her magnifying glass up to the page. "Ah, yes. The boy is right. *Cheluji tui kiraumo*. Snow leopard's crown." She continued to scan the page, deciphering bits and pieces. "The story tells of a young elvin warrior who went searching for this mythical treasure. Lots of details about the rituals he performed before leaving, and the possessions he brought with him."

Everybody was huddled around Edna now, hanging on the Sorceress's every word.

"Any clue as to what the Crown is or where it is hidden?" asked Marianne.

"Patience, young lady," answered Edna, who moved the reading lens slowly across every word. "*Tanah nok tahni*. He carried with him a crocodile-tooth dagger, and wore *mufahji* around his neck. Rain charms." She flipped to the next page.

That's when Aldwyn's attention was drawn to the librarian again. She was on her knees, muttering aloud before the three thumb-long bookworms.

"Uh, Jack." He nudged his loyal.

"Not now, Aldwyn," the boy replied without even giving him a look.

Aldwyn found the librarian's actions quite peculiar. Had she lost her mind? Was she trying to reason with the worms? Whatever it was, it wasn't normal. Maybe she—

Were the worms getting bigger?

Oh, yes, they most certainly were. They were now as thick as watermelons, and as long as pythons.

"Jack!" Aldwyn shouted, clawing at the boy's sleeve.

"Ow," cried Jack. "What did you do that—"

Then Jack saw it, too. In the short seconds it took to get the young wizard's attention, the slither of bookworms had expanded to the size of wine barrels. The librarian remained on the floor, reciting what sounded a lot like a magic spell.

"Guys," Jack called to the others, "you better look at this!"

Everyone turned around.

The once tiny and harmless-looking bookworms were now eight feet tall, their mouths surrounding a circle of teeth. The librarian stood beside the salivating creatures, her meek, shoulder-slouching demeanor gone, replaced with a scary confidence.

"What have you done?" asked Queen Loranella.

"The better question is *how?*" said Feynam. "How is a human still capable of casting magic?"

"They're not," answered the librarian.

Her body began to twist and contort; her ears started to grow and her nose shrank. Gray hairs sprouted from her flesh. Her brown eyes turned bright pink. She was shape-shifting. And when the transformation was complete, Paksahara was standing before them.

"Normally, bookworms only have a taste for parchment," she said. "But I think in this case they'll make an exception."

The three towering slitherers advanced on the wizards young and old and their familiars. The quickest of the worms charged at them with its mouth wide open, smashing aside chairs and scroll cabinets along the way. The group fled from the long wooden table where they had been sitting, hurrying to take cover behind the stacks.

"The book!" cried Marianne.

But before any of them could go back for it, the charging demon worm halved the table, sending the *Wizard's Almanac of Fables* flying, the pitcher of water rolling to the ground, and Edna's magnifying glass shattering on the floor.

"Last chance to surrender," Paksahara called out. "Join me, familiars!"

Despite these most dire of circumstances, Aldwyn would never accept her treasonous offer to betray Jack, and he knew that Skylar and Gilbert would never leave the side of their loyals, either. He focused on the fallen book and telekinetically lifted it into Dalton's hands.

"Quickly, this way," said Feynam to the others. "There's an exit in back."

The elder led them, running down the narrow aisle. He was the first to emerge out the other side, and he never saw it coming. One of the bookworms opened its giant mouth and swallowed him whole. It happened so suddenly that it almost didn't seem real. Everyone was left in stunned silence, except for Stolix, who had somehow remained asleep through everything thus far.

"Any of you want to reconsider?" Paksahara

asked the familiars with a sneer.

Ramoth looked to Loranella. "My loyalty had been teetering before," he said, showing his true colors. "Besides, I never like ending up on the losing side of a battle." The firescale snake darted out from the stacks and took his place alongside Paksahara.

"Children, run for the front door," instructed Queen Loranella. "Edna and I will distract the worms."

The wizards in training and their familiars sprinted for the entrance as the gigantic and clearly very hungry bookworms were bearing down on them. Queen Loranella and Sorceress Edna hurried in the opposite direction, throwing books at the purple beasts to bait them away from the children.

Skylar spread her wings and made a bookshelf stuffed with dusty tomes appear between them and the worms. Aldwyn hoped the illusion would fool the tiny minds of the oversize grubs, or at least buy them a little time.

Dalton flipped open the *Wizard's Almanac of Fables* as he fled, picking up where Edna had left off, searching the text as fast as he could.

"Dalton, what are you doing?" asked Skylar. "You can read the book later!"

"Not if I don't make it out of here alive," he replied.

Just then, a blast of electricity shot over his head, straight through Skylar's illusion. Apparently, Paksahara had grown impatient with waiting for the worms to finish off her opponents. They took cover behind a bookshelf. "*Niti wengi,*" Dalton read aloud from the Elvish fable. "A great big tree."

Aldwyn concentrated on a pear-shaped globe on one of the pedestals and flung it across the room, using only his mind. For a second he was quite pleased with his effort, but then Paksahara effortlessly shot it down. She didn't see the second globe coming from behind her, though, and it momentarily knocked her off her feet.

Aldwyn was starting to feel victorious when a sweat-inducing heat boiled up behind him. He turned to find Ramoth, scales aflame, ready to strike with his searing fangs.

"Traitor," shouted Aldwyn.

"I am a snake after all," replied Ramoth. He was about to strike, but his attack was thwarted when a splash of water doused the fire burning on his skin.

Jack stood with an empty pitcher in hand, the one that had fallen from the reading table but fortunately had not spilled all of its contents. Though stripped of his newly blossoming spell-casting abilities, Jack remained cocky in the face of the danger. He gave Ramoth a swift kick that sent him sailing across the room into a pile of scrolls. Aldwyn and his loyal shared a nod. No words were necessary to communicate their bond.

Dalton was still struggling with the foreign text: "The warrior traveled to some kind of tree, one whose branches . . ." he translated as the battle continued. "I'm not sure what these next words mean."

And he wasn't going to have time to figure it out. One of the giant paper-eating grubs shoved its head through the bookshelf and snapped the tome straight out of Dalton's hand. Even worse, its teeth caught one of his fingers as well, biting it clean off.

Dalton cried out with pain and stumbled away from his attacker. He shoved his injured hand to his chest and tried to stave off the bleeding with his tunic.

The loyals and their familiars tried to make a run for it once more, racing past the aisle of whisper shells as the creature chewed the invaluable book to shreds.

Paksahara was back on her feet, and she seemed quite entertained as she watched one of the other bookworms reach out to swallow Skylar.

"They say the early bird catches the worm," the hare said, delighted. "This time, it's the other way around!"

The bookworm was just about to bite down on the blue jay when a splintered stick pierced its throat. Queen Loranella had torn off the bristles and used the sharp end of a broomstick as a spear. She gave the handle a twist, and the beast's head collapsed limply.

Paksahara flew into a rage. She conjured two massive energy blasts in her palms, then shouted at her opponents: "This was fun. Now prepare to become food for the worms!"

"Food?!" a groggy voice called out. "Is it breakfast already?"

Aldwyn spun around to see that Stolix had finally awakened.

"Quick," said Edna to her familiar. "Immobilize her!"

Stolix breathed out her paralyzing mist, sending the cool vapors right into Paksahara's nostrils. The hare's muscles immediately tightened, and she was rendered motionless, a frozen look of anger on her face.

The two remaining giant purple worms encircled Paksahara protectively, preventing the wizards and familiars from attacking the defenseless hare.

"Let's get out of here," said the queen. "That spell doesn't last long."

Dalton grabbed Scribius off the floor, and then he and the others were running for the door without looking back. If the Archives held any other clues as to the whereabouts of the Crown of the Snow Leopard, they would soon be lost to the digestive juices of the bookworms.

4

FAREWELL TO FRIENDS

Dalton lay on a slender bed in the Royal Cleric's chamber as the palace healer's black raven ran a wing along his arm. During the whole trip back to the New Palace he had clenched his jaw, never once letting on how excruciating the pain must have been. Now Aldwyn watched as the bird's healing feathers worked their magic. The stump where Dalton's pinky finger once was began to pus and ooze as flesh and bone sprang forth, like a newly forming twig on a sapling. Within seconds, it had regenerated itself and looked as good as new.

Across the room, Marianne sat before a fireplace where wood crackled warmly in the hearth, having been lit by flint and stone rather than a magic spell. She traced her finger along a wrinkled parchment map, while Jack spun a globe in one and then the other direction.

"A great big tree," Marianne repeated. "That only narrows it down to, oh, every forest in Vastia."

"Could be in the mountains, too," added Jack.

Sorceress Edna let out a sigh of frustration as she paced behind them. "This is bad, very bad. Even worse than before, I'm afraid."

Aldwyn leaped onto the windowsill and looked outside. Night had fallen, and the moon was beginning to rise up over the Yennep Mountains. It was three quarters full, just seven days away from reaching the end of its lunar phase, when Paksahara's grim promise would be fulfilled and a new Dead Army would rise. In the court-yard below, Aldwyn could see Queen Loranella standing with a band of cloaked warriors, some the queen's finest soldiers, others disenchanted wizards—all beside their steeds. Many were accompanied by their familiars. Among them stood Urbaugh, the bearded spellcaster from the council meeting, and his brother. There had been rumors of suspicious activity on the northwestern border of Vastia, and while it was little to go on, in the face of such a grave threat, even the smallest lead was worth pursuing. The Queen touched each of the warriors' shoulders as they bowed before her, then they took to their steeds and rode off.

"Hmm-hm hm hm-hmm hm hm . . ."

Aldwyn spun around to see that the humming was coming from Gilbert yet again, the same melody that had been stuck in the tree frog's head since their encounter with Agorus.

"Gilbert," snapped Aldwyn, exasperated. "What's with the humming?"

"No, wait," said Skylar, suddenly taking great interest in Gilbert's out-of-tune music making. "Keep going."

"Hm hm hm hmm-hm hm?" continued Gilbert.

Skylar joined in, chirping along in harmony, "Hmm-hm hm hm-hmm hm hm. I know this song. It's a lullaby. They used to sing it to us at

Nearhurst Aviary." She searched her memory, then began singing, *"Hiding high upon its head, Draped in white shimmering gown, Lie the keys to the past, In the snow leopard's crown.* Gilbert, you've been trying to give us clues all this time!"

"I have?" asked the tree frog. "I mean, *I have!*"

"There's more to it, though," said Skylar. "That's just the end. How does it start again?"

Gilbert hummed to himself for a moment.

"That's easy," he said. *"When night falls hear the dog's bark, Howling to the tallest clouds. Secrets of yore buried, Beneath green needle shrouds."*

"Go on," said Skylar.

"That's all I remember. I always fell asleep right about then."

Some long-forgotten memory was bubbling up in Aldwyn, too, and when he opened his mouth, the words just tumbled out.

> *"When night falls hear the dog's bark,*
> *Howling to the tallest clouds.*
> *Secrets of yore buried,*
> *Beneath green needle shrouds.*

"Between the root of all roots,
Where every fear sinks away,
Are stairs with no bottom,
Unless eyes find sun's ray.

"Through brown mist stone arrows point,
To where the ladybugs rest.
A supper to be placed,
In the great spider's nest.

"Now comes a black crescent sword,
Cutting through the emerald night.
At last the waking moth,
Flies to the rising light.

"Hiding high upon its head,
Draped in white shimmering gown,
Lie the keys to the past,
In the snow leopard's crown."

Skylar and Gilbert both stared at him.

"I don't know where that came from," said Aldwyn, who was just as surprised as they were.

"Someone must have sung it to you, too," said Gilbert.

"But who?" asked Aldwyn. "I don't remember at all."

No one on the rooftops of Bridgetower had ever showed him any kind of tenderness, let alone soothed him to sleep with a lullaby. This memory must have been from before. From Maidenmere. Had he heard it from his mother or father?

"It's not just a nursery rhyme," said Skylar. "I think it's a puzzle, or rather a series of clues. Perhaps if we can decipher them, it will lead us to the Crown of the Snow Leopard."

Scribius had transcribed every word that Aldwyn had said so that the entire nursery rhyme was now written down neatly on a piece of parchment. Marianne, Dalton, and Sorceress Edna gathered around to study it.

"Black crescent swords," scoffed Sorceress Edna. "Dogs barking to the clouds! I think we'd be better off sticking to this great big tree that the *Wizard's Almanac of Fables* mentioned."

"Hold on," said Dalton. "What if Skylar's right?

Maybe this nursery rhyme does contain clues. It's possible the book and the lullaby are talking about the same thing."

"Yes," added Marianne. "We're looking for a great big tree, aren't we?" Then, turning to the parchment: "And the nursery rhyme talks about green needle shrouds. That sounds like a pine forest to me. What if this tree is in a pine forest?"

"And the only pine forests in Vastia," chimed in Skylar, "are the Yennep Wilds and the Hinterwoods."

"Unfortunately neither are inhabited by dogs," said Dalton.

"True," said Skylar. "But the Hinterwoods have *dog*wood trees!"

"What did she say?" Marianne asked Dalton.

"The Hinterwoods, they have dogwood trees," he repeated.

"And there's one whose bark stretches as high as the clouds," said Marianne. "The mighty dogwood at the center of the Hinterwoods."

The familiars and their loyals looked at each other, a sense of excitement brewing. Aldwyn

73

even felt his whiskers beginning to tingle, the way they always did when a new adventure was about to begin.

"You're getting ahead of yourselves, children," said Sorceress Edna, still skeptical. "This is all just speculation."

Suddenly, the door opened and Queen Loranella entered.

"Your Majesty, we believe we've figured out where the tree is," said Jack excitedly.

"Jack!" scolded Sorceress Edna. "What did I say?"

"Our familiars have recalled a nursery rhyme that was told to them," said Jack. "One that speaks of the Crown of the Snow Leopard."

"The first clue leads to the Hinterwoods," added Marianne.

"Then our search should begin at once," said the queen.

⁓⦿⁓

"But it's not fair!" cried Jack. "We didn't ask to lose our magic."

"I know, Jack," said the queen. "But I'm afraid this journey is for three, and three alone. The time of the prophecy has arrived."

The familiars and their loyals were standing in the grand hall of the New Palace. An early morning breeze was blowing in through the wide-open archway where the stained-glass window had once shimmered majestically before Paksahara destroyed it.

"Even without our spellcasting, I'm sure we could be of some assistance," pleaded Jack. "We could gather ingredients, carry extra supplies, stand watch at night."

"I'm afraid your presence would only be a bigger burden to the familiars," said Queen Loranella. "They will have enough to worry about without having to protect you. Besides, there is important work to be done here in Bronzhaven. Not glorious work, but crucial to the safety and well-being of all citizens. We're going to need to fortify the outer wall and build weaponry. Without magic to fight off Paksahara, we'll have to rely on sword and shield."

This was no consolation to Jack, who crossed his arms in a huff. Dalton was packing Skylar's satchel with powders and dried herbs, the finest components taken from the queen's own apothecary. Gilbert sat on the council table as Marianne filled his flower bud backpack and strapped a sharpened bamboo stick onto the tree frog's back.

"It keeps slipping," said Gilbert.

The tiny spear had fallen around his ankles. Marianne made some adjustments to the grass band and tried again.

"Maybe I shouldn't even bring it," said Gilbert. "My mother always discouraged me from carrying sharp objects. She said it was for my own safety."

Jack, still crestfallen that he wouldn't be able to join Aldwyn on his adventure, walked over to his

familiar. "Here, take this," he said as he held out his pouch. "It served you well on your last adventure."

Aldwyn looked at his loyal's leather bag and thought back on all that it had been through. There were singe marks from the fire in Kalstaff's cottage and remnants of yellow sleeping powder still staining its outside. He telekinetically lifted the bag out of Jack's hand and slipped his head through the pull strings. It had helped Aldwyn survive his first journey across Vastia, and even though Jack would be unable to join him on this next quest, it would be a constant reminder of his loyal's love.

"Children, you'll stay here at the palace," said Loranella. "Until this wretched curse is lifted, we'll stick close together."

The reality that the familiars and their loyals would be separated again was quickly sinking in. With the animals' preparations complete, all that was left now was to say farewell. Skylar flew atop Dalton's shoulder, and the two exchanged a few quiet words out of Aldwyn's earshot. It was clear there was tenderness between them, even though they never let their emotions bubble up and always kept their reserved demeanors. The same could not be said for Gilbert, who let his love for Marianne erupt like a volcano.

"I don't want to go without you!" he blubbered, wrapping his arms and legs around her ankle. "What if something happens to you? What if something happens to me?!"

"I believe in you, Gilbert," said Marianne in the gentle, calming voice she used whenever Gilbert was struck with a panic attack. "We'll be back together before you know it."

She peeled his orange fingertips one by one from her calf, and set him down on the ground.

Jack crouched down before Aldwyn, green eyes meeting green eyes. "Wherever you go, whether in Vastia or Beyond, I'll be with you." Aldwyn nuzzled his head up against the boy's hand and his tail curled happily. "And if you see Paksahara," added Jack, "punch her in the nose for me."

"It is time, familiars," interrupted Queen Loranella. "If you leave now, you should reach the Hinterwoods by late afternoon. I've drawn up an order, marked with the palace seal, stating that you are on a mission from the queen. Every man, woman, and child will respect its authority." She handed Skylar the folded parchment with the wax signet imprinted on the crease. "Now, you're just forgetting one thing." She turned to the doorway and called out, "Scribius!"

The enchanted quill shuffled its way into the grand hall, proud to be called to duty.

"I trust you know the way to the Hinterwoods," said the queen.

Scribius was already drawing a map on a piece of parchment.

"Does anyone else find it curious that every magic item in the land has ceased to function, yet Scribius continues to write?" asked Edna.

"Perhaps the spell that enchants him predates human magic," speculated Dalton.

"He was an heirloom in Kalstaff's family from centuries ago," said Loranella. "His origin is a mystery."

With a final stroke of his quill, Scribius completed the route to the dogwood tree, a full day's trip through the western Bronzhaven Plains to the Ebs, and then across its waters to the northern tip of the Hinterwoods.

Skylar placed map and pen in her satchel. Gilbert and Aldwyn stood on either side of her. Queen Loranella faced them.

"Find the Crown and bring it back to the palace," she said. "We'll assemble an army, and when the Fortress is summoned, animals and humans together will reclaim it."

The trio nodded.

"Familiars, for hundreds of years the safety of Vastia has rested on the shoulders of wizards," continued the queen. "Now its future rests on yours."

5

INTO THE HINTERWOODS

Aldwyn, Skylar, and Gilbert stood before the grand bronze portcullis for which Bronzhaven had been named. It took the strength of twelve horses to lift the heavy gate into the air, now that the queen's feather spells could no longer lighten the load. As the familiars passed beneath its shining bars, Aldwyn looked back to see Jack waving from the royal cleric's room. It was too far to shout, so Aldwyn lifted a paw instead, and loyal and familiar shared one last unspoken good-bye. With the gleaming parapets of the palace behind them, the trio headed down Bronzhaven's main artery, a thoroughfare paved with gold and silver taken from the Lilic Mines at the base of Kailasa. Unlike Aldwyn's former stomping grounds of Bridgetower, with its gritty back alleys and underground sewer markets, Vastia's capital city was befitting a queen, perfectly groomed and immaculate in every way. As a result of the council's recommendation to stay indoors, few citizens remained on the streets, but those who did stepped out of the familiars' way. Aldwyn assumed it was because they recognized him and his fellow companions as the prophesized ones.

"I'm still not used to this," said Gilbert. "When I see strangers staring at me like that, I always think I have food stuck in my teeth."

"Once word got out that a cat, bird, and frog were going to be the saviors of Vastia, what did you expect?" asked Aldwyn.

"I don't know," replied Gilbert. "Maybe a story written about us in the historical scrolls."

"Those aren't looks of reverence," said Skylar. "They're nervous that we're not capable of meeting such an insurmountable challenge."

Aldwyn glanced back at the people and immediately realized that her observation was on point. The citizens were watching them doubtfully, and Aldwyn, trying to see it through their eyes, could imagine feeling the same way. If he had been told that three animals an eighth of his size were all that stood between him and certain death, he wouldn't believe it, either.

Once they had reached the edge of the city, where the gold- and silver-flecked street became dirt, they turned west and headed down the fence-lined road that would lead them through the outer villages of the western plains. It was fast going, save for Gilbert, who Aldwyn noticed was hopping about rather strangely.

"Why the waddle in your step?" asked Aldwyn.

Gilbert hemmed and hawed a little. "This is how I always walk."

Aldwyn looked at the tree frog skeptically. They had traveled many miles together, and this was definitely a new gait for him.

"Okay, the truth is I've been practicing some of the spells in Marianne's pocket scrolls," said

Gilbert. "And it turns out I don't have much of a knack for this whole magic thing."

"What does that have to do with your funny walk?" asked Aldwyn.

"Have either of you counted the toes on my right foot lately?"

Aldwyn and Skylar glanced down at Gilbert's webbed foot. And sure enough, where there should have been four toes, there were seven!

"Gilbert," exclaimed Skylar, "how did you do that?"

"I tried to conjure a trio of enchanted bows. Apparently my b's sound more like t's when I'm chanting. I'm just lucky I didn't try to transform myself into a bird."

His two companions tried to keep from laughing.

"Did I ever tell you about the first time I tried to conjure a flame fairy?" asked Skylar. "It didn't go according to plan, either. Her hue was more yellow than orange."

"And then what happened?" said Gilbert.

"That's it. They're supposed to be orange. It was very embarrassing."

Gilbert shook his head. "Remind me not to have you cheer me up in the future."

"I haven't exactly mastered my telekinesis yet, either," said Aldwyn.

"Well I, for one, feel far more prepared this time," said Skylar. "This month of study and training has sharpened my spellcasting abilities considerably." Then, noticing her companion's looks, she added: "You're right. I'm not so good at the whole cheering-up thing, am I?"

For most of the morning, the three animals continued through the Bronzhaven Plains. Being fall, the weather was brisk, even more so given the disappearance of the queen's weather-binding spells. The outer villages were surrounded by squares of tall wheat, and if Aldwyn hadn't seen the portcullis at the palace's entrance, he might have thought the name Bronzhaven came from the brownish-gold color of the high stalks.

By the time high sun had arrived, the familiars were rounding a bend where they were treated to a kaleidoscopic rainbow of colors. There before them, to the right and left, was a patchwork of vibrant flowers—shimmering reds, electric blues, and tiny golden bulbs that sparkled as bright as any coin.

"A Xylem garden," explained Skylar, never one to miss an opportunity to show off her abundant knowledge of all things. "Every flower, herb, or spice a wizard would ever need is grown in these hills. Kalstaff often said if he hadn't become a teacher he would have tended one of these component nurseries."

Aldwyn, even though he hadn't been a familiar for long, could already recognize a few of the more popular varietals. There were orange mint leaves, cumin, and patches of gray rigor weed alongside pink-petaled flowers that looked like butterflies and bushes with white berries that jangled like bells in the breeze.

As they walked through the garden, the animals were careful not to step on any of the blossoming buds. But Aldwyn found himself undeniably drawn to a leafy green herb. Hypnotized by it, he stepped over some tendrils lying on the ground and reached out his paw. "Aldwyn!" called Skylar. "Don't touch that."

He was just about to grab the herb when he

felt something brushing up against his ankle. He looked down and saw that constrictor vines were twisting around his ankles. He backed away from the plant and the vines recoiled.

"I don't know what happened," said Aldwyn, hurrying away.

"Catnip," replied Skylar. "It's irresistible to you felines, but one should never steal it from a Xylem garden. Or anything else for that matter."

"Wish you had mentioned that before," said Gilbert, sounding strangely constricted.

Aldwyn and Skylar spun around to see the tree frog held tight in the grip of more constrictor vines. His webbed hands were covered in purple, and he had berry juice on his mouth and chin.

The vines began pulling Gilbert toward the undergrowth. Aldwyn's attention homed in on a rusty rake lying in a dirt patch of the garden. He lifted it telekinetically, swinging it through the air and causing its five metal pricks to impale the green tendrils. They let Gilbert go, and the tree frog made a giant leap and landed between Aldwyn and Skylar.

"Can we at least try to make it to the Ebs before

getting killed?" asked Skylar wryly.

The trio continued on. With the capital city far behind them, the roads became eerily calm. It seemed as if few humans were willing to risk all but the most necessary journeys during such uncertain times, preferring to lock their doors and keep their windows shuttered. Aldwyn couldn't help but wonder how useful that tactic would be if Paksahara decided to come knocking.

Aldwyn and Skylar had set a swift pace, but having seven toes on one foot didn't help Gilbert keep up. He complained incessantly about tiny pebbles getting stuck between his extra digits. It wasn't until Aldwyn suggested the tree frog hitch a ride on his back that they began to make up for lost time. Aldwyn didn't mind the additional weight; hearing Gilbert's haikus about lily pads and lost loves recited directly into his ear was a different story.

Later, with the afternoon sun no longer hanging as high in the sky, the Ebs appeared before the familiars, a thick wide swath of bluish green water that cut the land in two. Beyond it, Aldwyn could see the tall trees of the Hinterwoods, and towering over them the snow-peaked Kailasa mountains. The smell of the great river—a mix of fish and damp earth—reminded Aldwyn of his days spent in Bridgetower, whose western wall hugged the Ebs itself.

As they got closer, they could see that the river was littered with debris—capsized boats torn to shreds and wooden planks with giant bite marks in them. The familiars had ferried across this river once before, only this time on their crossing, it looked like the mighty Ebs would be inhabited by much more treacherous scaled creatures than river flounder.

The road that the familiars had been following led them to a small dock, or what little was left of it, where a half dozen floating rafts were tethered. A soldier armed with bow and arrow was ushering travelers aboard one of them, while a second ferry—empty save for a single oarsman—was preparing for departure as well. The animal trio was stopped at the foot of the dock by a second soldier, this one holding a sword.

Skylar reached her beak into her satchel and pulled out Queen Loranella's letter. She held it out for the soldier, who unfolded the parchment. It took him but a moment to read it.

"My apologies, noble familiars," he said and bowed deeply.

He returned the queen's letter and stepped aside, allowing Aldwyn, Skylar, and Gilbert to pass.

"Now this I could get used to," said Gilbert.

They hurried toward the passengerless raft, but before they got there, the sword-wielding soldier called out, "I wouldn't recommend taking that vessel if I were you. I'd stick to the other one."

Aldwyn wasn't sure why they were sending out a ferry with just a helmsman, but he and his companions would heed the soldier's warning. They headed for the crowded platform.

"I don't feel so good," said Gilbert as they were waiting in line to step onto the raft.

"Gilbert, we're not even on the ferry yet," said Skylar.

"It's the anticipation."

"You got any better ideas?" asked Aldwyn.

"How long would it take to get to the bridge in Split River?" responded Gilbert.

"Three days," said Skylar. "And three days to get back here. By that estimation, we'd have just a few hours left to find the Crown and defeat Paksahara."

"So I'm guessing that's out of the question," replied the tree frog queasily.

The single-manned raft left first, heading toward the other side, where the Hinterwoods rose up behind the riverbank. Aldwyn watched curiously as the vessel gathered speed. Then he noticed a massive bed of floating seaweed approaching the raft.

"Now!" hollered the armed soldier to the oarsman of the ferry still waiting at the docks. "Go! Go!"

Lurching forward, they began their trip across the Ebs. Aldwyn's eyes returned to the moving algae following the other raft. With sudden and alarming speed, the mass of floating vegetation lifted out of the water, and Aldwyn saw what it was clinging to: the dripping-wet head of a river dragon!

Nobody needed to tell the oarsman of their own vessel to paddle faster. He was already rowing furiously, as if their lives depended on it. Which, thought Aldwyn, they probably did.

The purpose of the other, empty, raft was now clear: it was a decoy. As the river dragon rose up in the air, Aldwyn got a good look at the beast's fish scales and gills, and the barnacles stuck to the underside of its neck. The dragon bared its teeth, but just before its ten rows of sharp incisors bit down on the wood planks, the helmsman took a flying leap off the empty raft, which splintered instantly and disappeared below the water. The helmsman came up for air thirty feet away and began swimming frantically toward the shoreline. By the time the river dragon realized there was no flesh to pepper the bland taste of varnished pine, the ferry the familiars were atop was already two-thirds of the way across and the helmsman had made it safely to the other side.

The vessel docked soon after, leaving the river dragon to trawl the deeper waters. Once they were safely on dry land again and Gilbert's face had more or less returned to its usual color, Skylar pulled out Scribius's map and oriented herself.

"We continue southwest from here, deep into

the heart of the Hinterwoods," she said. "If this dogwood we're looking for truly reaches to the clouds, it will be impossible to miss."

Skylar flapped toward the center of the forest, with Aldwyn and Gilbert trying to keep up with her. A cool, dry, pine-scented air filled Aldwyn's nostrils, and in that calming moment he thought back on how quickly and completely his life had changed since that day in the curious pet shop in Bridgetower. As they traveled through the woods, speeding as fast as they could toward their uncertain destination, all the trees started to look the same. It had already been a long day, and legs and wings were growing tired. But the trio was keen to get there before they lost the day's sunlight.

Sunset was near when, through the mass of brown and green, Aldwyn could make out a towering trunk of white that stretched vertically into the air. He didn't need to be told that this was the mighty dogwood tree.

The three animals came to a stop all at the same time. It was impossible not to be in awe of this massive, thousand-year-old natural wonder, with its pearly base as wide as ten cave trolls

standing in a circle. Every other tree in its presence looked like a mere blade of grass in comparison. Its branches were filled with leaves that had seen many seasons and with birds' nests that were long abandoned but that had withstood the trials of time in the tree's protective boughs.

"According to legend, the old tree's bark turned white a long time ago," said Skylar. "Just like Kalstaff's mustache. Nobody knows how long this dogwood has stood here, but it's said to be older than the queendom itself."

The familiars followed the tree's long, winding roots to its base, careful to avoid a bubbling and smelly sinkhole of mud in their path.

"So, either of you see the Crown?" asked Gilbert. Both Skylar and Aldwyn gave him a look. "Okay, I admit it—that was wishful thinking."

The familiars looked up and around, this way then that, but nothing stood out to them. Skylar took to the air, flying up through the branches, while Aldwyn circled the base, tapping his paw at the thick trunk. Gilbert inspected the roots for any sign of the Crown. The three expanded their search even wider, to nearby trees and neighboring boulders. Nothing. Absolutely nothing. They regathered at the dogwood.

"Maybe we were wrong," said Aldwyn.

Skylar repeated the first verse of the nursery rhyme: "*When night falls hear the dog's bark, Howling to the tallest clouds. Secrets of yore buried, Beneath green needle shrouds.* The dog's bark certainly seems to be reaching to the tallest clouds. And there are pine trees all around us. The only line left unexplained is *secrets of yore buried.*"

"You think the Crown is underground somewhere?" asked Aldwyn.

"I don't imagine it's dangling from the tree's branches," replied Skylar.

"Well, I didn't bring a shovel," said Gilbert. "And besides, where would we dig, anyway?"

"What about the second verse?" suggested Aldwyn. "Maybe it's the next clue. *Between the root of all roots, Where every fear sinks away, Are stairs with no bottom, Unless eyes find sun's ray.* What if the Crown is buried beneath the tree?"

"Then we may as well turn around right now," said Gilbert. "It would take the strength of a hundred gundabeasts to move that tree."

"I think the clues are trying to tell us something else," said Skylar. "Somehow, we need to get inside the tree. And the entrance is between the roots."

Skylar circled around the tree once, then flew over to the sinkhole of mud they had passed.

"*Let your fears sink away*," she said slowly, circling over the sinkhole. "This must be the entrance!"

"That's quickmud," said Gilbert. "You go in there, you don't come out."

"No, Skylar is right," said Aldwyn. "Think about it: it says, *let your fears sink away*. The lullaby seems to be asking us to take a leap of faith. To not be afraid."

"What?" exclaimed Gilbert. "Are you two crazy? What if your interpretation is wrong? What if we all suffocate and die in that sinkhole?"

"When has Skylar ever been wrong?" countered Aldwyn.

"But we don't even know if this nursery rhyme is anything more than a way to put restless tadpoles to sleep," muttered Gilbert.

"Then Aldwyn and I will go in on our own," said Skylar. "You can wait for us out here in case you're right. Someone will need to get word back to the queen should we meet our end."

By the look on Gilbert's face, Aldwyn could tell that Skylar's words weren't exactly the reassurance the tree frog was looking for, but before he could say anything else, Skylar sucked in a big lungful of air and dove beak first into the swirl of mud. Her blue feathers were quickly swallowed up as she disappeared. Aldwyn looked back at Gilbert, then to the sinkhole, wondering if his web-footed friend was the only one of them thinking clearly. But if Skylar was right, she would be inside that tree waiting for Aldwyn, counting on him. He took a deep breath, squeezed his eyes shut, and leaped into the hole. Immediately, he was swallowed up by the brown muck.

6

GUARDIAN OF THE SPHERIS

Aldwyn landed with a thud. He gasped for air and used the backs of his paws to wipe the thick mud from his eyes, then carefully opened them just wide enough to see. If he was dead, then Skylar had joined him in the Tomorrowlife, because she was right beside him, covered head to toe in slop. The two were inside a hollowed-out earthen tunnel. Ahead of them, Aldwyn could see the tunnel beginning to slant downward; lightning bugs were dimly illuminating the path.

"Luckily, it looks like you were right again," said Aldwyn.

"Whatever we're searching for must be down there," responded Skylar, gesturing beyond the flickering light.

The two picked themselves up and began their journey into the bowels of the tree, but they didn't get far before they heard a familiar voice echoing behind them.

"Ahhhhhhh!" screamed Gilbert as he came tumbling out of the mud ceiling, crashing to the floor below.

"Gilbert," cried Aldwyn, "what are you doing here?"

"Phantom lurkers," said the tree frog, out of breath. "I saw blades of grass moving all around me." He spit out a mouthful of mud. "Of course, it might have just been the wind. But I wasn't going to take any chances."

"Well, so much for our backup plan," said Skylar, although she didn't really sound annoyed at Gilbert. Aldwyn, too, had to admit that a part of him was glad that the three of them would be exploring the tunnel together.

The familiars started their descent, and soon the ground turned from hard mud to polished wood, carved and sanded with expert care. Aldwyn realized that they must have entered the base of the dogwood itself, and however great the tree appeared above ground, it was even greater beneath. The tunnel expanded into a large circular room with glyph marks carved into the walls and paintings of animals not unlike those they had seen hidden in the mountain cave of Kailasa on their previous adventure.

"I think we're headed in the right direction," said Skylar. She pointed her wing toward the image of a sleeping snow leopard—with the rolling curves of its back and a crown atop its head—drawn above the doorway on the far side of the room.

With all the fantastical beasts living within Vastia, it was curious to Aldwyn that none of the great cats of yore—lions, leopards, or tigers—still roamed inside its borders. Some said they had gone extinct, while others speculated that they had just left, seeking out grander hunting grounds. Aldwyn thought it would be a fine honor to meet one of these storied felines at the end of their quest.

They crossed the smooth floor of the richly decorated room. Aldwyn was certain that more forgotten animal history was depicted on these walls, but deciphering their meaning would have to wait for another time. He followed Skylar into a dark passageway that opened up before them right underneath the image of the snow leopard. There were fewer lightning bugs down this corridor, just enough for them to make out a wooden staircase at the end of the hall.

"It smells like the inside of Kalstaff's sweater closet," said Gilbert wistfully. "I caught a lot of moths in there."

Aldwyn couldn't suppress a smile: no matter how dangerous the situation, it was impossible for Gilbert not to think about food. At that very moment, he heard a high-pitched whistling sound, and his smile froze on his lips. A dozen arrows had shot out from the far wall and were zipping straight toward the familiars. Just a split second before the steel tips impaled them, Aldwyn stopped the arrows telekinetically in midair. They hung there for a beat before he let them drop to the ground.

"Thanks," squealed Gilbert. "I nearly got turned into a shish-kafrog."

Aldwyn glanced down at the fallen arrows and noticed what he hadn't before: that the ground was covered with bones. It was becoming increasingly clear that this was a sacred place and that someone had made very sure that unwelcome visitors would be kept out. A pair of lightning bugs landed on the skull of a nearby skeleton, its rib cage pierced with several arrows. The remains appeared to be those of a young boy. A string of clay charms was still dangling from his bony neck.

"These are rain charms," said Skylar.

Aldwyn got a chill down his back. This was no boy, but the elvin warrior from the story in the *Wizard's Almanac*. And if any more proof was needed, there, strapped to his belt, was the crocodile-tooth dagger the *Almanac* had mentioned.

"He, too, was searching for the Crown of the Snow Leopard," said Skylar. "But his quest ended here. And the traps of an ancient temple only get more devious, the deeper you go."

"I should have taken my chances with those phantom lurkers," moaned Gilbert.

The three tiptoed past the remaining bones. Clearly others beside the elvin warrior had risked life and limb for the same treasure they were seeking and had ended up just as dead. Aldwyn nicked his paw on an unexpectedly sharp fragment from a small mammal's skull. He decided to ignore the pain; there was no time to stop and lick his wound. He quickly caught up to Skylar and Gilbert at the foot of the stairs. The single beam of light that penetrated the gloom from some hole far above was the only thing keeping them from being in total blackness. They began their climb down into the darkness, only able to see five steps ahead of them and five steps behind.

"Nice work with those arrows, by the way," said Skylar to Aldwyn.

"Thanks," he replied, somewhat reticently.

"What is it?" asked Skylar, who must have sensed the doubt in Aldwyn's voice.

"It's hard to describe, but stopping those arrows was like trying to catch wind in my teeth. I still don't feel like I have any real control over my powers. You and Gilbert were trained since birth to use your natural gifts," explained Aldwyn as the familiars continued descending the stairs. "But I've had to figure this all out on my own."

"Guys, sorry to be interrupting, but does it seem like this staircase is going on forever?" asked Gilbert.

Aldwyn and Skylar had been too busy talking to notice, but Gilbert was right: they had circled down flight after flight after flight, but the steps appeared to have no end.

"They have to end at some point," said Skylar.

The next hundred steps down didn't help to prove her point. They seemed no closer than they were before.

"These must be the stairs with no bottom," said Aldwyn. "Remember the second verse? *Between the root of all roots, Where every fear sinks away, Are stairs with no bottom . . .*"

". . . *Unless eyes find sun's ray*," Skylar completed the verse. "Maybe we have to follow the ray of the sun."

"Up again?" groaned Gilbert. "We really need to start thinking about these clues in advance from now on. My extra toes are giving me blisters."

The familiars reversed course and began ascending the staircase. They took the steps two at a time, racing upward. Higher, higher, higher. Until they were back where they had started!

"Well, it sounded like a good idea," said Aldwyn.

"At least sharp, pointy things aren't flying at us," said Gilbert brightly.

"*Are stairs with no bottom, Unless eyes find sun's ray*," said Skylar to herself, repeating the verse in the nursery rhyme again.

Aldwyn thought to himself how none of these clues were what they first seemed. Barking dogs that turned out to be giant trees, quickmud that was actually a secret passageway. How else could this riddle be interpreted?

"What if we tried walking down the steps backward, while our eyes looked up, finding the sun's rays?" asked Aldwyn.

Nobody had any better idea, so the three familiars began to cautiously descend the staircase backward. Skylar, unable to fly in reverse, hopped from step to step, keeping her beak held high in the air. Aldwyn kept his eyes fixed on the tiny pinhole of light that seemed to be miles above them.

After a dozen stairs, Aldwyn fell on his butt. His feet felt for more steps behind him, but there was only flat ground. They had reached the bottom. Another puzzle solved!

"Hey, we're getting pretty good at this," said Aldwyn.

The trio found themselves in a kind of antechamber to an ornately decorated hall. Roots twisted through the ceiling, creating a latticework of delicate wood. Silver leaf was embedded into the walls, accenting the already elaborately drawn glyphs that covered them. Aldwyn had a hunch that they were getting closer to the Tree Temple's inner sanctum. As they stepped into the hall, Gilbert stopped by a patch of moss growing from a crack in the ground. His tongue plucked a mouthful of subterranean ants from the furry lichen.

"Really?" asked Skylar. "You have to do that now?"

"I skipped breakfast," replied Gilbert, mouth full of the colorless crawlers.

The animals reached a rectangular room with low ceilings that smelled of charred cedar planks. It immediately brought back a sense memory. Aldwyn wet his lips, thinking of the flame-licked fish he used to cook over the chimney tops in Bridgetower not so long ago.

Skylar flapped ahead and nearly got incinerated by a sudden blast of fire that shot down from the ceiling. It set off a chain reaction of a hundred flaming jets raining orange from above. She doubled back, with just the tip of her wing smoking, and quickly blew out the still-cindering feather.

"I should have sent out an illusion first," said

Skylar, frustrated with herself. "I was careless."

"I don't think one of your illusions is going to save us this time," said Aldwyn. "Did you see that? Even if you tricked one jet of fire, another would surely finish the job."

As Aldwyn and Skylar contemplated what to do next, Gilbert began to inch forward, his tongue preparing to lap up more subterranean ants from a stretch of moss growing out from the middle of the rectangular room's floor. Aldwyn reached out his paw and stopped him.

"Gilbert," scolded Aldwyn, "I don't think those ants are what you had in mind for your last meal."

"Wait," said Skylar. "This might be one time when it would be wise to follow Gilbert's stomach."

The tree frog seemed surprised but pleased by this. "It would?"

"Yes, look: there's a trail of lichen that winds all the way to the other side of the room. It must have found the only path untouched by the gauntlet of fire."

Aldwyn nodded. "You're right. I'll go first."

"No," said Skylar. "It was my idea. I'll go."

"Really, I insist," countered Aldwyn.

"Nonsense. Besides, fur is more flammable than feathers."

Then the cat and bird were talking over one another, with Aldwyn saying, "I'm faster," and Skylar arguing, "I can fly."

"I'll go!" cried Gilbert.

They both looked at him.

"Anything to make the two of you stop fighting."

Gilbert took the first jump along the path of moss. When nothing happened, he relaxed a little and leaped again. As his webbed feet touched the ground, a barrage of thousand-degree fireballs landed all around him, but Gilbert remained unharmed. Just as Skylar had speculated, the lichen was a safe zone, immune from the Tree Temple's fiery wrath.

Aldwyn and Skylar followed Gilbert, careful not to stray from the lichen path, and wound their way through the deadly trap. With every step, more flames shot out. Aldwyn could feel his skin baking just from the proximity to the extreme heat. The room was like a giant furnace, with only a narrow slit not consumed by the inferno.

Once they reached the other side of the lichen trail, safe from the fiery blasts, the familiars found themselves in yet another cavernous room. Just how far, wondered Aldwyn, did the inside of this tree extend? There was a calm in the air, and he was quite sure that they had overcome their last obstacle. Across from them stood a totem pole carved from stone. At the top of the eight-foot-tall statue was a double-headed eagle, identical to the crest on Bridgetower's flag. Chiseled beneath it was a bear, its eyes big and knowing. Below the bear sat a large tortoise whose granite head stretched out from its shell, with a jade bowl resting atop it.

They approached the idol cautiously. Aldwyn peered into the bowl, and he could see that its inside was stained red.

"It's an offering dish," stated Skylar. "And it looks like it requires a drop of blood."

Aldwyn lifted his paw and saw that the cut from where he'd stepped on the shard of skull was still open.

"At least this cut will be good for something," he said.

Aldwyn climbed atop the turtle's back and squeezed his paw until a few drops of blood fell into the jade bowl. At once the stone jaw of the bear opened wide and the statue sucked in a breath that sounded like wind blowing through a canyon. The two-headed eagle stretched its wings, while the turtle remained motionless.

"For what purpose do you awaken the Odoodem?" asked a thunderously deep voice that spoke through the mouth of the bear.

"We seek the Crown of the Snow Leopard," said Aldwyn. "It is the only way we can summon the Shifting Fortress."

"There is no Crown here," bellowed the totem bear. "And though we once protected that which could have guided you to it, you come too late."

"What do you mean, 'too late'?" asked Skylar. "What is it you speak of and where is it now?"

"We have defended this temple for over eight hundred years," said the totem bear, "acting as the sole guardian of the Spheris—made from the same ore as the Crown and forever magically linked to it. Whoever possesses it gets pulled to the Crown like iron drawn to a magnet. Together

113

with the Song of the First Phylum, the Spheris is the only way the quest for the Crown can be accomplished."

"Song of the First Phylum?" asked Gilbert.

"The nursery rhyme," said Skylar.

One of the eagle heads spoke up in a scratchy voice that sounded as if it had not been used in a very long time.

"Three years ago, another made his way through the traps of the temple. A clever and resourceful one, for many had failed before him."

"After he dropped his blood into the bowl, we deemed him worthy," added the second eagle head in a drowsy monotone.

"And then he took the Spheris from my paw," said the totem bear.

Aldwyn looked at the bear's raised paw and noticed the rounded indentation where the Spheris must once have sat.

"So that's it?" asked Aldwyn. "Isn't there another one?"

"No," said the bear. "There is not."

Aldwyn couldn't believe their journey had led them to this dead end. It seemed they had all risked their lives for nothing. What hope did they have of stopping Paksahara's sinister plot now?

"How could you just give it away?" asked Skylar. "All of Vastia is in danger. Finding the Crown is the only way to save the queendom."

"Tell us who you gave the Spheris to," said Aldwyn. "We'll track him down. We'll do whatever it takes to find him."

Then the turtle spoke up for the first time, in a whisper that made the animals lean in closer to hear him. "It was a cat. His was the blood of destiny." With these hushed words, the tortoise turned its stone eyes to Aldwyn. "The same blood that runs through you."

"I don't understand," said Aldwyn.

The turtle gave Aldwyn a piercing stare. "The one who came here seeking the Crown was your father."

7

A WELCOME RETURN

Your *father*. The turtle's words had been echoing over and over in Aldwyn's head, drowning out any other thoughts. Aldwyn had never believed in fate, but what other explanation could there be for his father, a complete stranger to him, setting off on the same quest he was on now? The probabilities were impossibly unlikely, yet here he stood, just outside of the Tree Temple, presumably not far from where his own father had stood three years earlier. But whether it was destiny or sheer coincidence mattered little.

Aldwyn's heart wanted answers to different questions: Who was this cat that he had never known, and why did he abandon him to the river Ebs?

The Odoodem had pointed the familiars to a secret exit—a tunnel that led from the Spheris's antechamber directly back to the surface. The group walked a short distance from the dogwood tree before Skylar spoke up.

"Do you want to talk about it?" she asked Aldwyn.

Aldwyn didn't know what there was to say, except for the obvious.

"Why would my father have been looking for the Crown?"

"Maybe he was searching for some stylish headwear," said Gilbert. Then he saw Aldwyn's look and added: "Sorry. Just trying to lighten the mood."

"Clearly he, too, was trying to summon the Shifting Fortress," said Skylar. "The question is, for what reason?"

Aldwyn hoped deep in his heart that it was a noble one, but he knew that in the wrong hands— the hands of someone like Paksahara—the

Fortress could bring terrible evils upon the land.

"Whatever the motive, without finding your father and the Spheris, we're back to square one," continued Skylar.

"How do you suggest we do that?" asked Aldwyn.

"We go to Maidenmere," she said.

The thought of returning to the plateau north of Kailasa, home of the telekinetic cats, filled Aldwyn with mixed emotions. He had been there once before, pretending to be magical, and was banished. Now that he knew he was one of them, what kind of welcome would he receive? Would his tribe greet him with open arms, or shun him?

Aldwyn nodded with a heavy but hopeful heart. "Let's go," he said.

They headed back toward the river again, and by the time they reached the waters, it was night. The trio camped along the bank, taking turns keeping watch, and awoke at the crack of dawn the next morning to resume their trek.

The familiars followed the Ebs north, walking along its rocky west bank as the hours of another day sped by. Their journey was peaceful and uneventful; at times it was easy to forget that the world was in peril. But in peril it was: Aldwyn knew that, throughout the cities and across the countryside, life was becoming more and more difficult as the effects of the disenchantment were making themselves felt. And somewhere, Paksahara was plotting to rain even more terror on the land. A terror that would plague the queendom just five days from now.

As the familiars came around the north side of Kailasa, they were presented with a majestic view of the grand Torentia Falls. The last time that Aldwyn had heard its mighty rumble, he had been in no position to admire the strength and beauty of this wonder of the queendom. Instead he had been tumbling through the air and paddling for his life through the water's fearsome rapids. He liked the view from here better, safe on dry land, only getting the occasional spray of mist.

Aldwyn, Skylar, and Gilbert climbed the sloping hill to the top of the plateau. Upon reaching the summit, Aldwyn could make out the floating rock formations that marked the entrance to the Maidenmere Pridelands in the distance.

His heart began to beat faster. His previous visit to the plateau had ended with him being outed as an imposter, but now that he had discovered his telekinetic powers, even if he was not completely in control of them, he was hoping his reception would be more welcoming.

After a short walk across the plateau, the familiars entered the village, passing below the hovering stone islands. Each island had rocks leading up to them that were suspended telekinetically in the air like stairs. These were the homes of the Maidenmere cats, hanging high above the ground, safe from predators, floods, or fire. Unlike the first time the familiars had crossed this plateau—when the dens were crowded with black-and-white felines peering down—now they were empty.

"Where are all the cats?" asked Gilbert.

Aldwyn knew that they could not be far, for his nostrils were filled with a comforting and familiar scent: that of baking river flounder, his favorite fish! It was dinnertime for the Pridelands' bicolors, and it was clear that their taste in food was similar to his. Apparently his culinary preferences were hereditary.

"This way," said Aldwyn, following his nose as much as his heart.

He led them beneath the maze of rocks, which reflected the golden light of a desert dusk. After rounding the community cave, they stopped behind a stout desert yucca tree. Up ahead, close to a hundred cats sat around a large bonfire. Above it, fish rotated on their own, slowly cooking with neither spit nor spear holding them aloft. If the flames began to dip at all, another stick would float into the pit, keeping the blaze raging.

Standing at the center of the gathering was a striped black-and-white cat with a spike through his ear and braids dangling from his tail.

"Do not feel guilty for being blessed with this bounty," he said. "Though man suffers now, time will bring things back into balance."

He spoke to the group with a persuasive purr, exuding a charm and confidence that left no doubt about why he had become their pride leader. This was Malvern, the cat who had exposed Aldwyn's lie during his first visit to Maidenmere and banished him from the Pridelands forever.

"Vastia has experienced many changes in its long history," Malvern continued, "and while this may seem like a dark cloud, perhaps there is light in it, as well."

Aldwyn looked at this band of cats with different eyes than on his previous visit. Now every face and fur in the crowd looked similar to his own. Was it possible that his mother or father was sitting among them?

As Aldwyn stood there, lost in thought, Malvern glanced over and made direct eye contact with him. Immediately, a dozen flaming branches from the bonfire lifted into the air and flew across, surrounding Aldwyn, Skylar, and Gilbert. Aldwyn swallowed hard. This was not how he had planned to make his entrance.

"What are you doing back here?" Malvern called out. "I told you never to return. Maidenmere is no place for imposters."

Every eye turned to the familiars. The heat of the hovering fire sticks inched closer to the trespassing trio, making Aldwyn break out in a sweat.

"Let this be an example to any who falsely claim the divine gifts of the bicolor cats," said Malvern.

Aldwyn nervously lifted a paw, and with the gesture a circle of sand swirled from the ground, rising into the air and engulfing each of the threatening, fiery torches. The burning embers were extinguished all at once, and the sand, along with the branches, dropped to the plateau floor.

Malvern's expression changed. "How did you do that?" he asked.

"I am a cat from Maidenmere," said Aldwyn. "I was born here, but I was sent away when I was just a baby, put on a pile of twigs and cast adrift on the Ebs. I am not an imposter, even if I didn't know it when I came to you the last time."

A murmur stirred through the crowd, then everybody fell silent.

Malvern studied Aldwyn closely, examining him, thinking. The silence seemed to go on forever until finally the leader of the cats of Maidenmere spoke: "That means you are Corliss's child. The one she never let anyone see. The son of Baxley. There is no other explanation." Malvern walked up to Aldwyn. Aldwyn wasn't sure what the imposing, intimidating cat was going to do. And then Malvern's paws embraced him. "You are my nephew."

123

Aldwyn remained in the clutches of this striped cat, the only blood relative he had ever known. It was safe there. It felt comforting to know he wasn't alone in this world.

"Welcome home, fellow Mooncatcher," said Malvern.

~~~

"I should start by saying that this is not a happy story," said Malvern. Aldwyn and his uncle were walking across the plateau in the moonlight; a strong wind was blowing in from the empty plains to the north. After Aldwyn's revelation at the bonfire, he and his companions had been welcomed warmly, with overjoyed hugs and a feast that took on a festive atmosphere. Given that the safety of the queendom was hanging in the balance, Aldwyn's mood was not entirely celebratory. But he was sure that even Jack would want him to enjoy this unexpected reunion. Having eaten until they could eat no more, which in Gilbert's case had meant until his stomach was as round as one of the driftfolk's crystal balls, Skylar and Gilbert had been escorted to the community cave to sleep. Aldwyn had remained awake to seek answers to the questions he had ventured from the Hinterwoods to discover, answers to the questions that had plagued him his whole life. Not only did he need to know why his father had been searching for the Crown of the Snow Leopard, but also who his parents were and why they had abandoned him.

"I need to know everything, Uncle Malvern," said Aldwyn.

Malvern nodded. "You shall. But understand that whatever you hoped your parents to be, I'm afraid the truth will only disappoint you." Then, taking a deep breath, he began:

"Your father, Baxley, was my older brother. We were the only two born to the Mooncatcher bloodline. Your grandfather was our village's elder lifter, your grandmother its den matron. Much was expected of us. I knew from an early age that protecting this tribe would one day be my responsibility. Baxley, on the other hand, wasn't born to lead; he was interested in more *independent* pursuits. Stealing from the community cave, playing practical jokes with his telekinetic powers, searching the Pridelands for secret passageways and unmapped territories."

Aldwyn felt a momentary sense of connection. He, too, possessed these very same mischievous traits.

"But these youthful follies took an ugly turn as he grew older," continued Malvern. "Playful curiosity turned into obsession. My brother's desire to possess unfound treasures consumed him. And ultimately it's what led him away from you."

"The Crown?" asked Aldwyn.

"Yes. The call of such a mythic artifact was too strong for him to resist."

"But why did he want to find it?"

"Glory. Fame. Selfish reasons with no merit."

Aldwyn felt a deep hurt at the thought that someone who should have loved him had left him for the pursuit of such a petty goal.

"And my mother?" Aldwyn asked hopefully.

"Her story is even more tragic, I'm afraid. Corliss was a great beauty. No tom could deny that, but only Baxley desired her as a mate, and she desired only him. She was a member of the Wind Chanter tribe, a family of bicolors whose mental powers extended beyond that of mere telekinesis, to firestarting, mind control, and astral projection. Unfortunately, they also had a tendency toward madness. Baxley ignored my warnings and pursued her anyway. Their love was strong, but not as strong as your father's ambition. He left Corliss immediately after your birth to search for the Crown. Alone and without the companionship of Baxley, your mother began to imagine things, growing paranoid and fearful. I tried to watch over her, but even I had to sleep sometimes. She had been keeping you hidden, and one night, gripped by delusion, she brought you to the river. I awoke to your crying and ran to your rescue. But it was too late. You were drifting rapidly downstream, and before I could restrain Corliss, she threw herself into the river as well. I jumped in after you both, but the currents were too severe. My telekinesis was no match for the rushing waters. You were gone, and your mother was swallowed by the river."

Aldwyn's insides were twisting. He felt anger and remorse, confusion and sadness. The emotions were almost too much to bear.

"But the gods have reunited us," said Malvern. "It's a miracle."

"Did Baxley ever come back? Is he even alive?"

"He was never seen again. Whether he's still out there is anyone's guess."

Aldwyn had spent his whole life fearing the worst about his parents, so in some sense Malvern's story felt more like validation than a crushing disappointment. He was quick to bury any lingering resentment, and tried to focus on the people he knew cared for him: Skylar, Gilbert, Jack, and now his uncle. And yet he was unable to completely ignore the feeling of abandonment that Malvern's story had left in him. But this was not the time to bemoan his fate.

"None of this changes the importance of finding the Crown," said Aldwyn. "I imagine word has reached Maidenmere about Paksahara's evil deeds."

"Of course it has."

"We must stop her, and we have discovered how we can. We need to summon the Shifting Fortress, and to do so we need to find the Crown of the Snow Leopard. Without it, Paksahara is going to raise a new Dead Army that will devastate all of Vastia."

"So the rumors that have been spreading are true," said Malvern. "These are indeed dark days for the queendom."

"But not hopeless," said Aldwyn. "Three years ago, Baxley discovered the Spheris—some sort of compass—that would guide him to the Crown. We need to retrieve it."

"I remember," said Malvern, his eyes suddenly lighting up. "After your birth, when Baxley returned to the Pridelands, he brought with him this ball. A silver metal globe that was pulling him to the north."

"Do you know where he was going?"

"I'm not sure *he* knew where he was going."

Aldwyn's shoulders slouched.

"Look at me, nephew," said Malvern. Aldwyn's eyes met his uncle's. "We will solve this problem. Together. But first, before you go to sleep, I want to show you something."

He brought Aldwyn to a sandy patch and put one of his striped paws on Aldwyn's back. "I'm going to guide you through your first sand sign," continued Malvern. "The way a father does with his son. It is a feat of extraordinary telekinetic artistry. Moving millions of grains of sand into a perfectly realized shape is not the same as lifting a rock. It takes true skill, not just brute force.

"Now, I want you to listen to the plateau. Feel the height of the earth and the sky resting on your back."

Aldwyn's senses began to open up to the elements around him—the rocks pushing up against the pads of his paws and the air hugging his body, rushing through his fur.

"Let your mind breathe. And let yourself be as calm as the Enaj River."

Aldwyn took a deep breath and relaxed his entire body, from the tip of his bitten ear to the end of his tail.

Suddenly, he felt something move through him, a surge of energy that strengthened and focused his mind. The sand on the ground around him began to rise, and a sign formed in the air: a paw reaching for the moon. It left him breathless. He had made objects float before, but had never achieved something of such beauty. Yet it was more than just a feat of artistry. This symbol hanging in the air represented the long line of Aldwyn's ancestors. He was a Mooncatcher. For good or bad, he had found his family.

❧

The following morning, Aldwyn could feel the red sting of a sleepless night in his eyes. He hadn't gotten a wink, lying on the cold stone floor of the community cave, waiting for the sun to rise. His mind had been racing from all the things Malvern had told him.

Across the supply den, Gilbert had snuggled up on a pile of woven blankets, while Skylar had found a place to perch atop a stack of boxes. Unlike Aldwyn, his companions had little trouble sleeping, exhausted as they were from the long travels of the previous two days. When the first morning light pierced the darkness of the cave, Skylar, who even during the peaceful days at the Runlet had been an annoyingly early riser, woke up.

"How did it go?" she asked when she saw that Aldwyn, too, was awake.

Aldwyn considered all that he could tell her—about his father's selfish abandonment, about how his mother had been destroyed by madness—but he just wasn't ready to bare his soul to Skylar. Not yet. So all he said was: "Malvern saw my father leave heading north with the Spheris."

"That's not much to go on," said Skylar, disappointed. "He could be anywhere in Vastia. Or even the Beyond."

Aldwyn walked over and gave Gilbert a nudge.

"Fruit fly casserole!" the tree frog shouted, still half asleep. Then his eyes opened and he seemed startled to find Aldwyn standing so close.

"Time to wake up," said Aldwyn. "I think we should return to the palace. We'll tell Queen Loranella what we've learned and see if we can come up with a new plan."

The familiars gathered their satchels, pouches, and spears and walked out of the community cave into the early morning sunlight. The steps on most of the floating rock islands had yet to be lowered, as only the most eager and youthful bicolors had risen. Some were getting an early start to the day's telekinetic training, maneuvering rocks through floating rings and lifting dew drops into the sky, like rain reversed. Others were performing chores around the Pridelands, hunting fish in the streams or gathering kindling for the evening's bonfire.

Aldwyn led the trio toward the largest of the hovering dens, the one Malvern claimed as his own. He called the floating stone staircase into formation, and he and Gilbert began to ascend, Skylar flying beside them. Once they reached the top, they found Malvern awake, deep in thought. A reading lens was held afloat in the air between his eyes and an etched stone tablet.

"Good morning, uncle," said Aldwyn. "Sorry to interrupt, but I think—"

"The idea came to me in the middle of the night," said Malvern, his eyes never turning from the slab of gray shale he was reading. "Something your grandfather used to say. *A father's path is never lost to his children.*"

The reading lens dropped to Malvern's side, and the striped cat looked at Aldwyn.

"The cats of Maidenmere believe that no generation can flourish without a strong remembrance of the past," he explained. "There are many traditions that keep the presence of yesteryear close. Each bead on my tail comes from one of my ancestors. This spike through my ear is a shard from the tip of a sword used by the first Mooncatcher. And there are spells that keep spirits from the Tomorrowlife in the today."

Skylar was peering down at the tablet, cocking her head so that she didn't have to read the glyphs upside down.

"*Rituals of the Felidae?*" she asked.

"Spells that have been collected for hundreds of years here in the Pridelands," said Malvern. "Our tribe uses them for religious celebrations, rites of passage, and during the mourning of loved ones. Their effects are mostly ceremonial, creating images of relatives in the stars and rainbows that lead to a proper burial spot. But then it struck me. What if one of these could be used in a different way? The *komi-pasu*, or spirit trail. In burial ceremonies, it's a spell cast on the child of the deceased to remind them that their parents walked the same land that they did."

"I don't understand," said Aldwyn.

"It reveals the paw prints of a father or mother to their child, and their child alone. We all try to follow in the footsteps of our parents. This allows a cat to actually do it."

"And you're suggesting that if you cast this spell on Aldwyn, he might be able to follow Baxley's path out of Maidenmere," said Skylar.

"Precisely," replied Malvern.

The idea gave Aldwyn new hope that their mission could continue after all. But the thought of walking in his father's paw prints also made him more than a little uneasy. What other ugly truths might he discover about Baxley if he went along with his uncle's plan? However, the well-being of the whole of Vastia was more important than his personal issues with his father.

"Show me how it works," said Aldwyn.

The pride leader led the familiars down from his airborne lair, with the ancient tablet floating beside him. They walked across the plateau to a sandy knoll.

"This was the last place I saw Baxley," said Malvern, "before he headed north. Now, I've never cast this spell before, but the instructions seem clear. Aldwyn, I need you to dig a hole in the sand."

Aldwyn cupped his paws and started shoveling.

"You don't need to dirty your paws, you know," said Malvern.

Aldwyn realized his mistake.

"I forget sometimes."

He stepped back and let his mind finish what his front paws had started, while Malvern looked at one of the engravings etched on the *Rituals of the Felidae.*

"Three thorns of a black cactus, petals from a golden rose," he read. As he spoke, a telekinetic breeze carried the very items forth, spinning them in a tiny whirlwind above the hole that Aldwyn had dug. "Moth's wings, cricket's legs, and seeds from an everwillow tree."

The remaining spell ingredients flew in from afar and were sucked downward into the hole. The sand buried them and all was calm.

"Let the steps of the past be present," Malvern called out. "Light up the *komi-pasu.*"

Malvern had hardly finished his incantation when, before Aldwyn's eyes, glowing paw prints started forming in the sand, each one a purplish-pink hue that was the color of a sunset. They pointed due north and stretched off far into the distance.

"It didn't work," said Gilbert. "Nothing happened."

But Skylar had noticed Aldwyn's intent stare and asked: "What do you see, Aldwyn?"

He was gazing off, speechless. His heart was beginning to skip beats, both from excitement and nervousness. He knew this trail could lead to answers he had so desperately sought, and so vehemently feared.

"Aldwyn?" asked Skylar again.

"I see the path of my father," he said.

Aldwyn was trying to restrain everything he was feeling inside. Once the pounding in his chest

subsided, he stepped forward cautiously, placing his paw on one of the glowing prints illuminated in the sand before him. It was a perfect fit. Even his pinky toe, which always stuck out a bit—a result, he had thought until now, of a back alley brawl in Bridgetower—matched Baxley's.

"The trail will either lead you to your father, or to where he took his last step," said Malvern.

"So long as it also leads us to the Crown of the Snow Leopard," said Skylar, "this world stands a chance."

"Will you come with us?" Aldwyn asked his uncle.

"The pride needs me here. Besides, this is your journey. And if what you told me about the prophecy is true, then the three of you are the only ones who can save Vastia."

"When this quest is over," said Aldwyn, "I hope to bring my loyal back here with me. Jack. I think you'd like him."

"Maidenmere will always have a den waiting for you."

Aldwyn nodded to his uncle, then tightened the strap on Jack's pouch.

"We'll follow you," said Gilbert, adjusting the spear that once again had slid down his back.

Aldwyn stared ahead, at the glowing trail of paw prints that was snaking its way north. Just a day ago, he had wanted desperately to know more about his father. Now, after what he'd learned, he wished he could go back, to somehow preserve the possibility of a father who loved him. But it was too late for that. He could only move forward, hoping that this path might reveal something good about Baxley. Something that would make Aldwyn hate him a little less.

8

PATH OF
THE FATHER

"Aldwyn, are you sure you're going the right way?" asked Gilbert, hopping behind him.

"We have to trust in the magic path, even if we can't see it," said Skylar. "And believe me, that's harder for me than it is for you. I start having a nervous breakdown when someone else even holds the map."

"The path is so bright and clear that it's amazing it only appears to me," said Aldwyn. "You don't have to worry. I'm not going to lead you astray."

Since they had left the plains of Maidenmere,

Aldwyn had continued to follow the path of the glowing purple paw prints along the edge of the Ebs River. Baxley's trail appeared before him like pink clouds at sunset lighting up a gray and dusty sky. The northern plateau was surprisingly uninhabited, not only of humans but of animals as well. Temperatures could be sweltering during the high sun hours, and during the summer you could fry a dragon egg on the barren ground. And if the climate wasn't reason enough, no one was eager to live so close to the border, especially at a time when sandtaurs and gundabeasts were making a habit of venturing into Vastia from the Beyond. Aldwyn had heard all of this from Skylar, which made it likely to be absolutely true.

Baxley's paw prints stayed steady and straightforward along the river's edge, except every mile or two when they stepped into the water—for what Aldwyn could only assume was a drink or to cool down—before resuming their path.

Gilbert peered occasionally into the stagnant pools dotting the riverbank, trying to aid his companions with a helpful puddle viewing, only to look up disappointed each time.

"Anything?" asked Aldwyn after what had seemed to be one of Gilbert's more focused attempts.

"Just my reflection," complained Gilbert. "Maybe Paksahara's curse took away my magic abilities, too."

"That must be it," said Skylar. "I'm sure you're the only animal in all of Vastia whose talents have been dispelled."

Gilbert hung his head low.

"It's possible," said Aldwyn, trying to cheer up the tree frog. "Unlikely, but possible."

The familiars continued their journey along the footpath until they arrived at a point where the glowing paw prints split off from the Ebs. Here the river veered west, while the trail remained steadfast to the north. As comforting as it would have been to have drinking water always just a few steps away, it was clear the Spheris's pull had no concern for the convenience of those it was guiding. The metal ball had but one goal: to reunite with the Crown of the Snow Leopard.

So north they traveled, leaving their own footprints behind them. Soon, hills began to rise up from the plateau floor, and the river was but a glimmering band of silver far in the distance. The wind picked up speed as gusts blew between the rocky channels formed by the curving landscape, kicking up dust clouds that made it difficult to see where they were going. Aldwyn kept his eyes on Baxley's path, whose ethereal light never dimmed, no matter how much sand was swirling around it.

By the time the sun began its afternoon descent from its zenith in the sky, the winds had calmed down somewhat, and the familiars could now see an isolated stone building up ahead. The structure appeared to be a small temple, surrounded by marble columns. Their true color was hidden beneath a film of thin brown created by the daily dust storms. Around the temple was a graveyard of tombstones, crypts, and mausoleums, all surrounded by a fence of twisted metal.

"This must be a Sanctuary of the Agate," said Skylar. "A house of worship for druids who pray to the cloud gods. They're kind and welcoming to man and animal alike, so long as you respect their customs. Everything within the fence is sacred, protected by a single spotted gemstone that keeps evil at bay. Somewhere hidden on these grounds is its altar. Very few of these sanctuaries remain standing. I would have been interested to explore it further."

"Well, you're in luck," said Aldwyn. "Baxley's paw prints lead right to it."

Aldwyn followed the glowing trail to the metal fence, which was no taller than the tip of his tail. Gilbert and Skylar remained at his side. Now that the sanctuary was in closer view, Aldwyn could see that it was in disrepair, the premises in a state of lonely abandon. The fountain out front appeared to be long dried up, and the silver doors of the temple were off their hinges.

"Well, I've seen enough," said Skylar, clearly not impressed.

Aldwyn's father seemed to have had the same thought, because his footprints didn't lead to the dilapidated entrance. They led around the back, past urns of dried flowers and fragmented tomb-stones.

When he rounded the far columns of the sanctuary, Aldwyn found that the prints headed straight toward a stone mausoleum. One side had been bashed open to reveal that it was hollow inside. Aldwyn took note of the paw prints, which traveled inside the crypt and then back out again.

"Baxley went in there," said Aldwyn. "He was looking for something."

"The Crown?" asked Gilbert

The blue jay flew inside. Aldwyn and Gilbert quickly followed, descending three steps into a small underground room. All that was there was a pedestal holding a bowl of water.

Skylar dipped her wing in the bowl and brought a drop of water to her beak.

"It's saltwater, from the Wildecape Sea," she said. "Agate stays pure within such waters. This bowl must have been where the sanctuary kept the gemstone. But it's gone. Whoever took it either wanted to bring harm to this place or valued the worth of the gem over the well-being of those kind souls who tended these sacred grounds."

Aldwyn looked down to see Baxley's paw prints leading directly to the pedestal, even scaling the stone stand, before retracing their way back out.

"Baxley stole it," said Aldwyn. "Malvern was right."

Skylar and Gilbert looked at him curiously.

"He told me that my father was nothing more than a selfish grave robber. He left my mother and me for this: to pillage treasure for his own glory. That's why he was seeking the Crown. Not to protect Vastia or summon the Shifting Fortress. He was just after a prize."

Gilbert looked at him with compassionate eyes; after all, the tree frog had his own experience with father issues. Even Skylar softened at the sadness with which Aldwyn had spoken.

"I'll be the first to admit," said Aldwyn, "I've stolen a fish or two . . . or a hundred in my day. But that was to eat. What Baxley did was different. He had a family. He should have been with us."

"Our parents aren't always the people we want them to be," said Gilbert, in one of his rare moments of wisdom.

"We should continue on. There's nothing left here for us," replied Aldwyn.

Aldwyn led the way out of the crypt, arriving back above ground where the paw path resumed once more. Suddenly, his nostrils flared and he sniffed the air.

"Do either of you smell that?" he asked.

"I'm sorry," said Gilbert, "I haven't bathed in two days."

"No, it's not you," said Aldwyn. "It's something else."

He didn't have the precise words to describe the odor, but it was like a combination of fresh paint and chopped grass, with a third element added that he couldn't wrap his nose around. Before he had time to take another sniff, Aldwyn heard a hissing sound coming from behind a tombstone and spun around to see a two-foot-tall, reptilian-faced humanoid with scaly skin and a forked tongue scampering toward him. Half a dozen more stalked out from the shadows of the crypts and mausoleums, carrying small shields and jagged rocks.

"Friendly?" Gilbert asked Skylar.

"Do they look friendly to you?" she shot back.

"I try not to judge by appearances."

"What are they?" asked Aldwyn, backing off the paw print path.

"Rumlins," said Skylar. "The scourge of the Northern Plateaus. I used to see them not far

147

from here, when I would take day flights outside the Aviary."

The rumlins seemed to be talking to one another by using a series of throaty warbles and clicks.

"I'm guessing neither of you can understand what they're saying," said Aldwyn.

He would have expected Skylar to pipe up, but to his surprise, it was Gilbert who responded.

"Actually, reptiles and amphibians have some lingual crossover," said Gilbert. The rumlins continued chattering, flicking their olive green tongues, while moving in on the familiars. "*Poison, carve, lunch* . . . I'm hardly fluent, but I'm getting a pretty good picture of what they have in mind for us."

The creatures began to surround the familiars on all sides.

"That's what the gemstone was for," said Skylar. "To keep evil like this away."

One of the ugly little monsters attacked, outstretching its claws and teeth at the same time, as if undecided whether to tear Aldwyn to shreds or bite a chunk out of his back. Aldwyn wasn't going to wait to find out. He lifted a large block of stone telekinetically into the air and hurtled it toward the rumlin, whose yellow-slitted eyes barely saw it coming. *Thrump!* The slab of granite knocked the creature flat out.

The other six rumlins didn't shed any tears for their fallen brother.

"I thought that would have scared them off," said Aldwyn.

"No," said Skylar, "they'll probably just eat him later."

"Don't worry. All the frogs of Daku are great snake hunters," said Gilbert, his voice croaking as he tried to convince himself of the truth of what he had just said. "A reptile like this should be no different."

He reached over his shoulder and grabbed for the spear tied to his back. But the sharpened bamboo stick got caught on the grass strap, and Gilbert stumbled sideways, colliding with a gravestone.

Aldwyn focused on some nearby burial urns with long-dead flowers shriveled inside that were resting in front of a family crypt. He mentally flung them through the air, sending them toward the approaching rumlins. But now they were prepared, using their shields to fend off the aerial assault.

The vicious lizard men were coming at the familiars with jagged rocks. One was ready to deliver a blow to Gilbert, who was still fumbling with his spear, which he had finally unsheathed. With all his might, the tree frog stabbed the attacking rumlin . . . with the blunt end of the stick!

"Gilbert," shouted Aldwyn, "you're holding it backward!"

Before Gilbert could reorient the weapon, the rumlin knocked it out of his hand with its small shield. The creature lifted his pointed rock in the air, but before he could bring the weapon down on Gilbert's head, he was distracted by a bright glow emanating from between Skylar's wings.

Aldwyn could see that she was holding a large red and black gemstone aloft in her feathers. All six of the scaly monsters began to back away, cowering in fear.

"You two better run," she commanded Aldwyn

and Gilbert. "When they realize this is just an illusion, they won't be happy."

Aldwyn and Gilbert didn't hesitate. Aldwyn sprinted for Baxley's path; Gilbert snatched his bamboo spear from the ground before hopping after him. Skylar waited until her two companions were a safe distance away, then took to the air, the gemstone disappearing as she did. The confused rumlins could only watch as their dinner made a hasty getaway.

With the sanctuary behind them, the three animals continued their trek through the northernmost reaches of Vastia. Evening was approaching, and the days of restless travel and the previous sleepless night had made Aldwyn exhausted. His eyes were bleary and his legs fatigued. There was no end in sight to the paw prints, and though the quest to find where the Spheris had taken Baxley was growing ever more urgent, Aldwyn would be a liability if he didn't get rest soon.

"I think we need to find a place to sleep for the night," he said.

Skylar pointed off the path to a large field of

grass that had sprung up around the burnt remnants of wooden buildings.

"That looks like as good a spot as any," said Skylar. "We can take turns keeping watch."

Aldwyn veered off the spirit trail and the familiars got closer to the expanse of green. As they did, Aldwyn could hear music, a triumphant battle hymn that filled him with a sense of adventure and purpose.

"Whistlegrass," said Gilbert fondly.

Aldwyn remembered passing such a field once before, on the way from Bridgetower to Stone Runlet, when Jack had first chosen him as his familiar. Kalstaff had explained how every rolling hill of whistlegrass played a different song, one that recounted the story of something that had taken place there days, weeks, or even years before.

When the three animals stepped through the blades, it felt as if they were suddenly surrounded by an orchestra of a hundred thousand instruments playing in perfect unison. They settled into the grass, and Aldwyn was sure that despite the music echoing around him, sleep would swallow him as soon as he closed his eyes.

"I'll take the first shift," said Skylar. "Gilbert, I'll wake you in an hour."

"Don't you think six-hour shifts would be more effective?" asked the tree frog innocently.

"By then the sun will have risen," she replied.

"And I will be very well rested," said Gilbert.

The music lifted to a crescendo as a strong breeze blew across the field. Pollen from every stalk of grass took flight, and as the melody settled into a quiet hum, the fine yellow grains, twinkling like stardust, began to form moving pictures in the air. Burnt frames of houses destroyed long ago appeared whole again, having returned to their original peaceful states. Between the buildings, human villagers walked, carrying buckets of water and going about their everyday morning chores.

Aldwyn wasn't sure if it was his weary eyes that were creating this vision, but as he looked at Skylar and Gilbert, he could see they were rapt, too.

"How rare and beautiful," said Skylar. "The whistlegrass is showing us the past of this place."

The grass symphony started to build to a

more ominous refrain, and from the nearby hill the pollen took to the air, forming a translucent army of men shambling forward. As they entered the town, Aldwyn could see that these men were in fact zombies, their faces nothing more than exposed flesh and skull, with muscles dangling limply from their arms. A few were even missing limbs. Aldwyn had heard many stories of the Dead Army Uprising, but now to see what this horrific mass of undead soldiers truly looked like gave him the chills. Villagers ran in terror as the zombies set the houses aflame with torches and lifted their rusty swords against the peaceful inhabitants.

High on the hill, watching over the army, were two ominous armored figures, masked and sitting atop two spectral steeds.

"Who are they?" asked Gilbert, their fearsome appearance causing his voice to tremble.

"Wyvern and Skull," replied an awed Skylar, "the two dark mages responsible for the uprising."

On the ground beside the evil wizards stood a two-headed coyote, what Aldwyn could only assume was one or both of their familiars.

The carnage continued. Why, Aldwyn wondered, had the whistlegrass at first sounded so triumphant, given the horrors that had occurred here? Though he didn't ask the question aloud, his thoughts were answered as the field's melody turned into a fanfare of trumpets. Six figures entered the battle from the other side of town: three humans and three animals. Aldwyn would not have recognized them, had he not seen pictures of them in their youth. It was Kalstaff, Loranella, and the Mountain Alchemist, looking young, vibrant, and heroic, and even more magnificent than anyone could ever imagine the Prophesized Three to appear. Following faithfully at their sides were their familiars: Zabulon, the bloodhound; Edan, the tortoise; and yes, Paksahara, the gray hare who was now plotting to raise a Dead Army of her own.

Skylar and Gilbert recognized them, too. They all watched in awe as they witnessed the true power that these great wizards of yesteryear once possessed. In a flash, they were in the fray of the battle. Loranella was first to strike, sending a bolt of energy from a ring on her finger, blasting a horde of charging zombies to smithereens. Kalstaff was next, cutting through an onslaught of decomposing limbs with a sword in each hand. Edan lowered his head to the ground, creating a time shell around the Mountain Alchemist and three torch-wielding soldiers of the dead. In the blink of an eye, the bubble was gone, and so were the zombies. Aldwyn had once wondered what this slow-moving turtle could do in the heat of battle, and now he knew.

A volley of flaming arrows flew toward the wizards, fired by a brigade of undead archers. Kalstaff was able to deflect the ones heading for him, but Loranella was not fast enough. The fiery tip of a bolt was coming right at her when Paksahara shape-shifted into a giant rhino. The arrow bounced off the transformed hare's toughened hide.

The music continued to swell as wizards and familiars—six against a thousand—decimated their foes. And then, with a gust from the north, the pollen was blown away and the song of the whistlegrass faded back into a quiet hum.

Gilbert was the first to say something.

"Wow," he said. "Kalstaff kicked zombie butt."

"I've read hundreds of history scrolls about the Dead Army Uprising," said Skylar, "and how the Prophesized Three fought them back. But no written word could ever do justice to the feats I just witnessed."

"If Paksahara succeeds," said Aldwyn, "and a new Dead Army does rise, how will the three of us ever be able to stop it?"

His words hung in the air. It was rare for Skylar not to have an answer, but this time she didn't.

"We should get some rest," said the blue jay eventually.

The funny thing was, even though he had been bone tired a few minutes ago, now Aldwyn was wide awake. As he stared up at the stars, all he could think about were the zombie hordes that Wyvern and Skull had unleashed upon Vastia, and how Paksahara—once noble and pure of heart—was preparing to do the same in a mere four days.

"Why don't you let me take the first watch," Aldwyn said to Skylar. "I don't think I'll be falling asleep any time soon."

Early the next morning, Aldwyn found the spirit path just where he had left it, glowing bright and stretching off to the north. He and his fellow familiars resumed their journey.

"Can you believe the way Kalstaff swung those swords?" enthused Gilbert. "It was like, *swoosh-clang-bam!*"

Gilbert had been reliving every moment of the whistlegrass vision from the minute he first woke up. No detail was too mundane to recount, from the drool dripping from the zombie soldiers' gums to the sandals the Mountain Alchemist was wearing during the battle.

"Paksahara was so selfless," said Skylar, "the way she put herself in harm's way to protect Loranella. There was no hesitation. I could see only compassion in her eyes for her loyal."

"Whatever good she possessed is gone now," said Aldwyn.

Baxley's paw prints led to a gorge, a hundred feet wide and extending to the east and west as far as the eye could see. Two wooden stakes marked the beginning of a rope bridge that was no longer there; only frayed twine swung from the posts.

Aldwyn arrived at the edge and looked across to see two similar stakes on the other side, where the bridge would have ended and Baxley's glowing trail resumed.

"The path continues across the gorge," said Aldwyn. "Something must have happened to the bridge since Baxley walked its planks."

"This is Liveod's Canyon," said Skylar. "It's the border of Vastia. Everything past this point is the Beyond. Even Scribius won't know what lies ahead."

The feather-tipped quill peeked out of Skylar's satchel upon hearing its name, then disappeared again inside the bag.

The three animals stood at the precipice, Gilbert's orange eyes peering over the edge at the sharp, sheer cliffs that flanked the bottomless chasm.

"Okay, now that you've proven your geography skills," said Gilbert to Skylar, "how do we get across it?"

9

NEARHURST AVIARY

Aldwyn was trying to clear his mind, the way Malvern had taught him to. He tried to feel the height of the earth and the weight of the sky. Three flat rocks were hovering like stepping stones across the first six feet of the gorge. A fourth rock was moving into place to extend the telekinetic bridge. Unfortunately, the rustling of some nearby leaves was enough to distract Aldwyn's attention and send the stones tumbling to the bottom of the canyon.

"Come on, Aldwyn," Gilbert encouraged him.

"Fifteenth time's the charm."

"It's no use," said Aldwyn. "My mind isn't strong enough yet."

The initial thought of circumventing the gorge by foot had been quickly dismissed by Skylar, who explained that Liveod's Canyon stretched over fifty miles to the west and even further to the east. By the time they would have made it all the way to the paw prints on the other side, the next full moon would have arrived and with it Paksahara's Dead Army. Of course, Skylar could have just flown across, but what good would that have done, seeing as how she was unable to see Baxley's path? Aldwyn had had the idea of using his telekinesis, but the way things had been going, crossing a bridge that depended solely on Aldwyn's powers of the mind would surely have ended with Gilbert and him plummeting to their deaths.

"Looks like our only option left is to create a bridge out of thin air," said Skylar matter-of-factly.

"She must be suffering from sunstroke," whispered Gilbert to Aldwyn.

"I heard that, Gilbert!" said Skylar. "But I'm

perfectly fine. I'm talking about an incredibly powerful illusion," she continued, "one whose manifestation is so convincing that it can even fool gravity and the laws of nature themselves."

"We would be walking over something that wasn't there?" asked Aldwyn.

"Yes, but it would be as solid as the ground we stand on now."

"So why did you let me waste all that time trying to lift those stones?"

"Because I can't cast such a potent illusion," said Skylar. "At least not yet. Only a five-feather master illusionist can create a phantasm so powerful."

Aldwyn had always thought Skylar *was* a master of her talents; he was surprised to learn that she hadn't reached her full potential yet, either. He was also rather worried what would happen when she did.

"We're closer now to the Nearhurst Aviary than we were before," said Skylar. "There are numerous birds under its dome capable of such a feat. If we hurry, we could get one to accompany us back here by high sun."

"Well, what are we waiting for?" asked Aldwyn.

Deviating from the glowing trail, the familiars set off for the Aviary. Skylar was visibly happy to be leading her companions once more. She was guiding them toward a small mountain range in the distance, and the closer they got to it the more chipper she appeared. She'd flap ahead and then spin back to Aldwyn and Gilbert, and if she could have carried them on her wings she would have.

"Slow down," said Gilbert, "I can't hop that fast!"

"Come on, we're almost there," she said.

Aldwyn had never seen Skylar so exuberant before. Usually she kept her emotions in check, but returning to her childhood home seemed to have brought out the chick in her. It was the giddy feeling a family reunion could bring out in some; it also was a feeling Aldwyn was now certain he would never have.

Skylar landed on a tree branch before a rocky hill and smiled warmly at the barren mound of earth.

"We're here," she said.

"Huh?" croaked Gilbert, as he did a three-sixty.

Aldwyn was equally confused: nothing

resembling an aviary or any kind of building was within sight.

Skylar flew to the base of the hill and pressed her feathers up to a block of stone. Much to Aldwyn's surprise, a door opened within the side of the mountain, and the blue jay entered. Aldwyn and Gilbert quickly followed.

Once inside, Aldwyn realized that this mountain was not a mountain at all, but a giant dome of glass and steel. The appearance around it had been an illusion, cast in order to protect the sanctity of this incredible place. Full-grown trees towered inside the translucent hideaway. Its size was as breathtaking as the polished beams of metal that arched like rainbows overhead.

Hundreds of birds flew among the vegetation, and nests sat on every branch of every tree. There were cardinals, blue jays, yellow-tailed swallows, parakeets—feathered fowl of every size and color—all of them practitioners of the art of illusion.

The Nearhurst Aviary was not only home to these magical birds, but to blossoming plants and flowers as well. The air was humid from the

sunlight entering through the glass ceiling, and the smell of lavender mixed with honeysuckle hung densely in the air like a warm, sweet fog.

Human caretakers, women wearing cotton blouses, linen trousers, and no shoes or socks, tended to the aviary. Some held wooden bowls filled with seeds and grubs, while others watered and clipped the vines. The grounds were kept pristine and immaculate, and it was clear where Skylar had gotten her tendency toward perfection.

"This is nicer than the Bronzhaven seaweed springs," said Gilbert. "Do they give out foot massages, too? My toes are killing me."

Aldwyn heard feet stampeding behind him and jumped out of the way of a charging tree ogre. Skylar let the large wood-skinned beast pass right through her.

"Don't believe everything you see here," she said.

A bright red cardinal flew to the ground. "Sorry, whiskers. Just a little Nearhurst welcome."

"Mason," said Skylar. "You've gotten bigger. But you certainly haven't grown up."

"I missed you, too, Sky," said the crimson-mohawked bird.

"These are my friends, Aldwyn and Gilbert. This is Mason." The animals acknowledged each other. "So, has anything changed since I left?" asked Skylar.

"I know what you're wondering," replied Mason. "And yes, all of your illusion records still stand. Biggest, longest duration, and most conjured at the same time. A lot of birds try to beat them, but nobody's come close."

Skylar tried to keep from gloating, but a smile crept out from her beak all the same.

"I don't see my parents' nest," she said, looking to the treetops.

"They relocated to the lower branches," said Mason. "Your pop isn't the spry jay he was when you last saw him. Come on, I'll take you to them."

Mason flew over a well-manicured rose garden full of hummingbirds and turtle doves changing the colors of the flowers with trembling wings. Aldwyn still flinched now and again as different illusions swept past his head; he was finding it difficult to get used to a place where winged pythons and vine-swinging trolls could appear at any moment. Gilbert was faring even worse, diving into some prickly shrubs to avoid a day bat that didn't exist and chomping through an illusionary hornet's nest, causing him to bite his own tongue. By the time a robin offered him a worm pie, he was too skeptical to accept.

"No thank you," said Gilbert. "I'm not falling for any more tricks. I've been made the fool enough today."

The robin shrugged. Within seconds, half a dozen birds landed and devoured the dessert, slurping up every last worm. By the time Gilbert realized the pie hadn't been an illusion, there were only crumbs of mud left.

While Gilbert was complaining loudly to Aldwyn about the lost meal, Mason had reached the trunk of a short magnolia tree, with several nests scattered through its lowest branches.

"I should probably get going, Sky," said the cardinal. "I'm late for scent summoning class."

Suddenly, a strong fragrance of roses overwhelmed the air.

"Professor Keel says a female bird can't resist

the scent of black roses," said Mason.

"I'm resisting," replied Skylar.

Mason smiled before taking wing to one of the tallest trees in the Aviary.

"You never told us you had a boyfriend," said Gilbert.

"He's *not* my boyfriend," said Skylar, looking a little less blue and a little more red as she dismissed Gilbert's comment.

"He called you Sky," teased the tree frog. "I thought you only let Dalton call you that."

"You know, Aldwyn still doesn't know about the lily pad wetting incident," said Skylar.

"Just kidding," said Gilbert. "Forget I even brought it up."

Then, from above, a voice called down: "Quickly, the four types of rain clouds."

"Heffinger puffs, white lingerus, cumula perspirants, and neb swirlums," Skylar answered without hesitating.

"That's my girl," said the voice.

A blue jay descended from the branch, his azure feathers speckled with silver but his beak still as sharp as that of any bird half his age.

"Daddy!" exclaimed Skylar, lowering her head into his feathers. He put a protective wing around her, holding her close.

A second jay flew down; this one arched her back the same way Skylar did.

"Welcome home, dear," she said.

Skylar moved from her father to her mother, hugging her as well.

"Hi, Mom."

"And this must be Aldwyn and Gilbert," said Skylar's father.

"How did you know?" asked Skylar.

"Word travels fast when your daughter is anointed one of Vastia's Prophesized Three," said her mother proudly.

"Then you know about Paksahara and her dispeller curse?" asked Skylar.

"Yes," said Skylar's dad. "Not since Wyvern and Skull has magic been used in such a corrupt manner, solely for the pursuit of power."

It was easy to see that Skylar had gotten her headstrong intellectualism from her father and her dignified, emotionally reserved demeanor from her mother. She was clearly the product of two loving and caring parents, and an environment that encouraged the greatness she had achieved thus far. Once again Aldwyn wished that his father hadn't been a useless and reckless treasure hunter.

"Why have you come here?" asked Skylar's mom.

"It's a long story," said Skylar, "but I need one of the five-feather masters to conjure us a bridge over Liveod's Canyon."

"So you saw that it was destroyed," said Skylar's father. "A sandtaur tried to cross it once the enchanted fence had fallen. Fortunately for us, the wooden bridge couldn't support his weight, and the beast plummeted to the rocks below."

"It's essential that we get to the other side," said Skylar. "And neither Aldwyn nor Gilbert can fly."

"I suppose it would take a healthy dose of Icari weed for them to sprout wings of their own," said Skylar's dad.

"Hepsibah is at Observation Perch," said Skylar's mom. "She should be returning soon."

"Our nest is certainly not big enough for five," said Skylar's dad. "Let's go down to the gazebo while we wait."

Skylar and her parents flew ahead to a white wooden gazebo just on the other side of the magnolia tree. The structure had been built atop a garden deck and resembled a large canary's cage. Benches for the caretakers sat around the perimeter, and a hundred metal perches hung from the trellised ceiling above. Aldwyn and Gilbert caught up to them.

"So, tell me, Aldwyn," said Skylar's father, "what kind of familiar is my daughter? I never imagined her as the assistant type."

"Her loyalty is unwavering, and her talents indispensable. But," added Aldwyn, "if you don't mind my saying so, she can be a bit of a know-it-all."

"You can blame her father for that," said Skylar's mom.

"Why blame? I'd say that's a compliment," said her dad.

"She's the best, sir," said Gilbert. "She knows things even wizards don't. Spellcraft history, the most obscure component charts . . . she's even learning how to raise the—"

"Gilbert," Skylar interrupted him curtly, "they

don't want to hear all of this."

"Did you think I wouldn't notice?" asked Skylar's father. "You're still wearing the anklet of the Noctonati."

"I told you it wasn't just a phase," said Skylar's mom.

Aldwyn's ears perked up at the mention of the bejeweled anklet of emerald and silver that Skylar always wore. He had suspected it wasn't the graduation gift she had once claimed it was, especially after seeing an identical one around the bony foot of Agdaleen, the gray-haired witch.

"I still seek knowledge above all else," said Skylar, "and there are things I have yet to learn."

"We know why you joined the cult of the Noctonati," said Skylar's father, "but no matter how long you study necromancy, it will be impossible to bring your sister back from the dead."

Information was coming in fast volleys, and Aldwyn was having a difficult time keeping up. He could see that Skylar was beginning to simmer.

"I won't let her go," she said, sounding a bit like a petulant teenager.

"She rests peacefully in the Tomorrowlife," said

Skylar's mom. "It's not your place to disturb her."

"I'm getting closer to unlocking the secrets of the dead," said Skylar. "How could you not want to see her again? Maybe even bring her back permanently."

"It's a knife's edge difference between what you're trying to do," said Skylar's father, "and what Paksahara has already begun. I know your heart is in the right place, but knowledge doesn't always lead to happiness. It can poison the soul."

Skylar was prevented from continuing to argue with her father when a nightingale soared into the gazebo through an open glass pane in the ceiling of the dome. In an urgent voice, she shouted: "Wolverines are approaching! Keep the young ones in the trees."

A bevy of birds took to the air, fleeing to the safety of the upper limbs. A quail with chicks too young to fly cast an illusion instead, concealing herself and the hatchlings within a noncorporeal flowerpot.

The brown-and-white bird who had called out the warning flew down to the familiars and Skylar's parents.

"Skylar, welcome back," she said. "I would love to hear all about your familiar adventures, but you and your friends need to be hidden at once."

"Hepsibah's right," said Skylar's father. "The wolverines have pledged allegiance to Paksahara and they've come to the Aviary once before asking us to join her. We refused, but they threatened to keep returning until we changed our minds. If they find you here, whatever quest you're on will be over. Paksahara will take any chance she gets to prevent the prophecy from being fulfilled."

"And if her disenchantment isn't reversed, things will change even more dramatically, and soon," interjected Skylar's mom. "Some animals have been waiting for a day like this, when humans could no longer protect themselves with magic. I fear that, unlike us, many will be unable to say no to Paksahara."

"How did the wolverines even find this place?" asked Gilbert. "I was standing right in front of it and didn't realize it was there."

"All wolverines are gifted with supernatural senses," explained Hepsibah. "Sight, hearing, and of course smell. They have the ability to see through illusions."

"You should probably go," said Skylar's mother.

"There isn't time," said Hepsibah. She pulled open a trap door on the deck with her talon. "Hide beneath here."

Skylar's father grabbed two sprigs of lavender in his talons.

"Cover yourselves with these," he instructed. "Hopefully the fragrance will muddle your scent."

The familiars did as they were told and quickly found themselves under the white wood planks, coated with the purple flowers. Skylar's father lowered the door back into place just as the metal entrance to the Aviary was pushed open.

Through the cracks in the wood siding of the deck, Aldwyn's green eyes peered out to see four wolverines saunter inside. He had never known an animal to look inherently evil, but these certainly did. He could even imagine their babies born with the same malicious grins and devilish eyes. The leader of the pack was slightly leaner than the others, which gave his walk more menace than his plodding followers. His sharpened lower fangs seemed to be permanently stained with blood. He approached Hepsibah, his claws scraping against the wood planks as he stepped up onto the gazebo.

"Have you changed your mind yet?" he asked, his voice calm but incredibly scary.

"No, Lothar," said Hepsibah. "We haven't."

The wolverines were standing just above Aldwyn, Skylar, and Gilbert, mere inches away from where the trio was hiding. Aldwyn was staring up at the bottom of the leader's foot and saw that a peculiar symbol was branded into his paw. It depicted a double hex, a five-pointed star inside of a circle, with two eyes squinting at its center.

"When the last human surrenders," continued Lothar, "Paksahara will not forget which animals stood with her and which against. It would be most regrettable to end up on the wrong side."

The familiars remained unmoving. Where was Stolix and her muscle-paralyzing talent when you needed it, because right now, staying completely still was a matter of life and death. To make matters worse, a line of prickly beetles were beginning to march up Aldwyn's leg.

"If it was my choice, I would have already burned the Aviary to the ground and feasted on the charred remains of those inside," said Lothar. "But Paksahara sees your flock as a valuable asset to her cause. She hoped you would have reconsidered by now."

"Sorry to disappoint," said Hepsibah. "The birds of Nearhurst refuse to raise their wings against the innocent. As you can see, we live a peaceful coexistence with our human companions. There's no reason all of Vastia couldn't do the same."

The beetles were now nearing Aldwyn's whiskers, and it was getting almost impossible for him to stay still: every little step of theirs felt like a small needle going into his skin. He flinched ever so slightly, sending dander flaking off his fur.

"I will report the unfortunate news to Paksahara," said Lothar. "This war will be won with or without you. And when it's over—"

He stopped suddenly, his nose searching the air. The wolverines beside him started sniffing as well.

"I smell the skin of a cat," said Lothar.

"Yes, one of the caretakers keeps them as pets at her home," said Hepsibah, thinking on her feet. "Perhaps you are breathing in the musk of her trousers."

Lothar inhaled the air a few more times before he was satisfied. It seemed the lavender had done the trick, as none of the intruders discovered what lay just below their noses.

"Now, where was I?" asked Lothar aloud.

"You were saying, 'when it's over . . .'" one of his pack reminded him.

"Yes, when this is over we'll return with torches and our appetites," said the wolverine, all too willing to show his blood-stained teeth. He stalked away from the gazebo, passing the illusory flowerpot cast by the quail. The slender wolverine halted before it and reached a claw inside. The illusion disappeared at once, and Aldwyn saw that Lothar had grabbed the mother quail by her neck. "And your illusions won't protect you from us."

He released the quivering quail and along with the other wolverines left the Aviary. None of the birds spoke or moved. Even though the danger seemed to have passed, Aldwyn stayed immobile and didn't dare pick off the beetles that were now dancing around on his nose.

After a short while, a parakeet flew into the glass dome through the same open pane Hepsibah had used to enter earlier and squawked.

"It's safe to come out now," said Skylar's father.

Relieved, Aldwyn brushed the prickly beetles from his nose and fur and pushed the trap door open with his head. The familiars emerged and rejoined Hepsibah and Skylar's parents atop the deck.

"Skylar and her companions need your assistance," said Skylar's mother to Hepsibah.

"I will do whatever I can to help them," said the five-feather master illusionist. "Just as I did with the first Prophesized Three sixty years ago."

Aldwyn was surprised to hear that the bird was so old, as she did not look aged at all. Then he wondered if an illusion was masking her true appearance.

"If we succeed in our quest," said Skylar, "then it will be those who sided with Paksahara who will regret their decision."

"Just promise us you will be careful," said Skylar's mother, with unexpected tenderness from one with such a stiff upper beak. "You might be a familiar first in your heart, but you will always be a daughter in ours."

"Good-bye, Mom," said Skylar, holding back a tear.

"Quickly, the two most dangerous wind currents in the southern Beyond?" asked Skylar's father.

"An erogale and a scimitar gust."

"That's my girl."

Skylar embraced her parents. Then she, Aldwyn, and Gilbert departed with Hepsibah, heading for the Aviary's steel door.

"Fly safely," called out Skylar's dad. "And remember, always keep your eyes on the horizon."

10

ECHOES FROM THE PAST

Skylar guided them back to the spot along Liveod's Canyon where the bridge had once spanned the gorge. Aldwyn was relieved to see that Baxley's trail still glowed brightly on both sides. He couldn't know for sure if all the birds of Nearhurst had a tendency for long-windedness, but Hepsibah certainly shared Skylar's fondness for lengthy lectures. The master illusionist had sounded off on the varying soil composition of the Northern Plateaus ever since they had left the Aviary, hardly pausing to take a breath and, more impressively, not letting Skylar get a word in edgewise.

Now Hepsibah perched herself atop one of the two wooden bridge posts and turned to the others.

"Once I've summoned the bridge, walk across quickly and don't question its existence," the nightingale instructed the familiars. "Disbelief weakens the strength of the illusion. I'd hate for your own skepticism to plunge you to the bottom of the gorge."

"If this is your idea of a pep talk, you might want to change your strategy . . . to one that doesn't include telling us how we're going to plummet to a horrible death," said Gilbert.

Hepsibah raised her wings, and at once a long bridge of wooden planks and rope appeared before the familiars. The detail of the illusion was simply astounding. There were swirls of grain on every plank and frayed fibers in the thick twine. There were even boot scuff marks every couple of steps. It looked like it had had years of use, even though it had never existed. And although Aldwyn knew that it was no more real than a daydream, he'd

soon be walking across it.

"Off you go," said the elder bird of Nearhurst.

Aldwyn noticed that, unlike Skylar's, Hepsibah's wing did not tremble while casting, which put him slightly more at ease. He decided to test a paw, well aware that if he waited for Gilbert to go first, the full moon would have come and gone. The pads of his foot made contact, and he could feel a firm wooden plank holding up his weight from beneath. Aldwyn continued until all four of his paws were on Hepsibah's bridge. Gilbert cautiously followed Aldwyn, while Skylar flew above them.

Hepsibah's illusion never wavered, and by the time Aldwyn had reached the final plank he had forgotten it was an illusion at all. Aldwyn glanced back and realized that once his paws touched the ground on the other side, he would no longer be on Vastian soil, but stepping into the Beyond. He and Jack often dreamed of venturing together across the enchanted fences, searching for treasure and exploring the unknown. But it seemed that his first journey outside of the queendom would be unaccompanied by his loyal.

Aldwyn and Gilbert completed their passage across the canyon and rejoined Baxley's path once more. Skylar soared in circles, eager to set off on the next leg of their adventure.

Skylar whistled a farewell to Hepsibah, who lowered her wings, causing the illusory bridge to fade into nothingness. And with that, the nightingale flew off in the direction of the Aviary, leaving the familiars alone on their quest yet again.

"Baxley went that way," said Aldwyn, pointing to a slowly rising hill of dense underbrush and rocks.

Aldwyn began the slow climb upward. Gilbert

followed behind, looking more nervous than usual.

"What is it now, Gilbert?" asked Skylar.

"I'm just expecting border monsters to jump out at any moment." He waited for her to respond, but she didn't give much of a reaction at all. "Hey, this is the part where you're supposed to say, 'Don't be ridiculous, Gilbert. Gundabeasts don't just sit around waiting for animals to wander by.'"

"I'm sorry, Gilbert. I'm really not an expert in the Beyond. In fact, I know as much about it as the two of you."

"In other words, *nothing?*" exclaimed the tree frog with a panicked croak.

Gilbert pulled out his spear, as if it would do him any good should a lumbering beast come out from behind a rock and attempt to squash him like a bug. He tried using it as a walking stick, but the tip got stuck in the ground, and despite his pulling, he couldn't yank it free. Aldwyn shook his head at the spectacle Gilbert was making of himself and walked ahead, following the path.

Skylar flapped over to a series of nearby bird droppings before circling back to Aldwyn.

187

"Interesting. Looks like a flock of geese stopped their southern migration here, where the enchanted fence once stood. Which makes sense, of course, given their—"

"I didn't know you had a sister," Aldwyn said, cutting her off before she rambled on any further. "You never mentioned her before."

Skylar became very quiet. Aldwyn's straightforwardness had caught her by surprise.

"I'm sorry," said Aldwyn. "It's just, if you ever wanted to talk about it . . ."

Aldwyn's words trailed off. Skylar flew silently beside him, as if considering whether or not to share her personal secrets.

"I shouldn't have said anything," said Aldwyn when the silence was beginning to get awkward.

"No, I've been keeping it bottled up for too long. I never even told Dalton." Skylar gathered some strength and continued. "It happened not long after I first began to fly. One afternoon, my sister and I took a trip outside the Aviary to collect flower petals. We stopped to eat some elderberries off the bush, and she accidentally ingested a few off a venom vine. I carried her home, but by the time we got her to a healing raven, it was too late."

Aldwyn could hear the grief in her voice.

"I mourned for her, and tried to hold her memory in my heart, to come to peace with the fact that she was gone. But I couldn't let go. I had heard that there were those capable of necromancy, but no one at the Aviary dared to dabble in forbidden magic. I plucked what I could from the scrolls, but it hardly scratched the surface. I had to learn more. Once, while I had snuck off to study a tome on portals to the Tomorrowlife, a human caretaker who tended the gardens of the glass dome spied what I was reading and approached me. She spoke fluently in the language of the birds. Her name was Lady Helenka. She was born to the Driftfolk clan. She had come to the Aviary at a young age after her caravan was burnt to the ground by her sister."

Aldwyn raised an eyebrow. He had heard the other half of this story from Skylar before.

"Agdaleen was her sister?" he asked.

"Yes, but Lady Helenka was good in every way that her sister was evil. One afternoon, when she sat cross-legged beside me, I spotted a bracelet of silver and emerald squares around her ankle. I didn't give it a second thought that day. We would meet several times a week in the shade of a birch tree, discussing matters of life and death and the ties between them. It wasn't until many months later that she first mentioned the Noctonati and explained their purpose. It was a secret sect of spellcasters, both human and animal, that believed in one thing more than any other: that knowledge should be pursued at all costs, because it was more valuable than gold, land, or a throne. The group gathered at the midnight hour in the caves on the western border of Mukrete. Lady Helenka said if anyone was capable of helping me bring back my sister, it would be the Noctonati.

"So one night, I snuck out of the Aviary and flew to the caves. There were sixteen crowded in the darkness—some wore hoods to hide their identities, even though all present took an oath to never reveal those who stood beside them. The complexities of the discussions often strayed beyond even my understanding, but with time I began to comprehend more. By the end of my first year, I had earned my anklet. I had gained so much insight into the mysteries of the dead, but these seekers of knowledge simply didn't have access to the spells I needed. And so I learned what I'd have to do if I wanted to advance my knowledge further: become a familiar."

Many of the questions Aldwyn had about Skylar—why she had stolen *Wyvern and Skull's Tome of the Occult* from Kalstaff's library, the meaning of the bejeweled anklet she wore, even why she had decided to become a familiar—had been answered. But it was clear she still had unfinished business, and there was no telling how far she would go to accomplish it.

Gilbert finally caught up to them, out of breath, the red mud-tipped spear in his hand. "Thanks for waiting up, guys," he huffed sarcastically, but then he noticed the somber mood Aldwyn and Skylar were in and fell silent.

The group continued their slow ascent, and soon it was past high sun. Aldwyn suddenly felt a bit queasy, and he thought it might have been because he hadn't eaten since waking up in the whistlegrass.

"I don't know about you two, but I'm starved," said Aldwyn.

He led the group off trail and sat down on top of a moss-covered rock. He dug into Jack's pouch and pulled out some dried salmon jerky with his teeth. Skylar found some fallen seeds on the ground and nibbled away. Gilbert, on the other hand, wasn't eating; he was unrolling one of Marianne's pocket scrolls that he had packed for himself.

"You okay, Gilbert?" asked Aldwyn, trying to cool down his body against the cold stone. "I've never seen you pass up a lunch break for study."

"Oh, I've been snacking along the way."

But Aldwyn could tell that there was more to it than that. Gilbert read one of the spells under his breath.

"What's that you're practicing?" asked Skylar.

"I'm going back to basics," said Gilbert. "Maybe I got ahead of myself with the enchanted bows. Thought I'd try a simple high-hop spell. It says here all I have to do is flick my fingers the right way."

Gilbert held a webbed hand in the air, making

figures-of-eight with his fingertips. Mid-spell, a horsefly buzzed by his ear and he swatted at it, breaking the pattern he'd been so intricately performing.

"Oh, I messed up, didn't I?" asked Gilbert, realizing his mistake.

Just then, four rocks enchanted by Gilbert's misdirected spell went hopping past them.

"I'm not cut out for this." The tree frog sighed. "I'd be better off—"

But before he could finish, a fifth rock leaped in from who knows where and clunked him in the head, knocking him to the ground.

Aldwyn and Skylar rushed to his side.

"Gilbert, are you okay?" asked Aldwyn.

The woozy tree frog opened his eyes. "Who's Gilbert?"

Skylar and Aldwyn shared a concerned look.

"You," said Skylar.

"Where am I? What happened?" he asked.

"You're Gilbert!" said Skylar. "Our fellow companion."

Still nothing seemed to be jolting his memory.

"You're Marianne's familiar," continued Skylar.

"One of the Prophesized Three, on a quest to save the world."

Gilbert's eyes lit up. Was there a spark of remembering?

"On a quest to save the world," he repeated, sitting upright. "Yes. It's all coming back to me." He looked himself up and down. "I'm a tree frog from Daku, a great amphibian warrior from the Swamps." He pulled out the bamboo spear and stared at the red mud-stained end. "And I can see my weapon has already seen the heat of many battles."

Uh-oh, thought Aldwyn. This definitely did not sound like Gilbert.

"If the world is at stake, we have little time to waste," bellowed the tree frog, in a bold voice Aldwyn had never heard before.

Aldwyn leaned over to Skylar and whispered: "What do we do? He's clearly not right in the head."

"Gilbert, I think when you bumped your head, you lost your memory," said Skylar.

"Nonsense. I'm fully aware of who I am and what I'm destined for." He hopped forward without hesitation, then stopped, confused. "Where are we going again?"

"To find the Crown of the Snow Leopard," said Aldwyn.

"Right. The Snow of the Crown Leopard. What are we waiting for?"

"Isn't there some kind of spell you can cast to get him back to normal?" Aldwyn asked Skylar.

"There are three types of brain coral that might do the trick, but without those components, my wings are tied. I think we're just going to have to wait it out."

"Come now, well-groomed bird and cat with the bite out of his ear," Gilbert called back to them. "There are trolls to behead and dragons to slay!"

Aldwyn shrugged, and the familiars resumed their journey. He was fairly confident that Gilbert would remember soon enough who he really was, although for now he seemed possessed by some legendary hero. One that Aldwyn could only imagine must have existed in Gilbert's fantasies.

"Creatures from Beyond, you can't hide from me," Gilbert shouted. "Show yourself and surrender before my spear."

"Is that really necessary?" asked Aldwyn.

"See these scars on my arms," Gilbert called to the hills, ignoring him. "You're probably wondering how I got them."

"Tripping into a bonfire, falling out of Marianne's bed, and accidentally jumping through a closed window," said Skylar under her breath.

"From fighting a scorpion-tailed lion with my bare webbed hands!"

"You don't know any silencing spells, do you?" Aldwyn asked Skylar.

"If I did, I would have already used one."

"Gilbert, we're trying to sneak up on our enemies," said Aldwyn, lying in an attempt to quiet the tree frog's dangerous boasts.

"Yes, of course," whispered Gilbert. "You will not hear another word from me until I see the whites of their eyes."

Finally, there was some peace and quiet as Gilbert began stalking silently beside Aldwyn. When the group reached an area where tall rocks jutted out from the ground, Baxley's trail suddenly veered left, then sharply to the right, then back and forth, twisting in circles, leaping from rock to tree branch and to the ground again.

"What is it?" asked Skylar.

"The paw prints," replied Aldwyn. "They're going every which direction. Almost as if Baxley was running from something."

"Can't you just pick up the path where it resumes?" asked Skylar.

"There are so many prints, it's hard to tell."

As Aldwyn was trying to make sense of the multitude of paw prints in front of him, he spotted a white cloth pouch lying on the ground at the base of one of the trees. Aldwyn moved closer and could see a symbol sewn into the outside: a cat's paw reaching for the moon. The sand sign of the Mooncatchers. This pouch must have belonged to his father!

"You should take it," said Skylar, eyeing the pouch as well. "While it's too small to hold the Spheris, it might have some clues inside."

But Aldwyn was hesitant. He didn't like what he'd learned about Baxley thus far, and he was quite certain that any personal effects within his father's shoulder bag would only disappoint him further.

Aldwyn felt a chill run down his back, and when he turned away from the pouch, he noticed that a thick fog had rolled in all around them. The gray mist was getting more impenetrable by the second, so dense that Aldwyn could no longer see his companions or anything but the footprints glowing through it.

"Skylar, Gilbert, where are you?" called Aldwyn.

"I'm over here," said Skylar.

"Over here," she repeated, but this time it seemed to come from the opposite direction.

"Follow the sound of my voice," commanded Gilbert. Aldwyn took a few steps toward it before he heard the tree frog call from behind him: "You're going the wrong way."

Another voice called out. It was Aldwyn's own: "Skylar, Gilbert, I'm over here!" Now Aldwyn was truly confused: he hadn't said a word.

"Guys, that wasn't me," cried Aldwyn. "Something's going on."

He spotted some shadows moving through the fog.

"Gilbert, is that you?" he asked.

"Yes." "No." "I'm not sure." Somehow Gilbert's

voice responded from three different places.

"Something must be mimicking our voices," said Skylar, or at least what sounded like her. "Just stay where you are. Don't move."

"Don't listen to it, Aldwyn," another Skylar said in response. "Come toward me. We only stand a chance if we're together."

"I'm holding my ground," said Gilbert.

Aldwyn almost tripped over Gilbert's webbed feet. The two had been just inches away from each other.

"*Gustavius rescutium,*" incanted Skylar, and a small whirlwind swept clear some of the fog surrounding them, enough for her to spot Aldwyn and Gilbert and flap over to where they were huddled.

The three looked around, then stared deeper into the fog. Out from the mist slithered a tentacle-like arm with a mouth on the end of it. Then another. And four more.

"I'm hungry," said one of the mouths, perfectly mimicking Aldwyn's voice.

"Me, too," added another, this one sounding just like Skylar.

Then the body of this strange beast appeared from out of the fog. It looked like a beached squid, short fuzzy feelers guiding it forward as it pulled itself along the ground.

"I think it's an echo beast," whispered Skylar. "They became extinct in Vastia during the reign of Brannfalk."

"How do we defeat it?" asked Aldwyn.

"If we coordinate our attacks perfectly, then perhaps—"

Skylar didn't get a chance to finish, as Gilbert leaped forward with spear in hand.

"Every one of your mouths will be screaming in terror when I'm finished with you," the tree frog shouted fearlessly.

One of the tentacle arms, its mouth slobbering, lashed out and gave Gilbert an unforgiving wallop, sending him airborne until he smacked into a boulder. Flat on his back, Gilbert was easy prey for the two other tentacles circling him.

"Mine," said Skylar's voice from a mouth.

"No, mine," said another, this time mimicking Gilbert.

As they stretched toward him, Aldwyn sent

a dried tree branch flying through the air that knocked the tentacles away for a moment, long enough for Gilbert to wake up. He took one look at the echo beast and let out a blood-curdling scream.

"Ahhhhh! I'm going to die!"

"He's back," said Skylar.

Gilbert hopped over to his companions. "What happened?! The last thing I remember is getting hit on the head by a rock. Then I'm waking up with a . . . *that* over me!"

Aldwyn kept flinging stones at the beast, but the slimy mass barely seemed to notice.

"That's the best I've got," said Aldwyn to the others.

"I'm not sure an illusion will do much," said Skylar. "Echo beasts don't have eyes. They just sense body heat."

"I vote for running," croaked Gilbert.

"You won't get away," Gilbert's voice called back from one of the mouths.

And it was true: by now, five of the tentacles had surrounded the trio on all sides, and the sixth was hovering threateningly in the air above them.

Drips of viscous saliva landed on Aldwyn's fur. One of the mouths swooped down, about to take a bite out of Aldwyn's still-whole ear, when the other mouths let out a horrifying wail. The echo beast recoiled, thrashing in pain. Through the fog, Aldwyn could see that the body of the beast was being attacked. He just couldn't make out by what.

"Come on, let's go!" shouted Skylar as the mouths retreated to assist the body.

The familiars made a run for it, Aldwyn leading them to where he saw Baxley's paw prints glowing on the ground. Along the way, he scooped up his father's fallen pouch with his teeth. The familiars looked back one last time at the echo beast, which was thrashing from left to right as its unseen attacker held fast to its back. The echo beast howled in pain, which was made all the more disconcerting by the fact that it was Aldwyn's, Skylar's, and Gilbert's own voices that were doing the screaming.

11

TIME STREAM

After escaping the rocky crags where the echo beast had trapped them, Baxley's paw print path led Aldwyn and his fellow familiars deeper and deeper into the jungles north of Vastia. Gilbert and Skylar had spent a good amount of time debating the intentions of whatever creature had fended off the echo beast's attack.

"It looked like it was coming to our rescue," Gilbert argued. "Maybe it was one of those angel beasts, bursting forth from the Tomorrowlife at our time of need."

"More likely some predator of the Beyond,"

Skylar countered with a shake of her head. "I'm sure if we stuck around long enough, it would have eaten us, too."

Aldwyn, though, had been less interested in his companions' theories than in what dangled around his neck: his father's cloth pouch. He had yet to look inside.

"Aldwyn, just open it," said Skylar, and it wasn't the first time she had implored him to do so since he had picked it up.

"We're going to keep following the path regardless of what I find," he replied. Still, a part of him knew that she was right, and that he should set aside his personal feelings for the good of the quest. But he wasn't quite ready yet.

"If it would be easier, I'll look," said Skylar.

"Give him a little more time, Skylar," said Gilbert. "You can be so pushy."

Skylar muttered something about Gilbert having no idea what pushy meant but eased off, keeping her beak shut as the familiars continued. They fought their way through thickets and vines for what seemed like hours, precious time with only three days left until Paksahara's promise of a new Dead Army would come to fruition.

The trail eventually rejoined the Ebs, and Skylar remarked that she hadn't realized just how far the great river stretched into the lands of the Beyond. They walked in silence along the footpath hugging the water's edge, but the jungle hardly shared their quietude. Their ears were greeted by a cacophony of birds chirping, snakes rustling through grass, and drops of water falling from leaves.

Although the air was thick with moisture, Aldwyn was incredibly thirsty. He spied a large corkwood tree with mouthwateringly clear sap dripping from a hole in its bark. Aldwyn stepped off the glowing paw prints and approached, thinking nothing could look more refreshing.

"I wouldn't drink that if I were you," warned Skylar.

Aldwyn retracted his tongue a split second before ingesting the liquid.

"Kalstaff had a saying about jungle fauna," she continued. "The ones that look the most inviting are the ones you should steer furthest from."

Aldwyn looked again at the inviting sap

dripping from the tree. It appeared more delectable than the cool waters of the Ebs that flowed nearby, but Skylar was right: now wasn't the time to take any chances. He watched a giant beetle scuttle over to the bark and take a taste of the sticky liquid. When it turned to creep away, the bug exploded, splattering beetle guts all over the ground. Quickly, worm-sized roots slithered out from the earth, grabbing chunks of beetle flesh and dragging them beneath the ground, and Aldwyn decided that he would be quite happy to stay thirsty for a little while longer.

He returned to his father's trail but didn't take a hundred steps before tripping over an unseen object that had been hidden beneath the dense flora on the jungle floor. He looked down at where he had stubbed his paw and spotted the shiny silver tip of a sword's blade. Aldwyn brushed away the leaves to reveal the rest of the weapon. It was a magnificent sword, its hilt made from solid ebony and carved in the shape of a black tarantula. Aldwyn was about to tell his friends about his discovery when he heard Skylar call out.

"Guys, look what I found."

She had made a discovery of her own: a helmet covered in thick brown hair with a horn at the center of it. Gilbert approached for a closer look.

"What kind of animal fur is that?" he asked.

"It's armpit hair," explained Skylar, "from one of the strongest creatures ever known to exist." She spoke as if she was in the presence of something awe inspiring. "This is a helmet of the Fjord Guards. It bestows the strength of giants on whoever wears it."

Gilbert stepped back, and now he stumbled across another abandoned artifact: a brass candelabra with five empty candle holders.

"What's a candelabra doing in the middle of the jungle?" he wondered aloud.

Gilbert reached out a webbed hand, and at once multicolored flames burst out from the candleless holders. He jumped back, but not before a greenish flame had set some twigs ablaze. Skylar quickly flitted over and batted out the burning branches with her wing.

Aldwyn's attention had already been drawn elsewhere.

"You two might want to see this," he said from up ahead.

Before them, the ground was strewn with objects of all shapes and sizes: a shield with a picture of a white beetle on its surface that seemed to frost the ground around it; a charcoal-black wand that appeared to quiver and shake as if it was scared; and a closed coffin double the size of any man. There were spyglasses, elephant saddles, and a rug woven with all the colors of the night sky. Some things looked like they had been there for years, while others seemed more recently arrived.

"Could the Crown of the Snow Leopard be here?" asked Aldwyn.

Skylar landed next to him, completely in awe of the treasures on display.

"Perhaps," she replied, her eyes searching. "Look, there's a dreaming rug, and Ebekenezar's cloak," she added excitedly, pointing at a worn and frayed piece of fabric. "And here, two of the three Swords of the Spider."

"I think I saw the third one back there," said Aldwyn.

"What is all this stuff?" asked Gilbert.

"Magical artifacts from all over the queendom and the Beyond," answered Skylar. "And someone or something brought them here."

For the next little while, the familiars were lost in exploring the items littering the jungle floor, looking for anything resembling what might be the Crown.

"I think this could be a mawpi's lair," said Skylar suddenly.

"Come on, mawpis are just make-believe," replied Gilbert. "There's no such thing as magic-sniffing goblins."

"No, they're real. I've read firsthand accounts of people who have seen them. They've just become increasingly rare."

"Well, no goblin could ever be strong enough to carry a coffin or an elephant saddle," said Gilbert.

"True, unless they were wearing one of the helmets of the Fjords."

Gilbert couldn't argue with her logic. "Okay, so let's say it is a mawpi's lair. Where's the mawpi?"

"Probably off collecting new treasures."

Aldwyn's eyes scanned past a curved mirror and a mesh bag filled with gold coins before landing on a crystal figurine of a squirrel in a terrified pose.

"What's this?" he asked his companions.

"Looks like a glass squirrel to me," said Gilbert. "Very realistic."

"That's because it was once alive," chirped Skylar, coming up beside them. "In fact, it might still be. But it's trapped for eternity in crystal. I've seen another statue just like this in the Museum of Bronzhaven, of a Beyonder who ventured into Necro's Maze."

"Necro's Maze," said Aldwyn, his ears perking up. "Jack told me about that before. He said no one has ever made it to the center."

"That's because Necro is a hideous beast that turns flesh to glass with the touch of its tail," said Skylar. "There is no spell capable of reversing the curse. Wizards speculate that the only way to return the statues to life is by killing the beast itself."

Aldwyn stared at the squirrel's frozen expression and felt bad for the little critter. He actually reminded him of a fellow rooftop dweller from Bridgetower who had roasted nuts in the hot smoke of the chimneys. Meanwhile, Gilbert had wandered off to the far end of the clearing, where he was playing with a silver chain of beads; two seemed to be shimmering a bright blue while at least a half dozen more were dull and colorless. And Skylar had already fluttered over to a crystal cube lying in the dirt.

"It doesn't look like the Crown is here," said Aldwyn. "And Baxley's path goes this way."

"Just give me a moment. If this cube is what I think it is, it could contain all the spells of the Elder Council," said Skylar, who was transfixed by the sparkling object. "Some were never transcribed to parchment." She pressed a wing against the side of the quartz block, and smoke started to stir inside of it. She closed her eyes, and to Aldwyn it looked as if she was attempting to draw the cube's knowledge straight through her feathers. Aldwyn watched as a swirling mist started to seep out from the quartz.

"Hey, Skylar, Aldwyn, I think I just found the mawpi," called out Gilbert.

"Not now," Skylar replied, deep in concentration, her eyes squeezed shut.

Aldwyn turned around and saw where Gilbert was standing. On the ground beside him, the decomposing corpse of a goblin lay facedown. What was worrying was that two giant fang marks were clearly visible on the dead body's back.

When Aldwyn returned his gaze to Skylar, the mist had taken the form of a ghostly snake. It didn't take long for Aldwyn to connect the dots and scream:

"Skylar, get away from that thing right now!"

But she had fallen into some kind of trance and didn't respond. Above her, the cube's serpent-shaped genie was about to strike.

"Skylar!" called Gilbert. "Skylar!"

She remained transfixed, leaving Aldwyn no choice but to give her a telekinetic push, jolting her awake.

"It hasn't spoken to me yet," cried Skylar, still unaware of the deadly inhabitant of the artifact hovering over her.

"I don't think it's going to do much talking," shouted Aldwyn.

Finally, Skylar looked up to see the misty fangs widening. Then the familiars ran. Gilbert shoved the silver chain of beads into his violet bud backpack as he fled. The trio dashed past the mawpi's corpse, leaving the goblin's lair and the rest of the stolen artifacts behind. The serpent genie, bound by the cursed cube, was unable to follow.

When they had caught their breath, the familiars made their way back to the river, and Aldwyn led them along the purple paw prints.

"I'm sorry about what I did," said Skylar. "I know it was reckless, but I thought that cube might contain spells that could aid us in defeating Paksahara."

Aldwyn had grown to know Skylar well enough to recognize when she wasn't telling the whole truth. First, there was the lack of eye contact; then there was the way she shifted her weight from talon to talon. He had a feeling that her temptation was less about the journey and more about following the credo of the Noctonati: knowledge above all else. But it would be hypocritical of Aldwyn to call out Skylar for letting her own personal issues interfere with the quest when he still hadn't looked inside the pouch pressed up against the black fur on his chest.

Thinking about it that way, Aldwyn could no

longer allow his own selfish reasons to keep him from opening his father's bag. He was about to do just that when the pouch was pulled straight from his neck by some unseen force. It was as if an invisible hand had reached out and grabbed it.

"Hey, did you guys see that?" he asked his companions, spinning around, looking for the thief.

"What?" asked Gilbert.

"The pouch! Somebody took it."

Aldwyn thought he heard something trip in the bushes nearby, and out of the corner of his eye he saw a flash of blue, but when he turned to look, there was nothing but dangling jungle vines.

"Maybe the invisible howler monkeys roam these jungles," said Skylar.

Gilbert clutched his flower bud backpack extra tight. "They better not lay a hand on my flies."

"Aldwyn, I told you you should have opened that bag sooner," said Skylar, who was flying about looking for it.

"How was I supposed to know it would get stolen like that?" asked Aldwyn. He was searching the tall grass and the reeds beside the river.

"Let's just hope Baxley's path and the Song of

the First Phylum are enough to guide us to the Crown," said Skylar.

Aldwyn gave one last glance around before following the path again. He experienced an unexpected emotion: a feeling of loss. Just a few minutes ago he had had no desire to see what was in Baxley's pouch, but now that it was gone, he would have given anything for a peek inside.

"What's the next verse of the nursery rhyme again?" asked Gilbert.

"*Through brown mist stone arrows point, To where the ladybugs rest. A supper to be placed, In the great spider's nest,*" sang Skylar. "We should be keeping our eyes peeled for stone arrows."

"And I'll be on the lookout for ladybugs," said Gilbert. "For the quest, of course. Not to eat."

The jungle seemed to breathe differently here by the river. This part of the Ebs was narrow and moved at such a crawl it almost appeared not to be flowing at all. A gentle breeze stirred the foliage around them, and Aldwyn observed how it blew some of the leaves on the ground upward, as if they were floating back to the branches from which they had once hung. The sun and the sky gave the impression of being out of sync as well, casting shadows of clouds that weren't there.

"Guys, I'm getting a puddle viewing!" exclaimed Gilbert, who was staring into a stagnant portion of the Ebs. "My uselessness on this journey has finally come to an end."

The others hurried to his side. Indeed: there in the water was the rippling image of Aldwyn, clearly in some kind of peril, taking refuge within a large circle of stones. A voice bubbled up from the stream and spoke: "Aldwyn is in terrible danger. If you wish to save him and all of Vastia, you must seek the Crown of the Snow Leopard."

"Great," cried Gilbert to the waters. "Tell me something I don't know!"

But the viewing had spoken its piece, and the image of Aldwyn slowly began to float downstream. Gilbert looked crushed with disappointment. "Even my puddle viewings aren't helpful," he said, then turned to the river and shouted: "Next time, why don't you tell me that the sun rises in the morning and sets at night? Or that Skylar is a bird and I'm a worthless familiar?"

"Gilbert, don't be so hard on yourself," said

Aldwyn. "If it wasn't for you, Paksahara would have turned us to dust in the Sunken Palace."

"I'm beginning to think that was just luck," said Gilbert.

Suddenly, a bamboo spear flew down from the trees, narrowly missing Aldwyn's feet. All three familiars ducked for cover.

"We're being attacked!" said Aldwyn.

Gilbert, who seemed angry with himself and with the world, reached for his own spear off his back and flung it straight up into the trees, from where the assault had come. The weapon disappeared in the branches. The familiars waited for a long moment, expecting another attempt on their lives. But none came. Then Skylar glanced at the bamboo stick impaled in the ground beside them.

"Gilbert, isn't that *your* spear?" she asked.

"What? That's impossible. This is the one that was thrown at us. Mine never came down from the trees."

Aldwyn looked more closely at the sharpened stick and noticed the engraving of a circle with a star inside it. There was no doubt about it: this was Gilbert's symbol.

"Okay, this is getting weird," said Aldwyn.

"You better be careful," a voice called out. "You could have hurt yourself."

Aldwyn's, Skylar's, and Gilbert's heads shot up in unison, and there, a little farther up the river, they saw a green iguana sitting atop a small waterfall.

"Welcome to the Time Stream," he said. "Nice to see you again."

"But we've never met," said Skylar.

"That's what you think. *Gesundheit.*"

The familiars looked at each other, utterly confused.

"Ha-choo!" sneezed the blue jay, to her surprise.

"You see, Skylar, the course of life is like a whirlpool here," said the iguana. "Sometimes it moves forward, sometimes backward."

"How do you know my name?" she asked.

"You introduced yourself the first time we met."

Aldwyn decided to cut through this interesting but confusing banter with questions they needed answers to.

"Did you see a black-and-white cat pass by this

stream, about three years ago?" he asked. "His name was Baxley. He was carrying a steel ball in search of the Crown of the Snow Leopard."

"I'm afraid I didn't," said the iguana. "But I look forward to meeting him."

Aldwyn was most confounded by this jungle lizard, who only seemed to talk in riddles.

"I don't understand," said Gilbert, who was just as flummoxed as Aldwyn.

"Place a leaf in these waters and let it drift downstream, and it could wash up on the shores of Vastia ten years ago," explained the iguana. "The waters of the Ebs begin their flow right here, and like the currents of time, they circle and spin before setting their path. Here and now is yesterday and tomorrow. Everything is connected. Past, present, and future. Now you better get going. You'll be arriving soon."

And with that, the iguana scurried up a tree and disappeared into the foliage.

The familiars were more than eager to leave this perplexing place. Aldwyn led them along Baxley's glowing trail as it curved around the base of the cliffs from which the waterfall descended.

It then slightly backtracked to the south, running almost parallel to where they had walked previously. Over by the river, the familiars could hear the sound of voices.

". . . but I thought that cube might contain spells that could aid us in defeating Paksahara."

It was Skylar's voice. Peering through the trees, Aldwyn saw himself, Skylar, and Gilbert walking along the path toward the Time Stream. It was a puzzling paradox he could hardly wrap his mind around. His eyes spotted Baxley's pouch around his own neck, and he knew full well that an invisible hand would be taking it from him any second. Unless he did first!

Aldwyn focused his telekinesis and pulled the bag from his other self, lifting it from his neck and tugging it through the air right to him. That's when he realized who had taken the pouch in the first place: himself. His head was spinning.

"Hey, did you guys see that?" asked the past Aldwyn, looking for the culprit.

"What?" asked the past Gilbert.

"The pouch! Somebody took it," said the past

Aldwyn, just as the present Aldwyn had a few minutes before.

"Quick, hide," said Aldwyn to his companions, who had now spotted the past versions of themselves as well.

Gilbert hopped for a tree, but tripped, smacking his face into the ground. Skylar was quicker. With a flash of her blue wing, she conjured an illusion of hanging vines to block them from view.

"Maybe the invisible howler monkeys roam these jungles," said the past Skylar. In the present, the three familiars stood silently and watched as their past selves continued toward the waterfall. Aldwyn had the pouch around his neck once more. And this time he wouldn't miss the chance to open it. Whatever lay inside that cloth bag was a piece of his father, and therefore a piece of himself. Like the iguana had said, the past and present were interconnected, and Aldwyn knew that he could never truly move forward without first looking back.

12

THE GREAT SPIDER'S NEST

Dried worms. Shriveled garlic. Blades of grass. A necklace with three shells on it. Two smooth stones. These were the contents of Baxley's pouch. Looking at them, Aldwyn felt silly for having been so hesitant to open the cloth bag in the first place.

Sitting in a quiet spot on some tangled roots away from Gilbert and Skylar, Aldwyn stared at the mundane items before him and realized they didn't tell much of a story at all. Worms to catch fish, stones to make fire. He had expected

incriminating evidence of the selfish and villain-
ous character Malvern had described. Perhaps
a journal that exposed how little Baxley cared
for his son and wife and how his only love was
seeking treasure. But alas, Aldwyn was left with
blades of grass, which told him nothing; neither
confirming his fears nor serving to counter them.

Skylar and Gilbert gave Aldwyn some time
before coming over beside him.

"Any clues that might help us?" asked Skylar.

"None that I see," replied Aldwyn.

"Anything tell you more about your father?"
asked Gilbert.

Aldwyn shook his head.

Skylar lowered her beak toward the string of
shells lying on the roots.

"I think these are whisper shells," she said.
"Have you listened to them?"

Aldwyn's heart began to beat a little faster. In
his haste, he had thought the necklace was just
that, a necklace. But now he remembered what
Jack had shown him at the Historical Archives:
that whisper shells contained voices, pieces of
the past recorded in time. Unlike the larger

conch and snail shells gathered on the counters of the Archives, these were no bigger than one of Aldwyn's toes.

He put his ear up to the first and heard the soft purr of a female voice. It was the same voice he had heard many times in his dreams, gentle and reassuring.

"Baxley," the voice said, "make sure you come back to us."

There was no question in Aldwyn's mind. This was his mother, Corliss. But she hardly sounded crazy.

"Who is speaking?" asked Skylar.

"My mother, I think," replied Aldwyn. "She said, 'Baxley, make sure you come back to us.'"

"That's not a very long message," said Gilbert.

"Well, it's not a very big shell," said Skylar.

Aldwyn moved on to the second shell and leaned his ear to it. This time, he heard the sound of a kitten mewing.

"It sounds like kittens," said Aldwyn. "Or maybe just one. I can't tell."

"Perhaps it's you," said Skylar. "Malvern said Baxley left Maidenmere just after you were born.

What if he brought along the shell to remember you?"

Aldwyn allowed himself for a moment to picture his father walking along this very path, listening to the sound of his voice. *Had his father been keeping him close this entire journey?*

No. He wouldn't let his mind start spinning fantasies that were most likely untrue.

"What does the last one say?" asked Skylar.

Aldwyn moved his ear beside it, but all he heard was silence.

"It's not saying anything," he told Skylar and Gilbert.

"A voice memory yet to be recorded," said the blue jay.

Aldwyn couldn't hide his disappointment. He secretly wished to hear the voice of his father. Good or bad, he was curious to know what Baxley sounded like, and if hearing him speak would bring back any memories from his earliest days.

Skylar looked through the gap in the trees above and saw that the moon was three nights away from being full.

"We should keep moving," she said.

Aldwyn used his telekinesis to gather up all of the contents of Baxley's pouch and add them to his own. Then the familiars marched on.

The paw prints sloped downward from there, making the journey a bit easier. Skylar seemed to enjoy gliding most of the way. The jungle became less dense, and once they had reached the base of the hill, they found a dirt road that was carving its way through the trees, and on it Aldwyn could see the marks left by horse carts. This was the first sign of any civilization at all in the Beyond.

Baxley's paw print trail intersected with the dirt road, giving the familiars a chance to examine the tracks more closely. Hooves and wheels had rumbled past recently. Where were they coming from? And where were they going?

"There were gundabeasts here, as well," said Skylar, pointing her wing to massive indentations cratered into the mud. "Big ones."

At that moment, a man's voice called out, "Help!" It seemed to be coming from around a bend in the road.

The trio followed the cry, and as they rounded a cluster of jungle palms, they found themselves face to face with the scene of a massacre. The bodies of a dozen armored soldiers and cloaked wizards lay strewn about on the ground, some wincing in pain, others unconscious and in desperate need of a raven's healing abilities. Aldwyn realized that these weren't just any warriors but the very ones that Queen Loranella had sent off from her palace. There was no sign of their horses anywhere.

"Familiars," beckoned the same man who had called for help. "It is you, the Prophesized Three." Aldwyn recognized him as Urbaugh, the bearded wizard from the emergency council meeting. He lay propped up against a tree, his leg bent in three places it shouldn't have been. "For the last two days, we were tracking a caravan heading north. We thought we had gone undetected, never using torches and staying miles behind. But we must not have been as stealthy as we thought, because hours ago we were ambushed. Out from the trees came two gundabeasts with chains wrapped around their waists. They were commanded by one of the tongueless cave shamans of Stalagmos. Our swords, halberds, and maces were no match for the two beasts' giant fists and horns."

"And this caravan?" asked Skylar. "What did it carry?"

"Forgive me, for my animal tongue is a bit rusty," replied Urbaugh. "My own familiar passed into the Tomorrowlife many seasons ago."

"The caravan?" repeated Skylar more slowly. "What did it carry?"

"This we still don't know, but it was something very valuable to Paksahara. Of that I am sure."

"How do you know?" asked Skylar.

"The wagons bore her symbol," said Urbaugh. "A double hex, with her wicked, gleaming eyes peering out from the center."

"I saw the same symbol on the foot of Lothar, the wolverine from the Aviary," said Aldwyn.

"Go on with whatever journey you've begun," said Urbaugh. "My brother's familiar ran off to find the nearest healing ravens. There's nothing you can do for us now."

Aldwyn felt guilty to leave such brave warriors spilling their blood on the ground. But Urbaugh was right. Their calling was the Crown of the Snow Leopard. Without it, nothing they did would matter.

"Here, take my maggots," said Gilbert, reaching into his flower bud backpack. "Besides being delicious, they're actually quite nourishing."

The tree frog left them in Urbaugh's hand.

"Gilbert, I think he'd rather go hungry," said Skylar.

This brought a smile to the bearded wizard's face. Then his eyes closed.

"No, don't leave us," croaked Gilbert. "It's not fair!" Gilbert leaped atop Urbaugh's chest and raised a webbed fist to the sky. "Curse you, Paksahara!"

Urbaugh's left eye opened slightly.

"I'm not dead," he said. "Just resting. Now get off of me. I have many cracked ribs."

"Right," said Gilbert, sheepishly stepping down. "Sorry."

The familiars left the wounded warriors behind and resumed the glowing path. The dirt road quickly disappeared into the trees behind them, and they again seemed to be all alone in the Beyond.

The journey so far had been exhausting for

Aldwyn, even with his two companions close by his side. It was hard to imagine that his father had come all this way on his own. Aldwyn didn't have a full appreciation for the distance they had covered until he glanced at the map Scribius had been busy composing along every step of their quest. Through the dusty plains of the Northern Plateaus, crossing Liveod's Canyon, reconnecting with the Ebs in the jungles of the Beyond, twisting toward the Time Stream and then back down to where they walked now, entering a narrow ravine.

"I really hope when we meet this snow leopard, he doesn't put up a fight over his Crown," said Gilbert. "Because after all we've been through, you'd think he would be pretty understanding."

"I'll pull it off her spotted head myself if I have to," said Skylar. "I can get very cranky after barely sleeping for a week."

Aldwyn noticed that the walls of the ravine were getting higher and that the chasm itself was leading to a giant, splintered stone wall—a dead end where Baxley's paw prints came to a sudden stop.

"Aldwyn, I hate to doubt your clarity of vision," said Skylar, "but unless Baxley had wings, I don't see a way out of here."

Aldwyn was just as confused. He doubled back to make sure he hadn't missed something.

"Kind of reminds me of Daku," said Gilbert, staring at the cracked wall.

"Gilbert, you grew up in a *swamp*," said Skylar.

"No, I'm talking about the spider web soufflé my mom used to make us," said Gilbert. "It used to look just like that wall."

Aldwyn looked up, and sure enough, the fissures on the stone barrier made concentric circles with lines stretching out from the center just like a spider web.

Through brown mist stone arrows point, To where the ladybugs rest. A supper to be placed, In the great spider's nest. The Song of the First Phylum's third verse played in Aldwyn's head.

"Are you guys thinking what I'm thinking?" asked Aldwyn.

"That a spider web soufflé would taste amazing right now?" said Gilbert.

"The nursery rhyme," said Skylar, nodding her

beak. "This must be the great spider's nest."

Aldwyn pointed to a circular hole in the wall, just outside the center of the fissure.

"*A supper to be placed*," he said. "Right in that hole, like a key."

"Wait, that's the second half of the stanza," said Skylar. "What about the stone arrows and the ladybugs?"

"We must have skipped an entire clue!" exclaimed Aldwyn. "We'll have to go back."

They all looked deflated.

"We don't have time for that," said Skylar.

"Besides, I've never seen a ladybug that would fill that hole," said Gilbert. "It would have to be as big as that red and black rock over there."

Aldwyn and Skylar looked down to see lying in a pile of gray stones a perfect sphere of red dotted with black.

"That *is* the ladybug," said Aldwyn.

"It is?" asked Gilbert.

"Yes," said Skylar. "The missing gemstone from the Sanctuary. Aldwyn, your father wasn't a grave robber. He was following the clues, too."

Aldwyn's mind flashed back to the paw prints

leading in and out of the crypt. "The arrows. They must have been obscured by the sandstorm!"

"*Through brown mist,*" said Skylar. "Of course."

Suddenly, everything Aldwyn thought he knew about Baxley was coming into question. If he hadn't stolen the druid's gemstone for selfish purposes, maybe the same was true of his search for the Crown. Had Malvern misjudged his own brother?

Skylar soared down and picked up the red and black stone with her talons. But just as she did, from above, four sharp-billed woodpeckers descended and alighted on the trees lining the tops of the canyon walls.

"Your journey ends here," one of them called out in a voice more booming and ominous than the woodpecker's small size would seem to allow. His yellow tail feather bristled. "You will never find the Crown of the Snow Leopard!"

With an unspoken command from their leader, the other birds began hammering away at the trees.

"How did they know?" asked Gilbert.

"It was only a matter of time before Paksahara's scouts discovered our quest," said Skylar.

The familiars glanced up to see that the woodpeckers had embedded their beaks within the bark of the trees—and that the trees themselves had begun to move!

"Skylar, quickly, fly the ladybug into the spider's nest!" shouted Aldwyn.

The trunks of the large oaks bent down, and their twisted branches reached out like arms, scooping up piles of rocks. Then the trees began flinging them at the three animals at the base of the ravine. Aldwyn nearly got crushed as a chunk of sandstone shattered beside him. Skylar and Gilbert only just dodged the first barrage of stone debris as well.

"There's nowhere to go!" cried Gilbert. "Skylar, quickly."

The blue jay flapped her wings toward the hole in the wall. The woodpeckers' beaks remained stuck in the bark, controlling the trees like puppets. The branches gathered a second round of jagged stones and launched them at the familiars. Aldwyn focused, trying to use his telekinesis to push back the assault, but the force of the rocks was too great. While their momentum was

slowed, the woodpeckers' attack still rained down on them, and it was only a matter of time until they would be crushed by one of them.

Skylar had to fly out of the narrow crevice in which Aldwyn and Gilbert were still trapped in order to reach her destination, but that didn't stop the oaks from trying to knock her out of the air. One of the rocks hit the gemstone and whacked it right out of her talons, sending it falling to the ground.

"Aldwyn, the stone!" cried Skylar.

Aldwyn concentrated on lifting it to the webbed wall telekinetically, but before he was able to guide it to the hole, a boulder six times his size—thrown by two of the trees together—hurtled down at him and Gilbert. There was no time to react. And even if there was, with his talents not yet strong enough to stop the flurry of smaller rocks, there was certainly no hope of holding back this one. He braced himself. This was it. This was the end. Gilbert threw his hands above his head.

And then the boulder stopped, frozen in midair.

Gilbert peeked out from between his webbed fingers.

"Aldwyn, you did it!" he croaked happily.

"It wasn't me," replied Aldwyn.

This was hardly the time to ponder what had just happened. Aldwyn refocused on the gemstone and sent it soaring straight into the hole in the wall. At once, the cracks lit up around it, and within the barrier's base a door revealed itself, opening into the darkness of a cave beyond.

The woodpeckers were still commanding the trees to attack, but now every rock they threw was mysteriously stopped in midair. Skylar swooped down to rejoin her companions, and the familiars hurried through the opening into the mountain.

Before they were swallowed up by the darkness, Aldwyn glanced back one last time. Standing at the top of the cliffs, he could make out a figure in the shadows. It was a cat.

13

STALAGMOS

Unlike Skylar and Gilbert, Aldwyn had been convinced that their escape from the echo beast had been a lucky break, another creature from the Borderlands arriving at just the right moment to settle some unrelated territorial dispute. But now, after getting saved a second time, Aldwyn was certain he and his companions were being watched over, protected by someone from afar. Someone who could lift objects telekinetically with his mind. A cat from Maidenmere.

"Aldwyn, come on," Skylar interrupted his musings.

It was difficult for Aldwyn to pull himself away: What if the cat stepped out into the moonlight and revealed his identity? But there simply wasn't time to wait, and so Aldwyn raced into the darkness, following the glowing paw prints of his father.

Quickly, whatever light had been coming in from the outside disappeared. Now the familiars had to find their way through the black using only the pale green luminescence emanating from a mold that hung to the cave walls; Aldwyn could use Baxley's paw prints for further illumination, but they weren't any help to his companions. Droplets of water dripped from the ceiling, and every time one hit the floor, a tiny sound bounced through the hollow subterranean halls. Every hundred steps there was a new branching passageway, and after having passed half a dozen of them, Aldwyn was confident that even if the woodpeckers followed them into the cave, they would almost certainly get lost in this maze of stalactites and stalagmites.

"Did you see who helped us back there?" asked Gilbert.

"No," replied Aldwyn—but at the same time his heart was full of hope that their protector was the same person whose path they were following: Baxley, his father. He was just glad that it was too dark in this place for his friends to see the wistful yearning on his face, his want for something so improbable.

"*Now comes a black crescent sword, Cutting through the emerald night. At last the waking moth, Flies to the rising light,*" said Skylar. "Let's be sure not to overlook any more clues. We're getting closer to the end of the song. Which means the Crown of the Snow Leopard shouldn't be far."

"I think my eyes have finally adjusted," said Gilbert. "If there's a curved sword to be seen, I will find it." A moment later, he hopped straight into a small column of limestone.

"I found two stones in Baxley's pouch," said Aldwyn. "We can light a torch to guide us through."

"I got a better idea," said Gilbert. "I'll conjure a flame fairy."

"Maybe you should let Skylar do that, Gil," said Aldwyn. "She's got a bit more experience in that area."

"Save your components," said Gilbert to Skylar. "I got this one."

The look on Skylar's face was more than skeptical, but Gilbert had already pulled Marianne's pocket scroll from his backpack and stretched his wiry green arms in preparation. The tree frog removed the necessary nightshade, juniper berries, and sage leaves from the pack, as well. He tossed them into the air and chanted: "Send a flame from whence you came!"

In a blink, a flame fairy formed, her tiny frame aburst in orange. A smile crept across Gilbert's face; this was a confidence-booster that he sorely needed.

"I did it!" exclaimed Gilbert. "The spell actually work—"

The flame fairy began to shake, and then turned into an out-of-control fireball. It rocketed off, leaving a puff of smoke in Gilbert's face. The spell bounced around the walls of the cave, nearly taking off Skylar's head as it flew by before shooting straight through Aldwyn's legs. They both dove for cover as the errant bolt finally crash-landed in a puddle on the ground and extinguished with an almighty hiss.

Gilbert wiped soot from his eyes.

"Here," said Gilbert, handing Aldwyn Marianne's spell scrolls. "Take these. We'll all be safer that way." Then the tree frog pulled his spear from his back. "You better take this, too." He set the bamboo stick on the ground. "Even my flower bud backpack could be dangerous."

"How could your backpack be dangerous?" asked Aldwyn.

"I don't know, but I'm not taking any chances," replied Gilbert, pulling his grass-strapped knapsack off his back. "Of course, there's no reason to waste perfectly good larvae. Or grubs." He reached into the pack and removed two bundles of squirming bugs, along with the silver chain of beads from the mawpi's lair.

"I've got no place here," said Gilbert. "I just wish I could go back to the palace and see Marianne."

Suddenly, one of the two remaining shimmering blue beads on the chain began to swirl with light. Gilbert squinted from the bright glare and then a large wooden door with a brass knocker at its center appeared before them.

"Gilbert, what did you do?" asked Skylar.

"I don't know, I don't know," he replied.

Skylar hurried over to look at what he held in his hand.

"Did you take those from the mawpi's lair?" she asked.

"Yes. Was that wrong?"

"Those are journey beads," explained the blue jay. "They'll take you to any destination, so long as you've stepped foot there before."

Just then, the knocker banged three times on the door and it swung open to reveal Marianne and Dalton sparring with swords in the fencing hall of the New Palace of Bronzhaven. Sorceress Edna and Jack stood on the sidelines watching.

"If you can't fight with your wand, you'll need to be quick with a saber," the familiars heard Edna call out.

"Marianne, over here!" shouted Gilbert. But his loyal didn't hear him.

"It's like one of your puddle viewings," said Skylar. "We can see them but they can't see us. Unless you walk through that door."

Gilbert was about to do just that when Skylar stopped him.

"But once you do, the door will close behind you," continued Skylar. "And each bead can only be used once."

Gilbert seemed quite conflicted. Aldwyn, too, could see how inviting the palace looked—far more so than the dark cave they were standing in now.

"We're the Prophesized Three, Gilbert," said Aldwyn. "Not the Prophesized *Two*."

"You might be excellent at telekinesis," said the tree frog as the wood door began to close, "but you're even better with guilt trips."

Aldwyn peered through the shrinking gap at Jack and could see that he was okay. Of course, he didn't know for how much longer.

Then the magic portal slammed shut, and once it did, it dematerialized in an instant. Aldwyn watched as the bead that had formed the door faded from blue to a dull, colorless gray. Now there was only one shimmering journey bead left on the chain.

Aldwyn gave his web-footed friend a pat on the back. He knew how he was feeling.

Clank-clank-clank.

"Did you hear that?" asked Aldwyn.

Clank-clank-clank.

"Sounds like human tools," said Skylar.

Aldwyn led his companions farther along the spirit trail, which, they quickly realized, took them straight toward the hammering. Soon they arrived at a hole in the tunnel wall, which looked out into a large cavern. It appeared to be some kind of mine, and Aldwyn could make out dozens of pale white albino dwarves with pickaxes who were chipping away at the stone walls of the cave. Others were sorting the ore, removing jet black fragments from the limestone and placing them in wheelbarrows. When they were filled, the wheelbarrows were brought by a third group of dwarves to an enormous cart and dumped inside. Instead of being pulled by horses, this wagon had a gundabeast harnessed to the front with leather straps and metal chains. Aldwyn remembered his hair-raising encounter with a baby gundabeast near Stone Runlet only too well—the ten-foot-tall, three-eyed, horned creature from the Beyond had been a fearsome sight and almost turned him into a cat pancake. But nothing could have prepared him for the sheer magnitude of a fully grown specimen, more than double the size of the baby and the armor plating on its back appearing tough enough to deflect even the sharpest sword. Then Aldwyn noticed that the entire mining operation seemed to be supervised by a number of mysterious robed figures. Some stirred vats of boiling liquid, while others walked the floor with shadow hounds at their side. Every so often, they would shout orders at the dwarves. Disconcertingly, the robed figures seemed to use not their mouths but gaping holes in their necks to do their commanding.

Aldwyn pinched himself to make sure he was awake, because what he was seeing felt very much like a bizarre nightmare.

"Where are we?" asked Gilbert, who looked absolutely terrified.

"I don't know," answered Skylar, which made Gilbert look even more terrified: if not even Skylar knew where they were, then what was this place?

"Stalagmos," said Aldwyn.

The two other familiars turned to him, clearly surprised that he knew something that Skylar didn't.

"I recognize those robed figures from the sewer markets of Bridgetower," he explained. "They're the tongueless cave shamans. They sell deadly concoctions and nefarious tools of the trade for assassins and bounty hunters like Grimslade. Olfax tracking snouts, spring-loaded soul suckers, arsenic arrows. I even had a run-in with a shadow hound once."

The three turned their attention to the vats of steaming magma below. Floating inside them were evil-looking contraptions with sharp edges and animal parts.

"This must be where they brew their dark

magic," said Aldwyn. "Rumor around the back alleys was that they were drained of their humanity a long time ago."

"Mine faster," commanded one of the tongueless shamans, striking an albino dwarf with a whip that crackled with black energy. "And take only the obsidian!"

The voice gave Aldwyn the creeps: it hissed and snarled like a snake with its tail cut off. Although it also sounded a bit like Gilbert croaking in his sleep.

"Obsidian," whispered Skylar. "That's the component used to raise the dead." She looked to the cart and spotted the symbol of a double hex burnt into the wooden frame. "They must be working for Paksahara. This is what she needs to bring forth the Dead Army."

"She must be smuggling shipments of obsidian across the border into Vastia," said Aldwyn. "That's what Urbaugh and his men stumbled upon."

"There's enough in that cart alone to raise a thousand zombie soldiers," said Skylar. "Who knows how many tons she's collected already?"

"Let's just follow the paw prints and get out of here," suggested Gilbert.

Aldwyn, too, wanted to leave this terrible place behind, but when he looked down again into the cavern, he saw his father's purple footprints go straight through the mine, past the gundabeast, and beneath a pair of pointy stalactites that hung above the sole exit on the other side.

"Don't even say it," said Gilbert. "I can tell by the look on your face that we have to go through that exit."

"Afraid so," said Aldwyn.

"And how do you propose we do that?" asked Skylar.

"We blend in," replied Aldwyn, gesturing to several long black robes hanging on hooks near the cauldrons.

They sneaked down the tunnel, staying low to the ground, until they reached the spare robes.

"Fly into the hood," instructed Aldwyn. "We'll take the feet."

But Skylar didn't need instructions. She knew just what to do. The blue jay soared inside one of the cloaks and flapped her wings, letting the hood drape over her. The effect was successful; it appeared as if a man was inside. Aldwyn and Gilbert crawled under the bottom, and together they began to move.

Aldwyn couldn't really see where they were going; he only hoped that Skylar could.

"I can't see where I'm going," whispered Skylar down to the others.

Aldwyn had no choice but to peek an eye out and guide her. "Straight, straight, a little to the left. Stop, stop, stop!"

Another cave shaman was approaching, and if Skylar had flapped her wings one more time, they'd have walked right into him. Luckily she halted just in time.

"We're behind schedule," groaned the shaman. "Tell the miners on the ridge there will be no rest until the full moon. Have I made myself clear?"

The familiars remained silent.

"Gilbert," whispered Aldwyn, "let out a croak."

"Why?" asked Gilbert.

"Because you sound like them when you're snoring."

"Is there a problem?" asked the shaman harshly.

"Ngrrugh," snorted Gilbert, letting out a sound that was indeed not so different from how the tongueless dark magicians communicated.

"Very well, then," said the shaman, continuing along.

The three animals let out a collective sigh, and Skylar resumed her flapping. They moved among the other cloaked figures without getting a second glance. The exit was approaching.

Aldwyn, back on the lookout, was momentarily distracted by an albino dwarf hurrying past, pushing a mine cart.

"Skylar, left," Aldwyn directed her. "No, no, right!" he corrected as the dwarf rolled by.

Skylar managed to reverse course, but Gilbert had already committed to Aldwyn's initial direction. He got tangled in the bottom of the robe, pulling them all to the ground. With a thud, they hit something. Aldwyn pushed the cloth fabric off his head to see that they had knocked a small cauldron to the ground. Black smoke was pouring out from it. Gilbert freed himself from the tangle and found himself face to face with a smoky creature forming just inches from his nose.

Oh, no, Aldwyn thought. He recognized this as the ghostly mist of a shadow hound, born from the very pot they had just tipped over.

Skylar freed herself from the robe last, and all three familiars witnessed the beast assuming its final shape. But this was no ordinary shadow hound. It was much, much . . . smaller. In fact, it looked more like a puppy.

The tiny hound of darkness immediately began licking Gilbert's face.

"Get off me!" said Gilbert, recoiling from the smoky slobber.

Fortunately, nobody had spotted the cauldron incident, and before they could be discovered, the familiars dove between a wash basin filled with ore and a smelting pot cooking limestone into molten rock to figure out their next move. An albino dwarf came by and picked up a poker, stoking the flames and coming frighteningly close to where the animals were hiding.

Meanwhile, the shadow pup was trying to get Gilbert to play with him, biting down on his flower bud backpack and tugging at it.

"Would you quit it?" whispered Gilbert.

The puppy let out a yip, causing the albino dwarf to turn in their direction. Gilbert immediately threw a webbed hand over the shadow pup's mouth. Everyone remained still and silent, except for the hound, who wagged its shadowy tail in the air, happy that Gilbert was finally paying attention to it and completely oblivious to the tension in the air.

After a moment, the dwarf dropped the red-tipped poker to the ground and moved on to tend to the other vats, but not before scooping up the fallen robe.

Once the coast was clear, the familiars relaxed. Now there was only the matter of escaping with their lives still intact. Then why was Skylar eyeing a nugget of fallen obsidian just out of talon's reach? thought Aldwyn. He knew of her desire to revive her deceased sister, but now did not seem the time to be collecting components. She flitted out from behind their cover and scooped up the black rock before returning with it.

"What about what Feynam said?" asked Aldwyn. "About there being consequences?"

"That's a risk I'm willing to take," replied Skylar

as she shoved the obsidian deep into her satchel.

Suddenly, there was a loud bang as the gundabeast lurched forward. Across the room, in the ore loading zone, the massive creature from the Beyond lunged at a passing dwarf pushing a wheelbarrow that was filled to the brim with obsidian.

"Keep back from the beast," snarled one of the shamans. "It's overworked and irritable."

The dwarf hurried away, keeping his distance from the three-eyed creature. Aldwyn took measure of the distance they still had to travel to the exit. He was quite certain that even at their fastest sprint, they would never make it there without being caught. His mind was racing. Luckily, it was precisely in situations like this when Aldwyn shone brightest: with his back against the wall and the odds stacked against him. He was still a scrappy alley cat at heart, and his greatest asset remained his street smarts; only now he had a new trick in his arsenal: telekinesis.

His eyes landed on the discarded poker, its tip still burning. Then he looked to the gundabeast, which was snorting disgruntledly through its nose.

"Just follow my lead," said Aldwyn to his companions.

He focused all of his mental energy on the metal poker and flung it through the air. Its glowing end landed squarely on the beast's exposed hind side, sending the creature into an instant fit.

"Arrrrrrr!" roared the monster, kicking its massive front legs into the air.

"Run!" shouted Aldwyn.

He sprinted out from behind the vats and made a dash for the exit. Skylar and Gilbert raced behind him. The gundabeast was thrashing angrily now. It lifted the cart attached to its back up over its head and tossed it across the room. Albino dwarves began scattering in a panic, while some of the cave shamans tried to maintain control. The flung cart toppled the vats of boiling liquid, sending a flood of red magma pouring in every direction.

The familiars' progress toward the cave's exit stalled when a fast-flowing rivulet of red-hot metal snaked past them. Skylar flew over it, but Aldwyn and Gilbert had to take a detour, heading back to the center of the room they were trying so

desperately to escape from.

"*This* was your plan?" shouted Skylar over the mayhem.

"It played out much more smoothly in my head," replied Aldwyn.

To make matters even worse, magma wasn't the only thing that spilled from the cauldrons; half-finished creatures the shamans had been conjuring up with their black magic took shape all over the cave as well.

A pair of crocodile skulls began chomping toward Aldwyn and Gilbert. *Lockjaws* thought Aldwyn, familiar with the deadliest traps the sewer markets had to offer. He knew well enough not to get a leg caught between those teeth, for once the jaws clamped down, they'd never let go.

One was closing in on Gilbert, opening wide. The tree frog hopped quickly, diving between the legs of a fleeing cave shaman. The lockjaw attacked, its teeth snapping shut not on Gilbert, but the shaman's leg. The shaman dropped to his knees, screaming in pain. The other croc skull was still pursuing Aldwyn, who found his escape cut off by another stream of red hot lava. But just as the lockjaw bounded forward, its skeletal mouth agape, one of the gundabeast's tree-trunk–sized hooves stomped it to the ground, turning the bones to dust. Aldwyn decided this was the first and only time that a close-up of the crashing foot of a gundabeast would be a welcome sight. He wondered briefly if the creature had suddenly become an ally, but the fist thrusting toward him made it clear that the border monster wasn't picking sides, just attacking indiscriminately.

The familiars were not far from the exit now. Though roundabout and potentially deadly in other ways, Aldwyn's plan had succeeded in creating enough of a distraction to make their presence in Stalagmos a mere afterthought to the chaos the stampeding gundabeast had wrought. The trio had a clear path to the opening until a shadow hound, menacing and ferocious, emerged from the darkness surrounding it. While Skylar remained safely above the fray, the canine apparition was stalking toward cat and frog, preparing to pounce.

"Nice demon doggy," said Aldwyn, trying to calm the vicious phantom.

The shadow hound didn't seem amused.

Just then, an albino dwarf sailed overhead, flung by the gundabeast. His metal helmet went crashing into the cave wall, and the small, pale miner landed on the floor with a thud, pickax gripped in gloved hand. It gave Aldwyn an idea.

He pulled the ax out of the dwarf's hand telekinetically and launched it through the air. Higher, higher . . . spinning toward the pointy stalactites hanging above them—coated with the same bioluminescent mold covering the cave walls. And with all his mental might, Aldwyn guided the sharpened metal edge into one of the rocky protuberances. It sliced the stalactite clean off the ceiling, sending the limestone dagger straight down. The gleaming tip impaled the shadow hound, vaporizing it instantly. But it wasn't the sharpened point, it was the lightness with which it was glowing that killed the beast.

With the path cleared, the familiars ran out of the darkness of the cave and into the darkness of the night. The clouds in the sky kept most of the moonlight hidden, but stray glimmers of white illuminated the deep valley of chiseled rock they found themselves in. Whatever vegetation had been here had long been blasted away; only blackened stumps rose from the valley floor, witnesses to the shamans' sinister arts. The cliffs, too, were cratered with holes, presumably where the albino dwarves had searched for rare stones and minerals like obsidian.

"Paksahara's not going to be happy when her obsidian doesn't arrive," said Aldwyn.

"If she wanted to kill us before, I'd hate to think how she's going to feel about us now," added Gilbert.

"It was just a single cartload we destroyed," said Skylar. "I'm sure many have already been delivered, and many more will."

Aldwyn picked up the glowing paw print trail of his father, and the trio began to climb the rocky embankment toward the exit of the quarry. Once they reached the top, they saw long wind-swept plains before them. They eased into a quiet stretch of their journey.

Aldwyn occasionally thought he heard the rustling of gravel behind him. He had the growing sense they were being followed. But every time he turned around, there was no one there.

14

SON OF BAXLEY

It was still dark when Aldwyn's eyes opened with a start. Skylar and Gilbert were curled up next to each other, and although Skylar wouldn't have admitted it, nobody could argue with the warmth of a tree frog's belly on a cold night in the Beyond. But Aldwyn's ears, trained to hear the tiniest sound even while he was asleep, had picked up what he was convinced had been quietly approaching footsteps.

Aldwyn sat up to find that it was still just the three of them here in the middle of this windswept plain north of Stalagmos. He remained very still, hearing only his heartbeat and Gilbert's snoring. Then, as quietly as he could, he rose to his feet and moved through the grass, in the direction from which he thought he'd heard the footsteps.

With all the excitement they had faced in Stalagmos, Aldwyn had had little time to ponder the mysterious cat who seemed to be both real and a spirit at the same time. Whatever, *who*ever it was, had saved them from a crushing death courtesy of Paksahara's woodpeckers and, more than likely, the echo beast, as well. If it was a cat from Maidenmere, why had it not shown itself? And if it was a cat from the Tomorrowlife, how was it able to cross over to this world to aid them? Either way, it was possible this cat was merely a few feet away, lurking in the tall weeds, just out of Aldwyn's sight.

Just then, he felt something on his back. Aldwyn barely had time to think. How had he been crept up on? Clearly, he had let himself get too distracted.

"Aldwyn—"

He spun around to find Gilbert.

"Gilbert." Aldwyn sighed. "Why are you sneaking up on me like that?"

"I called your name," said Gilbert. "What are you doing out here?"

"I think someone's following us," said Aldwyn.

A loud rustling in the grass, which Aldwyn was certain hadn't been caused by a gust of wind, seemed to confirm his suspicion. Gilbert jumped behind Aldwyn.

"Did you hear that?" he croaked.

Aldwyn put a paw up to Gilbert's lips and mouthed, "Shhhh."

Suddenly, bounding out from the tall grass, was a four-legged figure: the shadow pup from Stalagmos. He immediately leaped atop Gilbert and began licking him feverishly.

"What?!" exclaimed Gilbert, pushing him away. "You again? Stop it!"

Aldwyn let out a relieved breath, but inside he was disappointed. This definitely was not the mysterious stranger responsible for helping them.

"Get off me," croaked Gilbert. "That tickles."

The shadow pup bounded playfully back and forth.

"Why won't he leave me alone?" asked Gilbert.

"He must think you're his mom," replied Aldwyn.

Gilbert tried to reason with the smoke hound. "I am a frog," he explained. "You are a puff of black smoke shaped like a dog. We are not related."

The puppy responded with another lick of Gilbert's face.

"Aldwyn, Gilbert," Skylar's voice called from behind them.

"Over here," said Aldwyn.

The blue jay flew over to find them in the grass.

"We should probably get moving," she said, and then she also spotted the frisky shadow pup. "What's he doing here?"

"He followed us," said Gilbert. "I certainly didn't invite him."

Just then, the first beams of the sun crept up from behind the horizon. As they hit the plains, the baby hound darted into the shade of a nearby bush, whimpering miserably.

The familiars tried to ignore the pup's pitiful noises and got ready to depart, but then the puppy, which was still cowering beneath the shrub's cover, let out a loud yelp.

"What's he hiding from?" asked Gilbert.

"The sunlight," said Aldwyn. "Direct contact turns them to dust."

The pup whined, and even though it didn't have eyes or a nose, it definitely appeared sad and scared to Aldwyn.

"Oh, no," said Gilbert, shaking his head. "Don't look at me like that. You're not coming with us."

The hound let out another cry.

"Fine," said Gilbert. "But as soon as we find a dark cave, I'm leaving you there."

Gilbert hopped over to the bush and opened his flower bud backpack. The puppy gave him a slobbering lick, and his smoky essence wafted inside.

The tree frog caught back up with Aldwyn and Skylar.

"I couldn't just leave him out here," he said, apologetically.

Soon enough, the familiars were on their way again, and by the time dawn had given way to morning, they emerged from the tall grass to see an expanse of lowlands stretching downward to the edge of a great bay. There was something serene and peaceful about the scenery; it was nothing at all like the fearsome image of the Beyond Aldwyn had conjured up in his head. Baxley's paw prints led straight down until its purple glow disappeared into a line of trees that surrounded the large body of water.

"Looks like we've got a long day of walking ahead of us," said Aldwyn.

The group was about to resume their journey when Gilbert's attention was drawn to the east.

"Skylar, Aldwyn, what's that?" asked the tree frog.

In the foothills of a mountain range not twenty miles away stood a tall gray tower, with incredibly flat sides that tapered to a point at the top like the tip of a crossbow bolt. The polished bricks that made up its walls were so smooth they reflected the sunlight, with veins of red that stretched from its base to its peak. It stood there completely out of context with all that surrounded it, as if it had been dropped there completely at random.

"The Shifting Fortress," said Skylar.

"We found it!" exclaimed Gilbert.

They had spent the last five days on an epic quest to find a mystical artifact that they hoped and believed would be capable of summoning the impossible-to-find Fortress with its casting tower—and here it was, presenting itself like a gift just out of reach. Aldwyn couldn't believe their good fortune.

"This is what we've been searching for," said Aldwyn. "It's time to face Paksahara."

He wondered if at this very moment the gray hare was within those walls, staring at them, unsure what those dots on the horizon signified, unaware that those dots would be her downfall.

"Come on," said Aldwyn, veering from his father's path and running toward the foothills.

"The Fortress is constantly moving," said Skylar. "We could make it to its front door and it could disappear before we even knocked."

"Yes, but don't you think it's worth the risk?" countered Aldwyn. "We may never have this chance again."

Skylar hesitated, but eventually she relented. Aldwyn knew his blue jay companion was usually right, but there was no guarantee they were ever going to find the Crown of the Snow Leopard, and so this might be their only opportunity to restore human magic to the queendom and stop Paksahara from raising her Dead Army. That's if the three of them alone could overpower the hare and wrestle control of the Fortress from her.

The trio moved faster than they'd ever moved before, Skylar leading the way. Even Gilbert hopped double time. But as fast as they ran, it didn't seem they were getting there fast enough. It wasn't long before Aldwyn was panting. He was used to short bursts of speed, but marathon expenditures of energy were enough to knock him out.

"Look," gestured Skylar to the sky. "Spyballs."

A flock of Paksahara's winged eyeball spies

flew in from the south, not toward them but in the direction of the Fortress. They soared into the tower through one of the lone windows and quickly disappeared from sight.

As Aldwyn's paws pounded the dry earth of the plains, the only thing that kept him moving forward despite his aching muscles and heaving chest was the thought of defeating Paksahara. Queen Loranella's familiar had been a loyal assistant for over half a century. They had witnessed it in the epic tale the whistlegrass had told them south of Liveod's Canyon. But then something had changed—on the fateful day when the gray hare had stumbled into the caves of Kailasa and found the paintings on the walls, the ones that told of how animals had once ruled the land.

Aldwyn's feet still pounding . . .

Paksahara's plot had started taking shape when she assumed the form of Loranella, trading places with the queen. From the throne of Vastia, she had slowly crumbled the queendom's defenses, allowing the enchanted fences to fall and the weather-binding spells to weaken. Had it not been for the prophecy, human and animal would have been unaware of her traitorous deception until it was too late. But the three spinning stars in the sky had told of three young spellcasters who would rise up and defeat her, saving the land. And while at first all had thought those three were Dalton, Marianne, and Jack, it had in fact been them, the familiars, who were destined to be heroes.

Heart beating faster . . .

He, Skylar, and Gilbert had thwarted Paksahara once, in the bowels of Mukrete, but the hare had escaped, taking refuge in the Shifting Fortress that she could summon through the force of the queen's wooden bracelet. From the top of its casting tower, she had invoked a dispeller curse that left all the human wizards of Vastia magicless. And it was more than likely where she waited now, while the obsidian was being collected for the necromantic spell she would cast when the full moon came.

Wind blowing through his whiskers as he ran . . .

That's when the red veins of the Shifting Fortress began to pulse.

"What's . . . going . . . on?" wheezed Gilbert.

A checkerboard of bricks began to disappear from the tower. Giant stone after giant stone vanished, revealing the interior of the Fortress—the spiral staircase inside and the landings at every flight.

"The Fortress," said Skylar. "It's shifting."

Within seconds, save for the top of the tower, the outer walls were gone, and only the base, the curving staircase, and the top floor remained. For a moment, the steps disappeared, and it seemed as if the highest point of the Fortress hovered there on its own. Now exposed at the bottom was a globe the size of a large boulder, its smoky blue interior looking not unlike one of Jack's marbles. This, no doubt, was the teleportation device that Agorus had described, spinning round and round until every last inch of the tower had left for some faraway spot. The familiars watched as the globe disappeared, too.

There was little to be said. They had gambled and lost. Dejected, the three turned back for the trail. They had lost precious time and would have a lot of ground to make up.

272

Hours later, three exhausted familiars were approaching the tree-lined coast of the bay, once again in step with Baxley's path. They hadn't stopped to rest, but still the sun was already nearing the horizon, casting long shadows across the plains. Gilbert released the shadow pup from his backpack, allowing him to play and run alongside them, darting from the shade of one tree to another.

"He's good at that," said Gilbert. "He always seems to know where to find the shady spot."

The smoky hound wagged its tail and barked.

"Hey, he seems to like that," said Gilbert. "Maybe that should be his name."

"Yeah, Spot," said Aldwyn. "That's a great name for a dog."

"Spot?" asked Gilbert. "No, Shady. *That's* a dog's name."

They continued their march, walking beneath the coconut palms and other trees that formed a small grove near the bay. Before them they found a circle of mud huts—if you could even call them that, as they were more like giant mounds of dirt with holes dug out inside. Standing in the center of the village was the mud statue of a cat. Aldwyn moved closer—and it was as if he was staring into a mirror, albeit one whose only color was brown. The cat looked just like him, save for the bite taken out of his ear.

"You've come back," a voice called from within the huts.

Aldwyn turned to see eyes peering out from the darkness, seemingly cowering in fear, cautious of the new visitors entering.

"It's him," said another voice.

Suddenly, giant snouts were emerging from the huts into the cool evening air, and the familiars found themselves surrounded by dozens of white, hairless aardvarks. They were all looking reverentially at Aldwyn, barely giving Skylar or Gilbert a second glance. A few of the wrinkliest elders were even bowing their heads. Some of the youngest ran over and excitedly touched the fur of his leg as if he were a king.

Aldwyn glanced back at the statue again and realized in whose shape it had been sculpted: for the first time in his life, he was looking upon an image of his father.

"Baxley, our savior," said one of the hairless

aardvarks. "You have returned."

"You have me mistaken," said Aldwyn. "I'm not Baxley."

The aardvarks all seemed taken aback.

"But the white on your paws," said the aardvark, "and the rest of your coloring!"

"I'm not him. I'm his son, Aldwyn."

The aardvarks' disappointed eyes lit up again.

"It is the son of Baxley!" exclaimed a different aardvark. "The great mud mother has brought us another savior."

The aardvarks rejoiced. Many more poured out from their huts, carrying mud pots filled with ants. They pushed past Skylar and Gilbert, swarming around Aldwyn.

"No, no," said Aldwyn, increasingly self-conscious.

They began singing a hymn, dancing in a circle around the cat.

"Oh, mighty Baxley, you came down from the mountain, and brought with you peace on this plain!"

The aardvarks marched their feet and waved their snouts.

"Baxley from high above, glory never ending!"

The words faded out, but the stomping feet and humming continued, creating a steady beat for one of the elder aardvarks.

"I'm sure your father has told you the story many times," he said. "Of how the neighboring warthogs forced us to dig grubs and roots for them, and then came to collect the bounty each night. For generations, no one was brave enough to stand up to them, until that blessed day when your father arrived in our village. He saw the way we were being oppressed and would not stand for it. That evening, when the warthogs arrived, they had a mighty surprise awaiting them. While we remained hidden in our huts, Baxley lifted the earth into the air, forming a claw made of dirt and mud. Within moments, tens of them were on their backs. The others fled as the hand swiped at them. Your father had done what all of our people together couldn't—put fear in the hearts of our enemies."

Aldwyn listened with pride. Baxley had been a hero, and that he had used the sand sign of the Mooncatchers to fend off the evil warthogs was

276

an exhilarating revelation.

"After that night, the warthogs did not return for many, many moons," continued the aardvark. "We molded that statue in your father's honor, to remember the great animal who brought peace to our village." At this point, a plaintive note crept into the aardvark's voice. "Alas, after many years of peace, the warthogs returned three months ago. This time they came under the orders of an evil gray hare who they called Paksahara, attempting to recruit us to join her. We responded that we were mere mud farmers, capable of no feat that would aid her in whatever fiendish plot she was planning. Seeing that the feline warrior was no longer among us, they demanded we serve them again. And that is just what we have done. But here you are to change all of that, arriving in our hour of need once more."

"I wish I could stay and help, but we're on an urgent quest," said Aldwyn, feeling terrible as he saw the light of hope waver in the aardvark's eyes.

"Just like your father," he replied. "He, too, was in a hurry. But he refused to leave before aiding us."

Aldwyn looked to Skylar.

"We have to continue on," she said. "I'm sorry."

Aldwyn was wracked with guilt, but he knew that Skylar was right. If they delayed, this might cost them the Crown of the Snow Leopard, and all of Vastia would be faced with the same fate as these aardvarks: enslavement and suffering.

Aldwyn looked down at the ground, at the hundreds of paw prints that Baxley had left during his time in this village. There were wide leaping bounds that must have occurred during the heat of his battle with the warthogs, and quiet, peaceful steps that looked more like those taken in the victorious aftermath.

"I promise we will come back as soon as we have fulfilled our mission," he tried to comfort the old aardvark.

Then he led Skylar and Gilbert along Baxley's trail, which cut through the trees to quickly emerge onto a neighboring beach. As Aldwyn reached the sand he could see where Baxley's paw prints ended at the water.

"Maybe he swam the rest of the way," said Aldwyn, looking out at the sparkling green bay.

"The question is, where?"

No glowing paw prints could be seen in the dusk-tinted sea.

One of the younger aardvarks who had been walking behind them and eavesdropping piped up: "Your father left on the back of a traveling whale, following the pull of the metal ball he carried with him. If you like, we will call one for you."

The fact that these hairless mud dwellers would be so altruistic and offer their help while getting nothing in return made Aldwyn feel even worse.

Before the familiars were able to thank him, the aardvark reached its snout to the sky and let out a trumpeting blow. The sound carried across the bay.

"It will take some time for the call to reach the lower depths," explained the aardvark. "And longer still for a great blue back to arrive here. But they always do. Make yourselves comfortable here on the sands. I must return to the village and burrow into my hole with the others, for the warthogs will be making their nightly invasion soon. Good luck to you."

The aardvark turned and walked away through

the trees, with not even a judgmental glance back as he left.

As the familiars settled onto the beach to wait, the waves lapped gently against the shore, sending salty splashes against the sand, turning it from light brown to dark. Skylar seemed completely at peace with their decision not to help the aardvarks; Aldwyn couldn't say the same, feeling that he had not only let the aardvarks down but also his father's honor. *His father's honor?* Before yesterday, he had thought Baxley was the worst cat in the world, selfish and unloving. Now, suddenly, he had evidence that he was good and selfless. More and more, Malvern's assumptions were proving untrue. Whatever mischievous, treasure-seeking cat Baxley might have been, there was also nobility in him. And perhaps following in his father's footsteps wasn't such a bad thing after all.

Gilbert watched as Shady ran up and down the shore, safe to roam free under the sunless sky, getting his misty paws wet before bounding back to dry land. The tree frog eyed the wind-chopped waters.

"Guys," said Gilbert, turning to Skylar and

Aldwyn. "You've seen me almost lose my lunch on a boat. How do you think I'm going to fare on the back of a traveling whale?"

"Remind me not to stand anywhere near you," said Skylar.

Just then, the sound of shuffling feet and snapping branches could be heard from the direction of the aardvark village. Moments later, a nasty, wheezy voice called out: "This is it? You spent a whole day digging and that's all you could come up with?"

Aldwyn's ears pricked up, and he could hear the faint murmur of the elder aardvark speaking back to the voice. "The underground is not as fertile as it was in the past," he said. "Please don't punish us."

"Now what kind of message would that send, if I let you off without scars from my tusks," replied the unseen intruder.

Aldwyn moved carefully toward the tree line and saw through the bushes at least a dozen fat, sweaty hogs bashing in the mud huts with their hooves. That was it: no matter how little time they had left to save Vastia, he couldn't just stand there and watch the aardvarks being bullied by the intruders.

"Leave them alone," cried Aldwyn, bounding out from the trees.

The warthogs turned in his direction. Recognition, then fear appeared on the faces of some; others glanced to the mud statue and then back at him. The leader circled more cautiously now.

"Well, well, well," he said. "So you return after all these years?"

Aldwyn sneaked a glance at his father's statue. Then he puffed out his chest.

"That's right," he said confidently. "And I suggest you leave right now."

"If you thought his powers were strong before, wait until you see them now," bellowed Gilbert, who thought he was helping

Aldwyn shot him a look. "Let's not overdo it here," he whispered under his breath. Skylar and Shady had come up behind them.

"Something seems different about you," said the warthog. "You don't scare me. Bring forth your claw to prove that you are who you say you are."

The warthog had called their bluff. Aldwyn was being challenged to summon the Mooncatcher sand sign, an extraordinary feat he had only been able to achieve with his uncle's guidance.

Aldwyn concentrated, trying to relax his mind the way he had when Malvern had his paw on his shoulder, but while the dirt lifted off the ground, no sand sign was forming in the air. He wasn't yet capable of what his father had mastered.

The gruff warthog let out a mocking snort.

"I knew it," he said.

The other warthogs closed in around the familiars. Their tusks grew longer and sharper; it seemed their magical talent was gouging their enemies. Then a pair of the burliest hogs charged Gilbert.

And that's when Shady leaped out in front of him. The cute shadow pup transformed into a menacing hound, every bit as ferocious as the fully grown demon dog that had chased Aldwyn through Bridgetower when he had been trying to escape the notorious bounty hunter Grimslade. Shady snarled at the attacking warthogs, then lunged out for one, biting its sharpened ivory tusk

283

clean off. The other hogs stopped in their tracks. Aldwyn was amazed at what he had just witnessed; it was hard to believe this menacing beast had been slobbering all over Gilbert just minutes before.

Shady let out a bone-rattling growl, sending tentacles of mist toward the hairy swine. They fled off into the brush, squealing in horror. Seconds later, all was calm again, and Shady had transformed back into an adorable, innocuous shadow puppy and begun licking Gilbert's face. The hairless aardvarks came out from their huts and started cheering.

"I think it is time to build a new statue," said the elder aardvark. "Thank you, son of Baxley, and thank you, friends of the son."

But there was little time for celebration, as the sound of water blasting out of a blowhole could be heard from the bay: the traveling whale had arrived.

When the familiars reached the water, they were met with a majestic sight: a large blue whale was floating just offshore, its back full of ridges and bumps that looked comfortable to sit on.

Hundreds of silver lamprey eels clung to the whale's side and underbelly, making them sparkle in the moonlight. Gilbert opened his backpack and Shady leaped inside. Aldwyn and Gilbert swam out to the whale's extended dorsal fin and climbed aboard; Skylar simply flew the short distance across the water and perched beside one of the six blowholes that alternated shooting out waters like the queen's palace fountain. Once Aldwyn and Gilbert had found a comfortable seat as well, there was but one thing left to do: direct the whale to where they were going. But where exactly was that?

"Take us to the north," said Aldwyn.

It was just a guess. If they had to sit atop this whale as it swam along the entire coast of the bay while Aldwyn looked for where his father's paw prints began again, they would.

15

THE PROTECTORS

Riding on the back of a traveling whale felt to Aldwyn like he was flying. Unlike a boat, a whale didn't rock with every wave. It glided. The giant blueback cut through the water, barely leaving a wake behind it. Here, out on this great bay of the Beyond, Aldwyn couldn't help but feel a pang of bittersweetness. He was living out Jack's dream, riding atop one of these legendary marine mammals as it ventured toward unexplored lands. And without his loyal there at his side, it felt like a journey half taken.

Gilbert sat on a ridge above the whale's giant eye and didn't look the least bit sick, which was a welcome change from his typical seafaring queasiness. Skylar was a different story: no matter where she positioned herself, every time water sprayed from one of the blueback's blowholes, the wind blew it in her direction, soaking her from beak to claw.

"I might as well be swimming there," she complained as she was drenched yet again, shaking the wet off her feathers.

"I'm actually enjoying this tremendously," said

Gilbert. "Who knew water travel could be so delightful? All I need is a cup of juniper tea and it would be perfect. Ooo, look, dolphins!"

Gilbert turned his back to the others excitedly, taking a closer gander at a school of the aquatic mammals that kept leaping from the water.

"How would you like to be swimming with them?" muttered the blue jay.

"We should get some rest," suggested Aldwyn before his two companions got into a fight. "This could be a long ride."

Gilbert closed his eyes and immediately fell fast asleep. Aldwyn prepared to do the same but first looked over to see if Skylar was all right. The blue jay was sitting uncomfortably, her wings crossed. Whenever she shut her eyes, another blast of salty mist would douse her, making her look like a wet blue dishrag.

The familiars woke to the sun rising. Shady poked his head briefly out of Gilbert's backpack and immediately burrowed back in. Aldwyn oriented himself quickly and found that the whale had brought them close to the northern coast of the bay. It was all rocky cliffs, as if a giant had cut the hillside with a large knife. Skylar and Gilbert looked to Aldwyn anxiously.

"Anything?" asked Skylar, who didn't look like she had gotten a lot of sleep. Aldwyn scanned the cliffs, but he couldn't see a single purple paw print anywhere on the rocky embankment.

"We're still too far away," he said. "I wouldn't be able to see the trail even if it was there."

He knew his father must have gotten off somewhere—assuming he had made it across the waters alive—but where? He also knew that if they steered the whale as close to the shore as they would need to be for him to have a chance of spotting Baxley's prints, it would take them days to circumnavigate the entire bay.

Having nothing more to guide him than his gut and a fifty percent chance of being correct, Aldwyn leaned down to the whale's ear and called out, "Head east." Almost immediately, the whale shifted course and was now cruising parallel to the uneven shoreline of small inlets and towering cliffs.

"Look, up there," said Gilbert, after they had rounded a particularly prominent rock formation.

Aldwyn and Skylar turned to see a herd of mountain sheep, each with eight legs like a spider, hopping and jumping from rock to rock, peacefully grazing on tufts of grass that grew from the cracks.

"Now *there's* something you don't see in Vastia every day," said Skylar.

"Or ever," added Gilbert.

"What are they?" asked Aldwyn.

Skylar shrugged, but for once she didn't seem to mind not knowing. Instead, she appeared delighted to be seeing new things.

"Perhaps we're the first Vastians to discover them, whatever they are," she said. "Scribius, make a record of this." The enchanted quill sprang to attention, popping its tip out from Skylar's satchel. The blue jay began dictating: "Here on the northeast ends of the Bay of the Beyond, a herd of wool-covered mammals resembling sheep have been spotted. The creatures have eight hooves and silver horns, and seem to be vegetarians. No signs of aggression. And I believe they are a species yet to be named."

Aldwyn's eyes continued to search the coast,

surveying cliff after cliff. And while he was trying to find what he was looking for, his mind began to wander. He had often heard murmurings of the Beyond being a terrible and foreboding place, and in fact some of it was—the caves of Stalagmos, for example. But most parts were serene and beautiful, still unspoiled by roads or chimney smoke. It was hard to believe there had been a time when Vastia had been like this, too, before it became populated by humans, wizards, and familiars.

The whale continued its eastward journey, rounding one rocky outcrop after another, exposing the familiars to a forest of windswept pines here, a black-sand beach there, and a steep slope of rock debris around yet another corner. But nowhere did Aldwyn see the magic trail his father had left behind. Maybe he had guessed wrong; maybe he should have guided the whale to the west—

"Stop!" cried Skylar suddenly. "Go back!"

The whale slowed, and Skylar flew straight up into the air to get an aerial view of something.

"What is it?" asked Gilbert, as Skylar soared higher still.

"That beach," she replied when she had descended again, "it's perfectly crescent-shaped."

"So?" asked the tree frog.

"Remember the next clue in the nursery rhyme?" she said. *"Now comes a black crescent sword, Cutting through the emerald night. At last the waking moth, Flies to the rising light.* The beach is the black crescent sword, and the emerald night is the bay!"

Skylar was right: Aldwyn could see that there was a jetty of black sand that stretched out from the beach itself. The blueback rolled its body slightly before racing across the lightly crashing surf toward the shore. As they got closer, Aldwyn could see that the beach looked just like a sword, the black sandbar slicing through the green-hued water like its curved, sharpened tip. The whale slid its belly up onto the sandy bottom of the shallow waters, allowing Aldwyn and Gilbert to hop off without even getting their feet wet. Aldwyn wasn't sure what the proper way to wish farewell to a traveling whale was, so he just gave a thankful nod.

The black sand baked the pads of Aldwyn's feet with a heat so fierce volcano ants would have steered clear of it. Quickly, he darted toward a patch hidden in the shade of a cliffside, and from there was able to scan the inlet. And then he saw it: high up on the beach, Baxley's paw prints came into view. Three years earlier, when his father had set his trail in the sand, the tide must have been much higher. Without Skylar's discovery of the clue from the Song of the First Phylum, he never would have spotted the trail so far away from the water's edge.

"Found it!" exclaimed Aldwyn.

Skylar and Gilbert followed him as he ran toward the glowing prints, which quickly brought them to a path that led straight through a tangle of thorny underbrush.

"We're almost at the end of the nursery rhyme," said Skylar. "The Crown must be close."

Which was just as well, thought Aldwyn, because there was only a day and a half left before the full moon would arrive.

The familiars moved into the brambles, passing among low-lying flowering shrubs whose thorny branches held berries that looked sweet enough to eat. But there was no time for such pleasant diversions, and even if there was, Aldwyn had learned his lesson about trusting the appearance of friendly-looking vegetation.

The trio hadn't even exited the thicket before they heard the knocking of beaks against wood. Aldwyn recognized the sound: these were Paksahara's minions—the same woodpeckers who had tried to thwart them at the great spider's nest. It was too late to hide: already three of the gray birds, with their tail feathers of red and blue, had descended from the sky and embedded their beaks in the small saplings that surrounded the familiars. The prickly branches suddenly snaked to life, reaching out to ensnare them in their clutches. An especially long vine reached up into the air, gripping Skylar by her talon and pulling her down from the air before she could soar away. Aldwyn and Gilbert had no options for escape either, and soon they, too, were being held firmly within the berry-laden brush.

"We warned you once," said a fourth wood-pecker flying overhead, the one with the yellow tail feather who acted as their leader. "You will never find the Crown of the Snow Leopard." He excitedly hammered away at a sapling, and then commanded his minions: "Kill them!"

Aldwyn focused on the branches coming toward them, using his telekinesis to fight them back. But there were too many to stop them all: every time he deflected one, six more spiked tendrils took its place.

"Aldwyn, can't you do something?" croaked Gilbert, who was hopping desperately away from a vine that kept trying to wrap itself around one of his legs.

"I'm trying," Aldwyn replied, but in truth he was running out of ideas fast.

"Aldwyn?" repeated the yellow-tailed leader aloud. "That is a very uncommon name. I have only heard it once before."

"Probably from Paksahara," Skylar said defiantly. "And I imagine she said it in fear, knowing that it was the name that would bring about her demise."

But the woodpecker wasn't paying attention. "Cease your attack," he ordered his subordinates.

"What?" one of them asked. "This goes against the very thing we have been instructed to do."

The leader looked at the other sternly. "You are too young to remember.

"We are not in league with this creature you call Paksahara," he continued, turning back to Aldwyn. "The one who spoke your name was a black-and-white cat, just like you."

"My—my father? Baxley?" asked Aldwyn, incredulously.

"That was his name. Three years ago, he walked this very path that you walk now. He was seeking the Crown as well. And he believed that doing so would save your life."

"What? I don't understand," said Aldwyn.

Neither, it seemed, did the three other woodpeckers: they removed their beaks from the saplings they had controlled, and the vines that had ensnared the familiars fell lifelessly to the ground.

"The woodpeckers of the Beyond have protected the Crown of the Snow Leopard for over eight hundred years," explained the leader. "But the story of the Crown begins even earlier, during a time that has long been forgotten. A period of history rewritten by man. Before humans made themselves into kings and queens, it was animals who ruled the land. They were the great wizards—wielders of magic and accomplishers of miracles. In order to oversee the peace and safety of ancient Vastia, seven animals, each a different species, formed a council. They were called the First Phylum."

"Agorus began to tell us of them," Skylar interrupted the woodpecker's tale, "but his spirit left us before he could finish."

"The seven species asked Agorus and the Farsand lifting-spiders to build the Shifting Fortress, a tower from which their magic could be spread all over Vastia. It would never appear in the same location twice and so would be safe from any enemy who tried to claim it. Only the Crown of the Snow Leopard could summon the Fortress. All the members of the First Phylum agreed that this and this alone would be their shared key to bring it forth.

"And for many years, this was the way it stayed. The council was fair and just, making sure every voice was heard. When humans grew in number and asked for a seat beside the other species, the

First Phylum welcomed them warmly. For a while, man and animal governed Vastia in harmony.

"But as the years passed, the human population kept expanding, and some humans became adept in the art of magic; eventually, humans demanded a greater voice on the council. After a long debate, the majority of the animals agreed to the request; those that disagreed left the council, forming their own isolated communities, detached from the rest of society, in Vastia and the Beyond. And soon humans had a majority in this collective. But they still could not control the Fortress without the Crown. It was then that one of the council members—a man named Sivio, who studied animal magic with great interest—approached the woodpeckers. We lived a humble existence in the forest, as carvers and artisans. No other could mold wood the way we could. And the fact that humans were coming to us was an honor. He asked for something so simple that we thought nothing of it. A bracelet. Carved from black hickory and embedded with the hair and scales of the other animal species on the council, he said it would be a reminder of their unity. Too late did we learn that its purpose was something quite different: it was a replacement for the Crown of the Snow Leopard. Sivio had manipulated us, proving himself to be the worst of what humans were capable of. Now man was able to summon the Shifting Fortress on his own. Within a single year, the First Phylum was disbanded and a monarchy was put in its place. Sivio was anointed the first king."

"The animals never fought back?" asked Aldwyn.

"Some thought they should, others said that man seemed like a friend and only had the best interests of Vastia at heart," replied the woodpecker. "The wisest, however, knew that one day the Crown might be needed again. So they hid the Spheris, entrusting its safety to the Odoodem in the Tree Temple of the Hinterwoods. A spell was cast so that the great totem would only give the Spheris to one who had the blood of destiny. They also composed a song—the Song of the First Phylum—that to the uninitiated seemed a harmless nursery rhyme but in reality contained a series of clues that would lead to the hiding place of the Crown. Together, these precautions kept the Crown safe from most. Those clever enough to solve the riddle of the Song of the First Phylum and find their way to this place without the Spheris had us to deal with—woodpeckers who had been fooled and felt responsible for enabling man to rise to power in the first place. A final line of defense to balance man's corruptible nature. Only those who held the Spheris would be allowed to pass."

"How ironic then that it is Paksahara, a familiar, who uses the Fortress for evil," muttered Skylar.

"So you met my father?" asked Aldwyn. "Do you know why he was looking for the Crown?"

"Has the story not been told to you?" replied the woodpecker.

Aldwyn shook his head.

"When we first met Baxley, holding the Spheris, he recounted how he came to be on his quest. On a day like any other, he went down to the river Ebs in Maidenmere for his daily catch of fish. While staring into the waters, an image drifted past of a young cat cowering amid a circle of stones. And then a voice spoke from the river:

'Aldwyn is in terrible danger. If you wish to save him and all of Vastia, you must seek the Crown of the Snow Leopard.'"

"That sounds similar to the puddle viewing I had in the Time Stream," said Gilbert.

"Cats from Maidenmere don't have puddle viewings," said Aldwyn. "At least, I didn't think we did."

"Baxley thought it was a message from the gods," said the woodpecker.

"It wasn't a message from the gods," said Skylar. "It was a message from Gilbert."

They all turned to her.

"What Baxley saw in the Ebs wasn't similar to Gilbert's puddle viewing," she added. "It *was* Gilbert's puddle viewing."

Aldwyn had an inkling of what she was saying. Gilbert, though, looked completely lost.

"The Time Stream," explained Skylar. "Remember what the iguana said. If you put a leaf in the water and let it drift downstream, it could wash up on the shores of Vastia ten years ago. What if the same thing happened with Gilbert's puddle viewing? We saw it begin to drift downstream. Maybe the vision itself went back in time, to Maidenmere. Gilbert, your viewing was never intended to help us. The reason it came to you was to warn Aldwyn's father."

Aldwyn tried hard to make sense of what Skylar was saying. Time-stopping turtles like Edan, the Mountain Alchemist's familiar, were mind bending enough, but the paradox he was presented with now was even more of a brain twister. Still, Aldwyn realized one thing above any other.

"My father was risking his life to save me," he said aloud.

"Yes," confirmed the woodpecker. "You were all that motivated him. He had no idea what part the Crown would play in protecting you, but he wouldn't stop until he found it."

"Well, did he?" asked Aldwyn.

"We don't know," replied the woodpecker. "We've never seen the Crown. Its location has been kept a secret from even us. All we know is that the Spheris was leading Baxley toward Necro's Maze."

An image flashed in Aldwyn's mind of his

302

father frozen in glass, just like the squirrel he had stumbled up against in the mawpi's lair. Was Necro's Maze where Baxley's path came to its end? Or was he still wandering the farthest corners of the Beyond in search of the Crown? Or maybe, just maybe, had he been following the familiars this whole time, protecting them from a distance?

It was decided: Aldwyn and his companions would march north from there, resuming the glowing paw print trail. Though they would not be sure where exactly it would lead them, Aldwyn could now hold his head up high, for he knew his dad loved him.

16
NECRO'S MAZE

The spirit trail had taken on new meaning since Aldwyn had learned the truth about Baxley. No longer was he reluctantly following in the footsteps of some stranger who he thought to be a selfish charlatan. Now he was proudly walking in the path of his father, someone he could hold in the highest esteem. He looked down at the way his paw fit perfectly into Baxley's print, and took pride in even their matching crooked pinky toes. Gone was the worry and self-doubt of a cat who had always felt abandoned. In its place was a confidence that so long as he was guided by Baxley's trail, everything would turn out all right.

Aldwyn and his fellow familiars had left the woodpeckers behind and were winding their way up a hill, following the path of purple prints. As they continued to climb, Aldwyn looked behind and saw far in the distance—beyond the caves of Stalagmos and past the jungles of the Beyond— to where the Peaks of Kailasa towered high into the sky. It was the first time he had glanced back and seen a recognizable landmark since they had crossed Liveod's Canyon and departed Vastia. Above the mountain range, lightning jumped from cloud to cloud, an ominous reminder of the terrible danger the queendom was in.

Gilbert was staring at the lightning, too. Shady poked his nose out from the backpack to bark at the distant rumbling of thunder.

"I bet Marianne is watching from her bedroom in Edna's manor," said the tree frog. "She can stare at a storm for hours. She's always talking about becoming a weather wizard. I'm trying to push her in the direction of something that has its own unique brand of adventure: library wizard. Where the only danger we'll be facing is eye strain."

"Well, it would be nice if she could change the direction of those clouds, because I believe they're heading right for us," said Skylar.

Although it was sunny where they traveled now, Aldwyn could see that the cover of darkness was indeed slowly but surely moving toward the Beyond. Once the clouds enveloped them, gray sheets of rain would turn these hills into mud slides.

The three picked up their pace, and as they came up over the ridge, Aldwyn's eyes were blinded by the brightest of lights. Its source, however, wasn't the sun: something at the base of the hill was reflecting and intensifying the sunlight. As Aldwyn squinted for a clearer view, he could see that below them were miles and miles of twisting, covered corridors composed solely of opaque crystal, as if an overgrown hedge maze had long ago turned to glass. This sparkling labyrinth had to be Necro's Maze—and Baxley's paw prints led straight through its arched entryway.

"His footprints lead in, but not out again," said Aldwyn.

"Maybe he made it to the other side," said Gilbert.

"There's only one way to find out," replied Aldwyn.

They quickly made their way down to the entrance. From afar, it looked to Aldwyn as if he could have shattered the entire structure by throwing a pawful of stones. But up close, he could see that the glass walls were as thick and impenetrable as a cave troll's thigh. He remembered what Jack had once told him—that no one had ever made it to the center of the maze—and wondered why anyone would dare.

"This is the Beyonder's grail," said Skylar as the trio stood at the foot of the grand arch. "Explorers have traveled from all corners of the land to brave the perils of the maze. Many rumors have been told of the treasures that lie within, but the true pull is the challenge and glory of accomplishing what no other has."

In they walked. Before them stretched a long tunnel, with glass to the left, glass to the right, and glass above. Even the ground had been turned to glass. The suction pads on Gilbert's feet made especially loud blurping sounds with every hop. Each corridor split off into countless others. But unlike those who had entered the maze and gotten lost within, the familiars had a guide.

"Baxley's path goes in and out of nearly every passage," said Aldwyn.

"That must mean he hit a dead end and came back," replied Skylar. "We should only be looking for the trails with one set of prints."

Aldwyn did just that, and he was able to avoid the wrong turns that Baxley had already explored for him. He followed the path around a corkscrew turn, and he and his companions found themselves face to knee with their first crystal statue. A handsome young wizard, no older than twenty, stood with wand outstretched in one hand and shield in the other, with a look of sheer determination on his face.

"Necro is larger than I imagined," said Skylar. "Clearly, he was looking up at it."

Aldwyn turned and spotted a six-legged weasel with a medallion hanging around its neck, frozen in glass as well.

"Look," he said. "The wizard's shield and the weasel's medallion both have the face of Brannfalk on them. They must have been wizard and familiar."

"Probably sent on a mission by King Brannfalk of yore himself," added Skylar.

It was difficult to believe that this Beyonder and his animal companion had been standing here for two hundred years. Frozen in glass, they hadn't aged a day.

Aldwyn continued to follow the trail around another corner and down a different passageway. The air grew stale and windless. As they got deeper, more crystal statues began to appear. Some were human, wizards and warriors preserved in varying states of terror; others were animal, everything from a noble horse carrying leather bags over its mane to mice that looked like lost scavengers rather than brave explorers. It seemed the deeper one ventured into the maze, the more likely they were to run into the crystallizing touch of Necro's tongue.

As Aldwyn kept his eyes on Baxley's trail, he

saw scratch marks that looked like something had been dragged across the glass surface. There were also shards of shattered crystal statues that had been knocked to the ground, perhaps in the heat of battle. Once or twice, Aldwyn glanced over his shoulder, thinking he was being followed; but all he saw behind him was his own reflection staring back at him in the smooth, opaque walls.

"Not that I'm complaining, but how have we made it so far without running into Necro?" asked Gilbert.

"For one thing, we're moving much faster than anyone has walked this maze before," said Skylar. "Thanks to Baxley's paw prints. He's already made many mistakes for us."

Through the frosted glass ceiling, Aldwyn could make out the faint colors of the sky changing at dusk, and he knew that only one day remained until the full moon would allow Paksahara to begin her uprising.

The paw prints led into a wider passageway of the maze and then stopped.

Aldwyn had to look twice because his eyes couldn't believe it: Baxley's path had come to an end. Suddenly and without warning.

"What is it?" asked Skylar.

"The path," replied Aldwyn. "It ends right here."

"What do you mean?" asked Gilbert.

"I mean, there are no more paw prints."

"Baxley couldn't have just disappeared," said Skylar.

They all looked around, but there was no sign of the cat or a crystal statue of him anywhere. A deep uneasiness filled Aldwyn.

"Look, over there, in the corner," said Skylar.

The others turned to see a steel ball the size of a grapefruit pressed up against one of the glass walls. Gilbert hopped up to it and moved it slightly. When he pulled his webbed hands away, the ball rolled back to the wall, like it was being tugged by some unseen force.

"The Spheris," said Gilbert.

"But why would Baxley leave it behind?" asked Aldwyn, refusing to accept the obvious answer to his question.

Skylar and Gilbert both glanced away, as if they didn't want to say what was really on their minds.

Aldwyn walked up to the final glowing paw print that marked the end of Baxley's path. He looked down and saw faint but discernible scratch marks on the floor, similar to the ones he saw in other corridors of the maze. Four lines across the glass. Could these have been left by Baxley's clawed feet, turned to crystal and dragged some-place else in the maze? If so, then Aldwyn had a new path to follow, the one made by the trail scuffed into the glass floor.

Aldwyn was about to tell the others of his dis-covery, when from behind a nearby opaque wall he saw a figure approaching.

"It's Necro!" exclaimed Gilbert.

The three familiars turned to flee, when the figure revealed itself to be not the dreaded master of the maze, but a bearded explorer, with wrin-kled map in hand and backpack slung over his shoulder.

"Run!" cried the terrified man. "The vitrecore is coming!"

Vitrecore? Aldwyn could barely process all that was happening. The end of his father's path. The Spheris. Now a stranger charging toward them,

speaking in sheer horror of a beast he had never heard of.

"What are you waiting—" the explorer started to say, but he never got to finish. A milky white tongue lashed out from around the bend, striking the man on the back of his neck and instantly turning him to glass.

He looked just like the others they had passed, forever frozen in a state of desperate terror. It seemed an unfortunate final pose for one who had surely been a brave, fearless adventurer.

The beast came out into the passageway, and Aldwyn, Skylar, and Gilbert got their first look at Necro, the creature the man had called a vitre-core. It was a pearly white lion with what looked like the horns of a ram jutting from its forehead and the wings of a giant bat stretching from its back. It let out a vicious roar that echoed off the glass.

"Retrace Baxley's paw prints to where we came in," said Skylar. "We have to get out of here."

"Sounds good to me," said Gilbert, as he scooped up the Spheris in his lanky arms.

Aldwyn looked at the scratch marks heading

deeper into the maze, and then to the purple path that would lead them back to the entrance. He didn't want to leave without finding his father.

But they didn't have time to hesitate, not with Necro stalking toward them. The horned lion shot out his tongue, sending it snapping straight for Gilbert. The tree frog spun around, using the Spheris as a shield. The vitrecore's fleshy white appendage made contact not with Gilbert but the ball. In the blink of an eye, the Spheris—their best hope of finding the Crown of the Snow Leopard—was turned to crystal.

Having been denied its intended target only seemed to make the creature more determined to add Gilbert as its latest trophy. The tongue swiped back and forth, but Gilbert, who clearly knew a thing or two about the movements of a long tongue, managed to anticipate the beast's attacks again and again, valiantly defending himself with the Spheris.

Aldwyn turned his attention to the explorer and used his telekinesis to pull free the crystallized map held loosely in the man's hand. He lifted it into the air and flung it at the vitrecore's head. The glass parchment shattered on contact but did little to stall the creature's fury.

The lion changed its tactic, retracting its tongue and instead lowering its horns into attack position. It thrust its head forward, and the sharpened tip of one of the horns pierced the crystallized Spheris, fracturing it from the inside out and sending tiny pieces of glass to the ground. Gilbert was left exposed. Aldwyn and Skylar hurried to his side—if they were going to be turned into glass statues, they would stay together to the end.

The vitrecore sized up the cornered trio. Aldwyn knew that it would take just three lashes of its tongue and he and his companions would be spending an eternity trapped here in the maze.

Gilbert took a deep breath and smiled, an unusually large grin, especially given the dire circumstance.

"What are you doing?" asked Skylar.

"Well, if I'm going to be frozen for the rest of time, it might as well be in a flattering pose."

Necro's tongue began to show itself through the beast's closed lips. The familiars braced themselves. The lion opened its mouth. Aldwyn wondered if getting turned into a glass statue would feel anything like one of Stolix's muscle stasis spells, or if the sensation would be far, far worse.

Aldwyn, Skylar, and Gilbert huddled together . . . the beast's tongue cracked in the air like a whip . . . their journey would end here . . .

Then, from down the glass corridor, a black-and-white shape was moving like a blur. It leaped upon the back of the vitrecore, and caught by surprise, the creature retracted its tongue. As the beast tried to shake off its attacker, Aldwyn only saw glimpses of paw and tail. *Could this be . . . Baxley?*

Necro stood on its hind legs, throwing its attacker to the glass floor. When the cat looked up, Aldwyn could see who their savior from afar had been.

Malvern!

All this time it had been his uncle, not his father! It was Malvern who had jumped on the back of the echo beast to give them time to escape; he had used his telekinesis to hold off the boulders thrown by the plant-controlling woodpeckers; and here he was again, risking life and limb battling the vitrecore. Aldwyn's uncle was looking out for them, watching their backs, making sure nothing happened along their journey to the Crown.

"Uncle?" asked Aldwyn, still reeling.

Malvern did a somersault and roll, dodging out of the way of the beast's tongue and teeth as they came chomping toward him. He wielded a clawed paw and struck at the lion's underbelly, tearing out a clump of fur. When the vitrecore lashed out its tongue at him, all it managed to hit was its own shredded hairs, immediately turning them to crystal.

"I won't be able to defeat it alone," Malvern called out to the familiars.

Aldwyn had so many questions he wanted to ask, but with death's hot breath exhaling upon him, all he could think was how grateful he was to have Malvern at their side.

"Lend me your claws, Aldwyn," shouted Malvern as he swiped at the lion's paw, barely slowing it down.

Aldwyn dove into the fray, putting some of his old scrappy alley fighting skills into action.

"What are you going to do, scratch it to death?" asked Gilbert.

"Aldwyn, Malvern, stay clear of the tail," directed Skylar, who was eyeing the crystallized tuft of hair on the floor.

The two cats backed away and Skylar raised her wings. Suddenly the beast's furry tail looked as though it had transformed into a python, long, scaly, and hissing. Necro glanced back at the illusion and flew into a rage. It let out a growl and then directed a lightning quick tongue strike at the python or, more accurately, its own tail. At once, the entire creature turned to glass, frozen the same way it had frozen countless others over the centuries.

Gilbert, with his back still against the crystal wall of the hedge maze, slid down onto his bottom, breathing a big sigh of relief. Skylar lowered her wings and observed her handiwork. Once again, the familiars had escaped certain death by the narrowest of margins. Aldwyn was just as relieved as the others, but also in need of answers. "What are you doing here?" he asked his uncle.

"After you left Maidenmere, I decided to follow

you," said Malvern. "I couldn't let my only nephew wander into the Beyond without someone watching over him."

"But why did you keep your distance, stay hidden in the shadows?" asked Aldwyn. "You could have come along."

"And risk all of us meeting our end at once? In any feline hunting party, there's a core pack and the watchers who look out for them. It was safer for all of us to not let you know I was there. Had you been questioned or caught, I could have saved you that way."

Gilbert hopped over and wrapped his stringy arms around Malvern's body, hugging him a little too tightly. Malvern tried gingerly to push the tree frog away from him, but Gilbert wouldn't let go. Making it even more uncomfortable for Malvern, Shady stuck his head out of the backpack and began licking his face.

"Thank you, thank you, thank you," Gilbert kept repeating.

Skylar eventually had to pull him off by force.

"Finding the Crown of the Snow Leopard is as important to the cats of Maidenmere as to the rest of Vastia," continued Malvern. "I wanted to ensure that the prophecy was fulfilled."

"How did you follow us?" asked Aldwyn. "You couldn't see the path."

Malvern revealed an Olfax tracking snout inside his pouch. The disembodied nostrils, taken from the nose of a wolf, were an effective tool—Aldwyn knew this from his previous experiences with Grimslade.

"It picked up your scent when I guided you through your first sand sign," said Malvern. "I was never far behind. Sometimes I was certain you saw me."

Out of the corner of his eye, Aldwyn could see that the explorer's crystal form was changing. Color was returning to his face, the peach-ish hue of his flesh and the auburn red of his beard. What Skylar had told them and wizards had speculated before was true: upon defeating Necro, all who had been frozen by the beast would return to life.

Aldwyn looked toward the broken Spheris, but the shards of glass were not piecing back together or turning back to steel. Unfortunately, it appeared that once a glass statue had been broken, it would stay that way.

"If my father was frozen inside this maze, and his crystal statue was dragged somewhere, perhaps he is changing back to himself, too," said Aldwyn.

He was filled with hope yet again. It looked like he would be able to meet Baxley after all.

"You were wrong, you know," said Aldwyn to Malvern. "About your brother. Everything he did was because he loved me. He was on a quest to save me."

A pained look crossed Malvern's face, as if doubt had cast a shadow over everything he had believed to be true for these last three years.

"It sounds like we have a lot to catch up on," replied Malvern.

"I think these scratch marks will lead us to him," said Aldwyn. "Come on. Without the Spheris, he may be the only one who can help us find the Crown."

The group hurried through the maze, racing through corridors of crystal that were now transforming back into tall shrubs. The icy glass walls that had stood for so long were returning to their original state of leaf and branch. Like snow melting on a spring day, white slowly turned to green.

"We have to hurry," said Aldwyn, urgently. "Once the glass floor disappears, the scratch marks will be gone along with it."

Left and right and left again. The passageway twisted and turned in every direction. One thing was certain: if there wasn't an exit on the other side, they would never find their way back to the entrance.

The scratch marks led to a circular room at the center of the maze before coming to an end. Inside were dozens upon dozens of glass statues, all gradually turning back to their pre-frozen states. A whimpering sound could be heard from behind a row of crystal figures. There, watching the statues, sat an old, pruny man, muttering to himself. A whip, hammer, and rope hung on the side of his chair. Aldwyn wondered how this man could have remained untouched by Necro's crystallizing magic. Then the man looked up and did something very strange: he began to make animal noises. A common human would never have been able to comprehend him, but Skylar, Gilbert, and

Aldwyn could understand him perfectly, for he was speaking in animal tongue.

"You're a beast tamer," said Skylar. "What are you doing here in the center of Necro's Maze?"

The old man laughed, a chortle that went on way too long. The kind of chortle that makes you question someone's sanity.

"What am I doing here? Why, I am Necro," the man said once the cackles had subsided.

The animals all looked at each other, confused.

"But the creature, I thought . . . ," said Aldwyn.

"The vitrecore was merely my pet," said Necro. "And this is my family," he added, pointing to the statues all around him. "Five hundred years ago, I was sent on a quest by the third king of Vastia, in search of the rarest breeds of animal for his menagerie. After a storm left me without supplies here in the Beyond, I stumbled across a field of lifeseed and had only it to dine upon for weeks on end. I knew they were meant to be rejuvenating, but what I didn't bargain for was the immortality it bestowed on me. An agelessness that in the end made me outlive all those I cared about. So desperate and lonely did I become that I created this, a maze that would trap any animal or human who entered its walls. I brought with me a vitrecore, one that I had tamed for a wealthy spice baron but kept as my own, to turn anyone it touched to crystal. That way, no matter how long I lived I would have companions that would never leave me."

"My father," said Aldwyn, cutting him off. "He was turned to glass and dragged here. Where is he?"

"So many have been touched by the tongue of my vitrecore, it has been hard to keep track," said Necro.

"He was a black-and-white cat, just like me. Think!"

"Ah, yes," said Necro, staring at Aldwyn more closely. "I kept him right here by my side, for two whole years. 'Til he began to look at me funny. I could tell he was conspiring against me. Getting the other statues to join him."

"What did you do to him?" shouted Aldwyn, starting to get emotional.

"What I do to all of my glass brothers and sisters when I tire of them. I take a hammer to them."

Aldwyn nearly lunged at the old man, but

Malvern held him back.

Necro began laughing in the same high-pitched cackle as before.

"How could you be so cruel?" asked Gilbert.

"It was the only way I could ensure that I'd never be alone," said Necro.

When the rope hanging from the chair lifted telekinetically, Aldwyn knew it wasn't his mind doing it. It was Malvern, circling the twine around the old man's body and binding him to his chair.

"Now you'll be alone forever," said Malvern.

Necro struggled, but had no hope of escaping.

"When the statues turn back, they'll be merciless with me!"

"As they should be," said Skylar.

Beyond the center of the maze, the familiars could see a long, straight passage that led directly to the outside world. But Aldwyn remained frozen in place, even though he had avoided the touch of the beast's tongue. He was overwhelmed by sadness. Was his father truly gone? Had his path and his life ended here, in the company of a mad old man? Would he never get to meet his dad? He felt drops of water running down his face. He was crying.

17
DOUBLE HEX

Outside Necro's Maze, the Beyond stretched to the north, a vast expanse of hills and trees. The crystal walls of the labyrinth had become lush green hedges again, and soon explorers from eras long past would be stumbling their way out of the maze, only to find themselves in a bewildering world that had changed forever. The storm clouds the familiars had seen over the Peaks of Kailasa had blown their way, the winds were picking up, and the time between each lightning flash and its corresponding clap of thunder was getting shorter. And none of it seemed to matter to Aldwyn.

He had walked ahead of the group so the others could not see the tears he was shedding. He wiped them away with the back of his paw, but the pain and hurt that he was feeling could not simply be brushed aside. What a strange few months it had been, from being an orphaned alley cat, with not a whisker of family to speak of, to discovering that not only was he magical, but he got that magic from his parents. Now he had come to discover that they were gone forever and he would never get to know them.

"I'm sorry, nephew," said Malvern, catching up to him. "I know how difficult this must be for you. It's hard for me, too. You don't know the guilt I feel for having misjudged Baxley. And for not protecting your mother from her own sadness."

"I heard her voice in one of my father's whisper shells," said Aldwyn. "She didn't sound crazy to me."

"None of us knew how unstable she truly was," said Malvern. "Until it was too late." Malvern laid a comforting paw on Aldwyn's shoulder. "The best way to honor your father is to finish what he started. What the three of you started. We must find the Crown and stop Paksahara."

"Without the Spheris or Baxley's path, how are we supposed to know which way to go?" asked Gilbert.

"We still have the Song of the First Phylum," said Skylar. "The next clue. *At last the waking moth, Flies to the rising light.*"

"What does it mean?" asked Malvern.

"We don't know yet," replied Skylar.

"Well, before the Spheris was destroyed, it seemed to be pulling to the north," said Aldwyn.

"Then we'll keep heading in that direction, until the clue reveals itself," said Malvern.

Skylar, Gilbert, and Malvern continued on, but Aldwyn stayed behind for a moment. He opened his pouch and telekinetically lifted Baxley's necklace—the string with the three tiny whisper shells on it—and placed it over his head. He would wear it the same way he imagined his father had, with his mother's voice close to his heart.

◦⁓◦⁓◦

Raindrops were falling. It was still a light drizzle, but the dampness in Aldwyn's fur was becoming unpleasant. Ants and butterflies hid beneath mushroom caps, perhaps sensing worse things to come. Gilbert shot out his tongue and lapped up swallows of water. Shady was now walking on the ground beside them, splashing through puddles. It seemed that rain didn't bother shadow pups.

"In Daku we used to say, 'A rainy day is a happy day,'" said the tree frog. Aldwyn shot him a look. He didn't really see what anyone had to be upbeat about. "What? I'm just trying to look at the flower bud as half full here."

The steady pitter-patter suddenly let up, and the clouds parted enough for the nearly full moon to peek out. Its bright light even made a rainbow in the night sky.

"See," said Gilbert. "Things are looking up already."

"No, the worst is yet to come," said Skylar, pointing to what seemed like a whirlpool of gray overhead. "Look at how those neb swirlums are churning. If the winds keep increasing, we could see a full-on scimitar gust."

Aldwyn knew by the tone in her voice that the weather would be severe, and no matter how fast they moved, they'd never be able to outpace the clouds. Soon, they would be forced to do what the ants and butterflies were doing: take shelter until the storm passed.

They raced across the valley between the hillsides, trying to put as much distance as they could between themselves and the gathering tempest. In truth, they were running without a clear sense of direction, until one of them could decipher the second half of the next-to-last verse of the nursery rhyme.

At last the waking moth, Flies to the rising light.

Aldwyn puzzled over the meaning of the clue. Could it have simply meant that when you wake up, the sun is rising, and thus they should be heading to the northeast, the place where dawn first breaks?

"I never had a son of my own," spoke Malvern from behind Aldwyn. "My father and my grandfather before him tried to do both—be parent and pride leader—but there was only room for one. I never understood it before, but now I see why your father declined his elder birthright to guide the cats of Maidenmere. He chose you."

"Are the Pridelands safe with you gone?" asked Aldwyn.

"I have put the noble hunter Kafar in charge until I return," he replied. "I trust he will look after our fellow cats well."

"I just hope Paksahara's minions don't come to threaten them," said Aldwyn. "They were trying to recruit the birds of Nearhurst and a tribe of aardvarks we encountered. I imagine they're doing the same with many others."

"Traitors!" Gilbert chimed in. "All of them. What kind of animal would align themselves with Paksahara? They'd have to be heartless, soulless . . . no better than worms."

"I try not to judge," said Malvern calmly. "Different animals see the world in different ways. Of course no one should condone hurting innocents, but you'd be lying to yourself if you didn't see some beauty in a Vastia where animals ruled."

Aldwyn saw from out of the corner of his eye that Skylar was nodding in agreement. He couldn't argue with a society where creatures on four legs were no longer relegated to second-class citizenship, but the means by which Paksahara

332

was accomplishing her goal seemed unjustifiable.

Just then, a gust blew through the valley so strong and sudden that Skylar was pulled out of the sky and thrown to the ground with a thud. The rains were not far behind. Aldwyn helped Skylar up onto his back; the winds were heavy enough that she could not flap through the air. The group tried to trudge forward through the torrents, but their progress had been slowed dramatically.

"I think we should stop until the storm blows over," said Skylar. "Otherwise we could very well miss the moth or even the Crown itself like we did the stone arrows before."

Gilbert spotted a rotted log big enough for all four to crawl into. A few holes were letting rain in, but they could be easily covered.

"You two take cover," Aldwyn said to Gilbert and Skylar. "Malvern and I will gather some leaves and branches to complete the shelter."

All seemed in agreement. Bird and frog disappeared into the log. Aldwyn and Malvern moved across the mud-soaked ground toward some fallen timber and sycamore leaves.

"I can see how you three have come so far," said Malvern. "You make an admirable team."

Malvern raised a clump of branches with his mind, and Aldwyn did the same, nearly as skillfully.

"Your mental agility is getting better," said Malvern. "But you could still use the tutelage of an elder lifter."

The two carried the foliage telekinetically through the air, dropping it over the openings in the rotted wood.

"We just need a little bit more," said Aldwyn's uncle, as he walked back through the trees to find a fallen branch with enough leaves to keep them dry.

Aldwyn followed. He glanced down at the muddy paw prints Malvern was leaving behind. And then something caught his eye: an indentation within one of them. Two concentric circles with a five-pointed star at the center. It was the double hex. The very same emblem he had seen branded into the wolverine's paw at the Aviary and emblazoned on the side of the ore cart inside the caves of Stalagmos. What was this

symbol—which signified loyalty to Paksahara—
doing on the pad of Malvern's paw? A chill went
through Aldwyn's body.

Malvern had turned around and was staring at Aldwyn. Aldwyn tried to avert his gaze
from the ground, but that only seemed to make
Malvern more curious. His uncle's eyes flashed
to the ground, but luckily the rain had already
washed away the double hex.

"Is everything all right?" asked Malvern.

"Yes," said Aldwyn. "Just a shiver from the cold."

Malvern focused on a pile of twigs and lifted them through the damp air.

"We should join the others," he said. "Maybe we can figure out that clue before we sleep."

"Actually," said Aldwyn, wheels desperately turning in his head, "I didn't say anything earlier, but I think I have the answer."

"What are you waiting for, then?" asked Malvern, a little too eager, it seemed to Aldwyn. Given what he had just seen in the mud, Aldwyn was certain that his uncle's enthusiasm was not about helping the familiars in their quest. Instead it was for some nefarious purpose, yet unknown, but no doubt to aid Paksahara.

"I think it's quite simple," said Aldwyn. "When an animal wakes, the rising light is the sun, which climbs into the sky from the northeast. I think that's where the crown lies."

Malvern thought about it for a beat.

"Yes, nephew, that makes sense. Tomorrow morning, when we wake, we should all head east. Now let's sleep out this storm."

Malvern lowered the second gathering of bark and green atop the log and he and Aldwyn hurried inside. Skylar and Gilbert were already sound asleep.

"Rest well, Aldwyn," said Malvern. "I am confident that tomorrow we will find the Crown."

"Yes, uncle."

Malvern curled up and closed his eyes. Aldwyn stared at him. The pieces hadn't all fallen into place yet, but there was no question that his uncle was a traitor. To himself, his pride, and all of Vastia. He couldn't look upon his black-and-white stripes with anything but disgust now. Malvern had deceived him about Baxley and his own allegiances. What other lies had he spun?

Aldwyn shut his eyes, too. Not to sleep, though. To wait.

It was hard to tell how much time had passed. The sound of rain, thunder, and wind continued incessantly outside the log. Aldwyn had been lying there silently, pretending to sleep, since he and Malvern had said good night.

The noise was almost inaudible, but still he could hear it. Aldwyn's eyelid opened just a hair, and he could see Malvern tiptoeing out of the shelter. Aldwyn moved some leaves away from the top of the log and peered out to see his uncle, through the driving storm, heading northeast. Once Malvern had disappeared into the forest of tall sycamores, Aldwyn shook Gilbert and Skylar awake.

"What is it?" asked Skylar.

"My uncle is in league with Paksahara," said Aldwyn. "I saw him leave a paw print with a double hex embedded within it."

Gilbert's sleepy orange eyes snapped wide open.

"How is that possible?" asked the tree frog. "Why was he protecting us then?"

"Think about it," said Aldwyn. "The only way to stop Paksahara is by locating the Crown. I'm the only one who could do that, by following Baxley's path. What if Malvern was using me to get to it, so that it could be destroyed forever?"

"But Aldwyn, if you were the only one who could find it, why didn't he just kill you when we first arrived in Maidenmere?" asked Skylar.

"I don't know. I haven't figured it all out yet."

"Where is Malvern anyway?" asked Gilbert.

"I told him I deciphered the last clue," said

Aldwyn. "That when the moth wakes, the rising light is the sun coming up from the east."

"Why would you do that?" asked Gilbert.

"Because a moth doesn't wake in the morning," said Aldwyn. "It wakes at night, when the moon rises."

"In the northwest," said Skylar, quickly catching on.

"Exactly. I tricked him. But I'm guessing we don't have much time before he realizes it."

"What are we waiting for?" said Skylar. "Let's go."

The three familiars quickly gathered their belongings, left the shelter of the fallen log, and headed northwest. It was just the three of them again, and that's how Aldwyn liked it.

18

THE CROWN OF THE SNOW LEOPARD

Familiars, for hundreds of years the safety of Vastia has rested on the shoulders of wizards. Now its future rests on yours.

Queen Loranella's parting words were echoing in Aldwyn's head. So much faith had been placed in him and his fellow companions, the animals they called the Prophesized Three. But now the driving rains seemed to confirm the lingering feeling that Aldwyn, Skylar, and Gilbert were up against an evil that was more than they could handle on their own.

Skylar had been right about the storm: it was only getting worse. The night was even darker in the absence of moon and stars, which the thick layer of clouds obscured. The familiars were at the center of a full-blown scimitar gust, and it was all too clear why it had earned that name. The winds cut through the branches like sharpened blades, leaving splintered limbs strewn about the ground. Aldwyn heard a loud crack above him as the heavy bough of a sycamore tree snapped and came crashing down, nearly flattening Gilbert if Shady hadn't tugged him out of the way.

"Leopards are reclusive creatures," said Skylar. "They're not like lions, who live out in the open plains in family groupings. No, they could be camouflaged in the trees or hidden in crevices between rocks. They would be difficult to spot in daylight or on a clear night, never mind during a full-blown scimitar."

"Okay," said Gilbert, trying to take control of an impossible situation. "If it's so difficult to find, maybe instead of searching for the snow leopard, we should try to get the snow leopard to come to us. Aldwyn, you didn't happen to pack a really big jar of cat food, did you?"

"At this point, I don't even think we're looking for a leopard," he replied wearily. "Perhaps not even a crown."

"Yeah, that makes sense," said Gilbert sarcastically. "It's called the Crown of the Snow Leopard. Why would we be looking for a crown or a snow leopard?"

"*Hiding high upon its head, Draped in white shimmering gown, Lie the keys to the past, In the snow leopard's crown,*" said Aldwyn. "Think about it. Nothing in the Song of the First Phylum has been what it appears."

"Even if you're right," said Skylar, "where does that leave us?"

Aldwyn didn't have an answer to that, and so the familiars continued silently through the rain-soaked valley in the unnamed stretch of the Beyond. The denseness of the trees thinned, and the group could at least take some solace in escaping the threat of timber toppling upon their heads.

Then they came up over a rise—and were met with a glorious sight, one that rivaled the majestic beauty of Torentia Falls. Across the valley that spread out below them, they saw a hillside that was completely covered in white-petaled flowers, with only a few patches of black earth visible beneath. The curve of the hill's crest resembled two rolling waves coming into shore. On second glance, they seemed even more like . . . the back of a reclining cat. On the taller of the two peaks stood a circle of seven gray rocks. Aldwyn had seen these rocks before, in Gilbert's puddle viewing. They were the ones he had been cowering among, clearly in danger.

Aldwyn and Skylar looked at each other. Then they turned to Gilbert.

"Even I figured this one out," said the tree frog.

There was no question that they had found the Crown of the Snow Leopard. And it wasn't a precious object, but a place. Aldwyn knew that hidden somewhere high atop that hill lay the keys to the past and the power to summon the Shifting Fortress.

"We did it," said Skylar proudly. "And with a day to spare, too."

They hurried as fast as they could across the

valley and up the flowered slope. There was such joy in Aldwyn's step that he momentarily forgot the downpour drenching him. Skylar flew for the rocks, so eager she could not wait for Gilbert and Aldwyn to catch up. Aldwyn's paws crushed white petals underfoot as he dashed to the edge of the crown.

Skylar was already standing at the center beside a pedestal of steel, which had a grapefruit-sized hole carved out of it.

"The Spheris would have fit perfectly here," she said. "That must have been what the Odoodem meant when it said the Spheris was one with the Crown."

A rapid succession of lightning flashes illuminated the sky and the stone circle, and Aldwyn could see that the inner face of each of the seven rocks was covered in glyphs. The etchings reminded Aldwyn of the symbols he had seen on the glyphstone outside Bronzhaven and the one in Bridgetower.

"What does it mean?" asked Aldwyn.

"The symbols on the seven rocks are in a script I've never seen before," replied Skylar. Another

344

series of sparks in the sky allowed the jay's eyes discover something else. "But there's writing here on the steel pedestal, not unlike the language used in the oldest spells recorded. It appears to be instructions."

Gilbert huffed his way up to the others, his wiry legs sleeved in wet mud, Shady at his side. "You two save the queendom yet?"

"We're working on it," said Aldwyn.

Skylar leaned in closer to try to translate the words, which had worn away with time. "'Noble possessor of the Spheris,'" she read. "'Carrier of the blood of destiny. You have deciphered the secrets of the Crown and stand here hoping for the Shifting Fortress to appear. But your journey is not yet complete.'" Skylar's voice grew anxious, and she continued to read faster. "'Now, all that is left for you to do is gather the seven descendants of the First Phylum. Bring them to one of the three glyphstones and stand together, side by side in a circle, just like the seven stones surrounding you here. Then the Fortress will summon forth, and order can be restored to this great land.'"

"Hang on," said Gilbert. "I think I misheard,

pretty sure you just said, 'Your jour-
...omplete.'"

...eyes were speeding over the words
...n the pedestal again, as if even she could
...lieve that what she had read was true. But
...lwyn could feel in the pit of his stomach that
...his was not the end of their adventure, only a
halfway point. And another realization was
quickly setting in: they would never be able to
summon the Shifting Fortress in time to stop
Paksahara from raising her Dead Army.

"We don't even know who the seven descendants are," said Skylar.

"We need to get word back to the palace, to
warn them," said Aldwyn.

"It will be too late by then."

Aldwyn didn't even need to turn around to
know who had spoken these words: Malvern had
found them.

"Very clever, nephew," the traitorous pride
leader continued. "I would have kept going, too,
had it not been for the moth I saw flying toward
the moon."

Malvern stalked around the circle, looking at

the stones and the steel pedestal at the center.

"So this is the Crown of the Snow Leopard?" he asked. "I never doubted that you'd find it. You have the same annoying persistence as your father."

Malvern opened his pouch telekinetically, removing a small vial of gold powder. The vial uncorked itself and the powder flew up into the rainy sky. It swirled about before taking on the ominous shape of the double hex, glowing brightly in the darkness.

Aldwyn understood that Malvern was sending out a signal, a bright gold against the night sky. Many would see it, but it was only intended for one: Paksahara. And once she saw the burning eyes at the center of the five-pointed star, she would be coming for them.

"Why did you do it?" asked Aldwyn. "Why did you betray us?"

"What you see as betrayal, I see as justice long overdue. Before you were born, when I first became pride leader, Paksahara came to Maidenmere. We met secretly. She promised a day was coming when animals would rule Vastia again. She was looking for allies who would be there at her side to rise up against humans when that time finally came. Humans, who pushed our pride to the dusty and deserted plateaus. There was a day when the bicolor cats could roam all the land, before cities and castles infested it. I promised to do whatever I could to help."

"Everything you told me about my father was a lie," said Aldwyn. "I deserve to know the truth about my parents."

"The truth is simple: Baxley and I never saw eye to eye. I lived constantly in the shadow of his virtues, even when he was off on his adventures and I was in Maidenmere helping our tribe gather food and shelter. He had a chivalry and romanticism about him, but you can't lead that way.

"Shortly before you were born, your father came to me. He told me of a vision he had seen in the Ebs. It was of his son in danger, and the only way to save him was by retrieving the Crown of the Snow Leopard. At the time, none of us knew what the Crown's meaning or purpose was. But Baxley was unwilling to risk your safety, and he set out to find it. He remembered a nursery rhyme told to us as kittens, and followed the clues to a great tree in the Hinterwoods. He brought a steel ball back to Maidenmere. By that time, Corliss had given birth to you, and your father was able to say his good-byes to both of you.

"I promised him I would look after you and your mother. It was during this time that Paksahara and I began meeting more frequently. But it was of the utmost importance that our alliance remain a secret. Then I noticed Corliss acting strangely around me. And I knew what I had worked so hard to keep hidden had been exposed. It was impossible to keep anything from your mother. All the Wind Chanters like Corliss had special gifts. Your mother's was the ability to read minds. She was telepathic."

"Her death wasn't an accident, was it?" asked Aldwyn, doing everything he could not to jump forward and claw his uncle's eyes out.

"I tried to reason with her. Tell her that what I was doing would be for the good of the Pridelands. But she was just like your father. Righteous to a fault. Besides, she could read my thoughts, and no matter what I said aloud, the voices in my head said something different.

"She sent you down the river to protect you from me. I was too late to stop her. We struggled, and I pushed her into the river."

A blind rage took hold of Aldwyn. A sharp rock flew up from behind him, directed right at Malvern. But it was blocked in midair by an even bigger shard that Malvern had lifted with his own mind.

Gilbert and Skylar watched helplessly as nephew confronted uncle.

"I would be angry, too," said Malvern, sensing his nephew's fury. "But proceed with caution. My powers are strong, and I will show no mercy."

The two stones hovered between them, locked in telekinetic duel. Malvern, with a quick twist of the mind, sent Aldwyn's rock flying to the ground. Then, just by raising his chin, Malvern lifted Aldwyn off his feet and threw him into one of the seven stones in the circle. Aldwyn cowered there, the same way he had in Gilbert's puddle viewing.

Aldwyn put a paw up against one of the rocks and got slowly to his feet.

"*Mongoose*," whispered an ancient-sounding voice.

Where had it come from? He listened, his paw still up against the rock, and there it was again:

"*Mongoose.*"

He had hit his head pretty hard, but surely not so hard that he was hearing things.

"It sounded like it was coming from the stone," said Skylar, erasing any doubts Aldwyn might have had about whether what he was hearing was real. He pulled his paw away and the rock went silent. Then he put it back up to the smooth surface, and there it was a third time: "*Mongoose.*"

"The stones, they must speak the names of the seven descendants upon being touched," said Skylar excitedly. "We need to learn them all!"

Just then, the sound of beating wings could be heard overhead. Aldwyn looked up to the sky to see a bird the pale tint of indigo slicing through the air. It was almost as if the droplets of rain bent around it, the wings moved so quickly.

"A periwinkle falcon," shouted Skylar with relief in her voice. "The fastest of all avian creatures. Noble and just, and a vicious fighter, too."

The bird came swooping down toward Malvern, ready to carry the traitorous cat off in its sharp talons. But then it landed beside Malvern—and began to transform. Claws turned to paws and beak to gray fur nose. There standing before them was Paksahara.

"I want to thank you," Paksahara said to the familiars. "I could have never found the Crown without your help."

Aldwyn and Skylar exchanged a quick look and a nod. They both backed away slowly, inching toward the neighboring stone in the circle.

"Get the names!" whispered Aldwyn through his whiskers. "Gilbert and I will cover you."

Skylar didn't hesitate. She flew up to the next rock and pressed her wing against it. The stone spoke out a second species' name, and Aldwyn was close enough to hear it:

"*Golden toad,*" said the same mysterious ancient voice.

"The seven stones must be destroyed," Malvern told Paksahara. "They must never reveal their secret to the Prophesized Three."

Skylar was already at the third rock. "*Wolverine,*"

the blue jay called out just as a blast of emerald energy shot out from Paksahara's paws. It twisted through the air like a corkscrew and struck the side of the third rock, obliterating it. Skylar was caught in the blowback, landing on a pile of debris.

Aldwyn lifted the rubble off her telekinetically and sent it hurtling toward Paksahara. The hare twitched her ear and a black hole of darkness formed before her, sucking up the attack. She then flicked her wrist, shooting out two bolts of lightning that turned the first two rocks to dust.

Gilbert was hopping for the fourth stone, with Shady bounding behind him. His webbed hands reached out and made contact. "*Howler donkey!*" he shouted excitedly.

"I think you meant '*howler monkey*,'" observed Skylar, who was getting dizzily back to her feet.

"Right," said the tree frog. "It's kind of hard to hear with the storm and Paksahara blowing stuff up next to my ears."

Paksahara turned her attention to the stones that remained standing, and Aldwyn could see the energy beginning to crackle at her paw tips. He sprinted for the rock, hoping to distract her long enough for Skylar and Gilbert to gather the last three species' names. But before he could make contact with the stone, he felt a tearing sensation rip through his back. Aldwyn tumbled end over end, looking up to see Malvern atop him, claws digging into his flesh.

"I told you I would show no mercy," hissed Malvern.

Out of the corner of his eye, Aldwyn saw Gilbert whispering in Shady's ear. The next thing Aldwyn knew, the shadow pup was throwing itself at Paksahara, distracting her before she could send out the blast.

Malvern pinned Aldwyn to the ground, pushing him into the mud and holding him down. A large piece of loose rock flew for the back of Malvern's head, but was stopped in midair.

"Come now, nephew," scoffed Malvern. "You're no match for me, not in strength and certainly not mind versus mind."

While he tried to fight off his uncle, Aldwyn could see Shady nip at Paksahara's leg and Skylar, who was still a bit off balance, sailing toward the fifth stone. She was able to touch her wing to the surface, and although Aldwyn couldn't hear what the rock said, he was sure Skylar had learned the name of the fifth species they needed.

Malvern had taken control of the piece of rock that Aldwyn had initially lifted, and it was now hovering directly above his nephew's head. Aldwyn pushed with all his mind to hold it back, feeling his temples strain and eyes burn.

"If I was the only one who could find the Crown, why not just kill me when you first had the chance?" asked Aldwyn.

"After you came to Maidenmere and revealed who you were, I contacted Paksahara. She directed me to follow you and your companions at a distance, to ensure that you would make it to the Crown safely. I couldn't take the chance of traveling at your side, in case you possessed the same mind-reading ability as your mother."

Despite Aldwyn's own precarious situation, he could see that Paksahara had cast a light spell, surrounding herself in a bright glow of sun that forced Shady to retreat.

The evil hare addressed Skylar: "You disappoint me the most," she said to the blue jay. "I see a lot of myself in you. Your thirst for knowledge. Your want for more. I was just like you once."

"You're nothing like me!" cried Skylar, who had almost reached the sixth stone when Paksahara conjured a glider cage in the air and sent it hurtling toward the bird, entrapping her in mid-flight. Aldwyn tried to attract Gilbert's attention, but the tree frog was fumbling through his pouch, removing some nightshade and juniper berries.

"Gilbert, get to the last two rocks," called Aldwyn. "What are you doing?"

"Stopping Paksahara," he answered.

"But you can't cast spells!" Aldwyn said.

"I know. But nobody's better at miscasting them." With these words, Gilbert threw the components into the air and shouted: "*Send a flame from whence you came!*"

Just like in the cave, a glowing fairy started to form but quickly became an explosive firework. It blasted up and down, from rock to mud, zipping straight over Malvern's head and into Paksahara's back. She was knocked facedown into the mud. The glider cage came crashing down to the ground.

Aldwyn and Malvern continued to wrestle tele-kinetically as the rock lowered toward Aldwyn's face. He knew that its weight would crush him if he wasn't able to keep it hovering in the air.

"You still haven't answered my question," panted Aldwyn. "There would have been no need to destroy the Crown if only the child of Baxley could follow the path here."

"You're not the only child of Baxley," said Malvern. "You have a sister."

Aldwyn couldn't believe what his uncle had told him. For a split second his concentration wavered, and the large rock descended closer toward him. But then Malvern's revelation gave Aldwyn an unexpected surge of strength. He was able to win the tug or war with Malvern's mind and toss the rock aside. Aldwyn leaped up and thrust his head into Malvern's nose, causing his uncle to stumble backward just as Skylar busted out from the now weakened cage and flapped to the sixth stone, touching it with her wing. This time Aldwyn was able to hear the rock speak: *Bloodhound.*

Now only one stone remained before all seven of the stones would be revealed to the familiars.

Paksahara, back on her feet. shook off the last burning embers clinging to her fur from the flame fairy. Looking more annoyed than angry, she turned to Gilbert, who could hardly believe that his miscast spell had actually struck its intended target. But there was no time for gloating: Paksahara conjured a wind gust and hurled it at the tree frog, picking him up off his feet and throwing him off the crest of the hill and down the white-flowered slope.

Skylar, meanwhile, was charging for the final stone. But before she reached it, Paksahara fired a trio of ruby needles toward the blue jay's wings. Skylar darted out of the way and chanted, *"Shieldarum resisto!"* and a shield spell intercepted the flying needles.

"Your magic has grown stronger since we last met," said Paksahara. "But even a student of the Noctonati cannot withstand me for long."

Her pink eyes stared coldly, much like those in the circles of the double hex, and sparks of energy bubbled in her paws.

Aldwyn wanted to come to Skylar's aid, but he still had his uncle to contend with. Malvern was licking blood from his lip, smiling at the taste of it.

"You're unworthy of calling yourself a Mooncatcher," he snarled. "Just as your father was."

Aldwyn's mind and body were exhausted, and he wasn't certain he would be able to withstand another of Malvern's attacks. His uncle leaped, paws outstretched toward his neck. *Let your mind breathe. And let yourself be as calm as the Enaj River.* A swirl of dirt and mud whipped up off the ground and formed the Mooncatcher sand sign— a paw reaching for a crescent moon.

Out of the corner of his eye, Aldwyn saw that Paksahara had summoned a spear of white energy and was pointing it at Skylar.

Aldwyn's mind gave life to the paw, and as if it was his own, he thrashed its claws across Malvern's eyes. The pride leader was blinded by the sand, causing him to veer off course . . .

. . . directly into the path of Paksahara's death blow!

The bolt meant for Skylar ripped through Malvern's chest, evaporating flesh and leaving only bone. He collapsed dead upon the ground.

Aldwyn felt a momentary pang of sadness for this close relative, but Malvern's death would not be mourned for long. He wasn't worth Aldwyn's tears. He was a traitor and a murderer.

Gilbert had pulled himself up from wherever he had fallen and rejoined his fellow familiars. Now Aldwyn, Skylar, and Gilbert were left face to face with Paksahara.

"The final stone!" cried Skylar.

The familiars made a dash for it. Aldwyn's paws bounded across the mud, kicking up sprays of wet dirt behind him. Paksahara lifted her paws above her head and brought them to the ground with furious might. A shock wave of energy pulsed through the earth, and like a shark through water, it sped to the stone. Aldwyn's paw reached out and touched the surface of the seventh rock. A voice began to speak, but before Aldwyn could hear the words, the stone exploded.

Aldwyn flew backward, hitting the ground hard. He hadn't heard it! The final species that needed to be collected around one of the glyph-stones remained unknown. Their whole adventure had ended in total failure.

In rapid succession, Paksahara fired a series of blasts from her paws until all seven stones had been turned to rubble.

Once the ringing in his ears subsided, Aldwyn got back to his feet.

"Now you will never be able to summon the Shifting Fortress," said Paksahara. "My Dead Army is going to lay waste to Vastia. I just wish the three of you could have seen it."

The gray hare raised her paws one last time—and the familiars ran. They sprinted behind the steel pedestal still standing at the center of the crumbled Crown. When they came out around the other side, Paksahara incanted, *"Ekonpiske v prave!"* and a double blast of energy shot from her paws.

The two bolts struck the familiars, sending electricity coursing through their bodies. By the time the energy dissipated, there was little left of the bird, frog, and cat but dust.

Paksahara shape-shifted back into a periwinkle falcon and disappeared into the stormy night sky.

19

FULL MOON RISING

S hady, who had been hiding behind the rubble of one of the stones, came out and approached the pile of dust. The shadow puppy hung his head low and let out a little whimper for the fallen familiars.

"Hey, cheer up, Shady," shouted Gilbert.

The shadow pup spun around with a confused look on his smoky black face to see Gilbert, Aldwyn, and Skylar emerge from behind the steel pedestal, alive and unharmed.

"It was only an illusion," explained the tree frog,

welcoming Shady into his arms.

Aldwyn and Skylar looked around at the devastation.

"Did you hear anything before the stone was destroyed?" asked Skylar. "Even just a sound?"

"Nothing," said a dejected Aldwyn.

"Unfortunately, six of the species won't do us any good," replied Skylar.

Aldwyn ran his paws through the dusty debris of the seventh stone, hoping to hear what he hadn't before. But there was only silence.

"I don't think there's anything more for us here," said Skylar. "It's time to return to Bronzhaven. Gilbert, now might be a good time to use that last journey bead."

As Gilbert dove into his pouch, Aldwyn let out a heavy sigh. "My mother and father are dead. My uncle betrayed me. I have a sister, but I have no idea where she is, or if she is even alive. At least before, I could imagine a day when we'd all be together again. Now I'm truly alone."

"You're not alone, Aldwyn," said Skylar. "You've got us."

"We're your family now," said Gilbert.

Aldwyn felt a webbed hand on one shoulder, and a wing on the other.

"Come on, Aldwyn. Let's go home," said Skylar.

Gilbert held up the silver chain of beads from the mawpi's lair and rubbed the only one that still shimmered blue between his suction pads.

"Take us to the New Palace of Bronzhaven," he said aloud.

Again, the wooden door with the brass knocker materialized before them. Again, the knocker banged three times, and again the door swung open. Just on the other side was the magnificent throne room of the palace. The familiars stepped through the opening, and just like that, they were returned to where their long journey had started six days ago.

The door immediately closed behind them and vanished. Aldwyn, Gilbert, and Skylar hurried through the halls, shouting the names of their loyals. Soon, young wizards and familiars were reunited in a flurry of hugs and tears. Queen Loranella joined them and was briefed on all that had happened: of their trip to the Beyond, Baxley's path, the Crown, and how their urgent quest was far from finished. And they of course told her how the only way to summon the Shifting Fortress was to gather seven descendants of the First Phylum around one of Vastia's three glyphstones. The Crown had revealed six of the seven species—mongoose, golden toad, wolverine, howler monkey, king cobra, and bloodhound—the seventh, however, remained a mystery. Without it, there was no purpose in collecting the six.

"I'll have every wizard, soldier, and familiar protect the glyphstones," said the queen. "I refuse to surrender without a fight. Somehow, we'll find the name of the last species."

But Aldwyn was not so certain. There was a reason the Crown had been hidden from humans, and he was sure that its secrets had died when the stones had been destroyed.

⁘

Jack and Aldwyn sat by the golden eel pond in the courtyard of the palace. It had become their special place, where loyal and familiar could talk in private. Jack told Aldwyn how he had spent the last six days building fortifications around the outside walls of Bronzhaven. The carpentry and handicraft lessons his uncle had taught him before he began his wizard training were hardly a substitute for magic, but better than nothing. Dalton had been out helping the farmers, stockpiling crops in case the city came under siege. And Marianne had assisted in the smithies, smelting swords and shields.

"It wasn't as exciting as riding on the back of a traveling whale, that's for sure," said Jack.

Aldwyn's paws stroked the whisper shells, which were still hanging from the string around his neck. He had been touching them often without even realizing it, as if the voices from his past were bringing him some comfort in the aftermath of all he had experienced.

"I found these in my father's pouch," said Aldwyn. "One has the voice of my mother. Another sounds like my sister and me."

Aldwyn leaned his head down so Jack could take the necklace from him. The boy put his ear to the first shell.

"Your mom has a nice voice," said Jack.

The boy then moved to the second shell. He smiled.

"Is that really you?" he asked.

"I think so. And I'm pretty sure you can hear a second kitten, too."

"What about the third one?" asked Jack.

"It's empty."

Jack brought the shell to his ear.

"I hear something," he said.

Aldwyn looked at him with disbelief.

"It's hard to make out," continued Jack. "There's a lot of commotion. It sounds like *lightmare*. What does that mean?"

Aldwyn climbed onto Jack's shoulder and leaned his ear toward the shell. He could hear the battle atop the Crown of the Snow Leopard. The sound of rain and crackling energy filled the air. The faint cry from Skylar: "The final stone!" A loud explosion. And through it all, there was a single word being uttered in that ancient, mysterious voice.

"*Lightmare*."

It was the seventh stone revealing the last species.

Aldwyn could hardly believe it. The whisper shell had captured what he feared was lost. And suddenly new hope coursed through his body.

"Skylar, Gilbert!" he shouted across the court-yard.

From beneath the colonnade, his fellow familiars ran, with Marianne and Dalton following behind them.

"What is it?" asked Skylar.

"The whisper shell," said Aldwyn. "It recorded the voice of the final stone. *Lightmare*. The seventh species of the First Phylum is *lightmare*."

"Then we have them all," said Skylar. "We need to seek out a descendant from each at once. There's no time to waste."

"Great," said Gilbert. "And just how do we do that?"

"Some of these species have not been seen on these lands for hundreds of years," said Skylar. "It will take a master tracker. A tenacious hunter of all creatures that walk on four legs. Someone who will search every corner of Vastia and the Beyond for an animal that does not want to be found."

The group stood quietly for a moment.

"I know just the person," said Aldwyn.

The streets of Bridgetower had not changed much since Aldwyn had last seen them. He would have liked to give Skylar, Gilbert, Jack, Marianne, and Dalton a tour of his favorite rooftops and alleyways, but the six of them had a far more pressing matter at hand. They had rushed to the white-walled city in the royal carriage, accompanied by two of Queen Loranella's soldiers. It had been early morning when they left Bronzhaven, but by the time they arrived it was already dusk. And once the moon rose over the northwestern horizon, it would be full.

The group stood across the street from the Tower Pub tavern. Aldwyn had sneaked into the cider house before to lap up bits of cheese that had fallen to the floor. It was an establishment frequented by the shadiest characters this side of the Ebs: elvin pirates, sewer market vendors, even the occasional Gordian mindcaster. It was hardly a place for young wizards and their familiars, but few would ask questions once they revealed the queen's decree they were carrying.

Escorted by the soldiers, the group entered the pub. They got more than a few sideways glances from tattooed driftfolk and long-bearded beast tamers. Aldwyn's eyes scanned the room. They quickly fell upon a figure sitting by himself in the corner, cloaked in shadows.

"There he is," said Aldwyn.

Jack pointed him out to Dalton and Marianne. They all approached.

"Excuse me, sir," said Jack. "We have a job for you."

The figure turned to reveal a claw-scarred face.

It was Grimslade, the infamous bounty hunter.

Aldwyn's old nemesis was dressed the same as he always was. Pouches dangled from his belt. A crossbow was slung over his back. His bronze-tipped boots shined bright beneath the table. The only new piece was a six-inch black dragon tooth that hung around his neck. He glared at Aldwyn and the other familiars. They had outsmarted him once before, leaving him asleep beside the Hydra of Mukrete.

"Give me one good reason I shouldn't noose that cat right now," he snarled.

One of the queen's soldiers dropped a heavy burlap bag full of gold coins on the tabletop before

Grimslade. The stray hunter wrapped a gloved hand around the drawstrings and pulled the bag toward him. He looked inside.

Just then, a loud horn blared outside, followed by the sound of people screaming. Pub patrons began crowding at the windows.

"What's going on?" asked Gilbert.

"I have a suspicion," replied Skylar, and Aldwyn could tell she was truly terrified.

"Stay close," said one of the soldiers to the young wizards.

Grimslade pushed out his chair and stood up from the table.

"Follow me," he said.

He moved swiftly through the bar, elbowing past ale swillers and kicking open a door that led to a stairwell. Aldwyn and the others hurried behind Grimslade as he took two steps at a time. The stray hunter pushed open a hatch to the roof and climbed out. The others followed him as fast as they could.

From the roof of the Tower Pub, Aldwyn could see that the full moon had risen. The screams were coming from citizens who were huddled

atop the city walls and looking out into the distance. There, advancing across the plains, was an army of thousands. Skeletal wolves, zombie bears, and ghoulish animals of every size and shape marched in step. It was Paksahara's Dead Army. The uprising had begun.

"When night falls hear the dog's bark,
Howling to the tallest clouds.
Secrets of yore buried,
Beneath green needle shrouds.

"Between the root of all roots,
Where every fear sinks away,
Are stairs with no bottom,
Unless eyes find sun's ray.

"Through brown mist stone arrows point,
To where the ladybugs rest.
A supper to be placed,
In the great spider's nest.

"Now comes a black crescent sword,
Cutting through the emerald night.
At last the waking moth,
Flies to the rising light.

"Hiding high upon its head,
Draped in white shimmering gown,
Lie the keys to the past,
In the snow leopard's crown."

Can the Familiars defeat Paksahara once and for all?
Don't miss what happens next!

THE
FAMILIARS
CIRCLE of
HEROES

Adam Jay Epstein
Andrew Jacobson

Art by Greg Call

HARPER
An Imprint of HarperCollinsPublishers

1

ESCAPE

Aldwyn cringed from the foul stench gusting in over the eastern wall of Bridgetower. The full moon cast a glow on the macabre parade of approaching zombies, bathing every skull, rib cage, hoof, and paw in a harsh yellow light. Dead animals of all sizes, from great elephants down to swarms of vermin, were ready to attack.

Such a fearsome sight would have caused a lesser familiar to tremble, but Aldwyn's paws remained steady. He stood firm on the Tower Pub rooftop, exchanging glances with his equally stalwart animal companion, Skylar the blue jay. The third member of their heroic trio, Gilbert the tree frog, appeared far less bold.

"Go to your happy place, go to your happy place," Gilbert chanted to keep from panicking. "I'm picturing a bug-infested lily pad."

"An undead army never tires, never grows hungry, and never knows fear," said Skylar, a bit ominously.

"How do you kill something when it's already dead?" asked Aldwyn. His question hung in the air.

"If I still had my magic, I'd blast them back to the Tomorrowlife," said Aldwyn's loyal, Jack.

"Well, thanks to Paksahara's dispeller curse, we don't," said Marianne to her younger brother. "No human does. Not even Queen Loranella."

Aldwyn looked back out at the dead animal army to see a line of skeletal rams bashing their horns against the outer city wall. Decomposing corpses of bears slammed their claws into the battlements, trying to rip open holes large enough to force their way through.

"It won't be long before they reach the

glyphstone," said Dalton, the eldest of the three apprentice wizards.

Aldwyn turned his attention from the outer wall. At the center of the city, a large stone pillar covered in runic symbols stood outside Bridgetower's House of Trials, guarded by the queen's soldiers. This pillar was one of Vastia's three glyphstones. These ancient monoliths had the magical power to summon the Shifting Fortress, but a glyphstone alone could not bring the Fortress forth. It needed to be surrounded by seven animals. And not just any animals. Magical animals. Descendants of the seven species that formed the First Phylum.

These were the animals that Aldwyn and his companions were going to search for, and the reason why they had enlisted the help of Grimslade, Vastia's most notorious animal tracker.

Despite the rams' continued charge, the strong stone barrier resisted crumbling, but it did not escape damage entirely: a few small gaps began to form in the wall.

"So long as Paksahara remains hidden away in the Shifting Fortress, she'll continue to command her Dead Army without fear of retaliation," said Dalton. "Skylar, the map."

The blue jay reached a talon into her leather satchel and removed a rolled-up piece of parchment. She set the map down on the rooftop and smoothed it out with her wing.

"We need you to find some animals," Jack told Grimslade.

"A mongoose, golden toad, wolverine, howler monkey, king cobra, bloodhound, and lightmare," said Skylar.

"We know where a few of them are, but most are a mystery to us," said Jack.

Dalton continued, "We already know a howler monkey who lives in Split River and a bloodhound who lingers in the Gloom Hills. But we'll need your help with the other five."

"What's a howler monkey doing in Split River?" asked Grimslade. "Last time I checked, most of them spend their days banging their drums high up in the Forest Under the Trees."

"She's a familiar to one of our mentor's former wizard apprentices," answered Marianne. "They've been protecting Split River for years now."

Aldwyn had heard many stories about Banshee and Galleon from Skylar and Gilbert. He even remembered seeing some of the letters that Galleon had sent to Stone Runlet, bragging about his adventures.

"If we pick up the howler monkey and blood-hound first, I suggest we then head north to the Abyssmal Canyon," said Grimslade. "That's where the mongooses and king cobras reside, deep within the broken crevices of the Kailasa mountains. I've tracked them once before with my Olfax snout. Give me that pen of yours."

The bounty hunter reached for Skylar's satchel and tried to grab Scribius. But before he could tighten his grip, the frightened pen leaped from his hand, glided across the map, and ducked behind Gilbert. Shady, the shadow puppy who had adopted Gilbert as his dad, let out a fero-cious bark at Grimslade, his smoky snout and ears peeking out from the tree frog's flower bud backpack.

"It's okay," Gilbert assured Shady and Scribius. "He's with us now."

Scribius cautiously reappeared from behind the

frog, before moving over to the map. Following the bounty hunter's instructions, the magic pen then began charting a course from the Gloom Hills to the Abyssmal Canyon.

"After we pick up a mongoose and king cobra in the crevices of Kailasa," continued Grimslade, "we'll let this do the rest."

Grimslade held up a disembodied wolf's nose that was attached to his belt. Aldwyn knew only too well what this was: an Olfax tracking snout, one of the black magic specialties of the cave shamans of Stalagmos, able to sniff out any prey. Grimslade had used this very snout to track Aldwyn through Vastia only a few short weeks ago. How ironic that now it would be used to aid the former alley cat and his companions, rather than hunt them.

"If I may make a suggestion, perhaps we should save the wolverines for last," said Marianne. "They are allied with Paksahara. One won't come without a fight."

"No animal puts up a fight when it's dead," said Grimslade.

"We must not have made ourselves clear,"

said Dalton. "All of the animals need to be brought in alive."

"That's going to cost you extra!" replied the bounty hunter.

Aldwyn heard a loud crack and looked up from the map to see that the rams had turned the small gaps in the eastern wall into bigger holes. The vanguard of the Dead Army began to squeeze their way through.

"I don't need to look into a puddle to see that this is going to end badly," said Gilbert, whose innate magical talent was seeing the future in pools of water.

Then, from across the city, the Sun Temple's bell started to chime loudly. Aldwyn had heard it ring only peacefully, to announce the rising sun, but now it was clanging madly, sending a warning to the residents of Bridgetower. And the people heeded its call, running for the safety of their shops and houses.

"Come on," said Grimslade. "We should get moving."

Grimslade led their retreat, leaping feet-first through the hatch on the roof and into the stairwell below. Loyals and familiars followed, and it was just a matter of seconds before they were back in the Tower Pub. Only the most committed ale swillers remained, the type of rogues content to die with drink in hand. Grimslade pulled a coin from the burlap bag he had been paid off with and flicked it onto the table where he had been sitting not long ago.

Two of Queen Loranella's soldiers, who had chaperoned the young wizards and familiars from Bronzhaven, immediately took their places on either side of the group. Grimslade pushed through the pub doors and led them all down a twisty cobblestoned side street toward the major thoroughfare. As they made their way, Aldwyn could hear the sounds of windows being slammed shut and tables scraping across floors to barricade doors.

The group came to the main road: to the west, it led to the House of Trials, where the glyphstone stood; to the east, Bridgetower's entrance gate. The gate was the only official way in or out of the city and certainly the quickest—that is, when there wasn't an army of zombies laying siege to it. "I know another way to get out," Aldwyn said to Jack. "Follow me."

Jack related the message to the others, and Aldwyn took off in the lead. Not for the first time, he was thinking back to his days as an ordinary alley cat and the beginning of his adventure. Then, he'd been running away from Grimslade. Now they were running together, looking to leave the city before Paksahara's zombie army made escape impossible!

From above, a terrifying cackling seemed to be coming closer and closer. Aldwyn glanced up over his shoulder. Two zombie chimpanzees were running along the canopies and tapestries that lined the outdoor markets. Loranella's soldiers stopped and pulled their swords.

"Keep going!" ordered one of them. "We'll fight them off."

The loyals, the familiars, and Grimslade continued to flee. With every step, Aldwyn could feel his father's whisper-shell necklace—which he hadn't taken off since the day he discovered it—brush against his fur. He turned back one last time to see the soldiers fighting valiantly against the vicious zombie chimp attack.

Aldwyn led his companions down a street lined with shops that sold copper pots, swords, and other metal goods. Candles in glass bowls atop waist-high lampposts had been lit, illuminating the darkness. They ducked down an alleyway filled with piles of junk and stopped so Jack and Marianne could catch their breath.

A skinny rat emerged from one of the piles.

"Oh, no, you don't!" The rat recognized Aldwyn. "Every time you come through this alley, trouble's not far behind." Not a moment later, Grimslade appeared.

"Wh-wh-what's he doing here?" the rat asked in a panic.

"It's not what you think," said Aldwyn, trying to sound reassuring. "He's on our side."

"Grimslade?"

Aldwyn nodded.

"Huh," said the rat. "I never thought I'd see the day."

Just then the alley wall shattered. A zombie bear pushed aside the rubble, oozing green stomach acid from a large hole in its rib cage. The beast looked ready to attack.

"Aldwyn, do me a favor. Find a different alley!"